A

WOLF

OF

WAR

A

WOLF

OF

WAR

A DARK MAFIA WEREWOLF ROMANCE
JUNIPER HARTMANN

JUNIPER HARTMANN

JH

YOUR FANTASIES GIVEN FORM

ALSO BY

BUNNY TALES
Run, Rabbit, Run
The Hare in His Snare

THE TOOTH & CLAW DUET
A Wolf of War

STANDALONES
Darkness and Spice

COLLECT THEM ALL

PLAYLIST

HAPPY TOGETHER
the turtles

DU HAST
rammstein

WAIT SO LONG
swdish house mafia

HIGH
stephen sanchez

THE FALL
half alive

OH, PRETTY WOMAN
roy orbison

DU8T·STARS
rogue vhs, tima

DAY OF DEAD
konrad oldmoney

WARNING

The content in these pages may be disturbing to some readers. Please take caution and read these TWs before continuing this book.

NOTE:

This is not an exhaustive list, and may be missing topics or potential triggers that I am unaware of or might have missed.

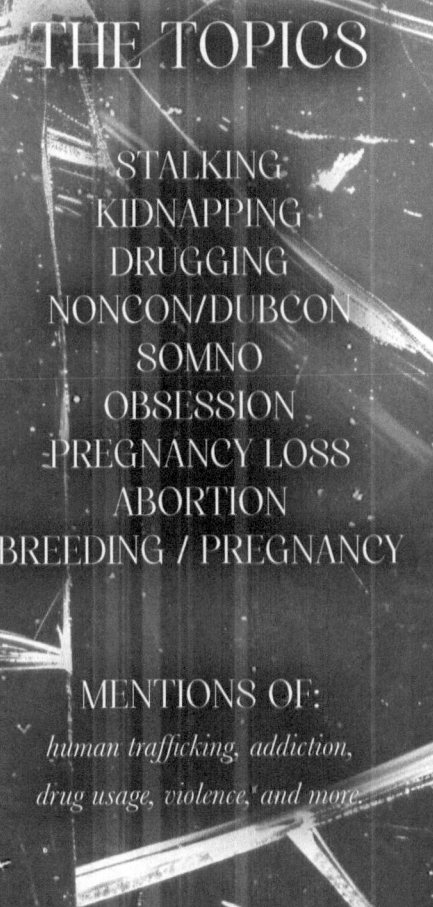

THE TOPICS

STALKING
KIDNAPPING
DRUGGING
NONCON/DUBCON
SOMNO
OBSESSION
PREGNANCY LOSS
ABORTION
BREEDING / PREGNANCY

MENTIONS OF:

*human trafficking, addiction,
drug usage, violence, and more.*

To the first creative director
I worked under as a copywriter:

I'm not a very "creative writer," huh?

(READ THIS AFTER THE
BOOK BECAUSE OF
POTENTIAL SPOILERS)

Well, cum is stored in the knot.
Bet you feel *so* dumb right now.

PART ONE

WILLOW

CHAPTER ONE

The end of the month always hit hard.

Reports piled up, meetings drained her bandwidth, and her vastly varied tasks converged in a maddening rush. But for Willow, it was in these moments that the repetition became both her burden and reprieve. Each task had a rhythm that made it easy to fall into step, a steadying force she waltzed in time with.

"Hey, quick question."

Broken from her trance, Willow sucked in a shallow breath, flinching at the words, though they had been softly spoken.

"Don't scare me like that, Poppy." Her tone was unintentionally sharp.

"Okay, okay. I didn't mean to."

Willow eyed her older sister, who stood in the doorway, hands up as though in surrender.

Poppy recognized that there was a boundary she had crossed. She knew that no distraction was welcome when it was nearly time to rip another page off the big calendar on Willow's office wall.

"I just wanted to let you know dinner will be ready soon."

"That's why you're in here bothering me?"

"Look, you need to eat. It's been twelve hours since you locked yourself in here. So, yeah, I'm bugging you about dinner."

Willow exhaled slowly, her eyes closing as she tried to release the weight pressing against her chest.

It wasn't really Poppy that was irritating her—it was the crushing awareness of how little time remained to finish everything. The flurry of tasks left her drained and hollow with exhaustion. She reached beneath her, fingers brushing against the cool edge of the mini-fridge tucked beneath her desk. With a soft click, she opened it and pulled out a long-necked bottle.

Poppy eyed the beer but held her tongue, instead quirking an eyebrow and saying, "It'll be ready in an hour, toots. I'll be back, and you will be leaving this office and eating."

With that, her sister turned and walked back down the hallway on the second floor of their little three-bedroom condo. Willow had picked it out because of the all-season room she turned into her office, getting a fourth room in the process. The third bedroom was an art studio for her sister to do crafts, a favorite pastime—of which she had many, almost all projects left abandoned after the fixation ended.

Having all of those windows letting in sunshine made her heart brim with joy. She had never seen an all-seasons room on the second floor. It was a lovely place for it, she had decided.

Except, of course, when she was writhing with anxiety because of her ever-growing to-do list.

Willow sighed between sips. Each bitter mouthful was easier to swallow than the last, and soon she had downed the entire bottle.

"Alright, break's over," she muttered, straightening her back as she pulled her chair closer to the monitors. The first task was to record the KPIs, and then she'd dive into assigning articles once she'd figured out which writers were hitting the mark the previous month. Her position as editor-in-chief kept her busy, but it paid well, and the money was well worth it.

That's what she told herself, anyway.

***

When Poppy returned to collect Willow, she had managed to get halfway through updating a spreadsheet, while her inbox continued to ping in the background. With great hesitation and quite a lot of sighing, she dragged herself away from her desk and followed her sister out into the hallway.

The wooden floors were still faintly slick beneath her socks, the result of Poppy's meticulous washing and polishing. The floors gleamed under the soft light, pulling gold instead of brown. Even so, she wished her sister would take it easier on her aching hands.

Willow gripped the banister as they descended the stairs, which opened into an airy, open-concept living space. The kitchen was separated from the living room by a long counter, which had stools lined up against it. It was sleek and modern, black and white with small splashes of color here and there. Poppy thought it felt sterile. Willow simply thought it looked clean.

A mouthwatering scent filled the air, and despite her reluctance to admit it, Willow had to concede that Poppy was right. She needed to fuel herself. Her stomach grumbled, flipping over.

She trailed Poppy into the kitchen, her fingers brushing the smooth surface of the granite countertop. A feast awaited her—a golden spiral ham, creamy au gratin potatoes, sweet candied yams, roasted asparagus, soft rolls, and a bowl of ruby red cranberry sauce.

"You've been working hard lately. You deserve a nice dinner to celebrate all your success this month."

Willow scoffed even as she smiled. Her sister knew she had a weak spot for cranberry sauce.

"Don't give me that. You know as well as I do that you're doing great."

Willow grabbed a plate from the counter and began loading it with food, each scoop guided by the whims of her stomach. She piled her plate high with enough food to hold her over for the next few days, let alone a single meal. She doubted she'd finish, but she'd give it her all.

After they assembled their meals and moved to the other side of the counter, they fell into a comfortable silence. After a few years of living together, the sisters had settled into a routine, the days flowing by effortlessly. At first, they were constantly in each other's way. Something changed, though, as they grew accustomed to each other, and soon their laughter was as frequent as their spats. There were still plenty of disagreements to be had, however, and Willow found that half the time she wanted to wring her older sister's neck.

The first bite of ham nearly sent Willow into space, sweet brown sugar glaze melting into the wonderfully tender pork.

"It's incredible, Poppy. Thank you."

"You're welcome, sweetheart."

Their relationship was tangled, complicated by the weight of shifted responsibilities and flipped roles. Though Poppy was technically the older sister by a stretch, it was often Willow who stepped into the shoes of the eldest.

She was the one who carried the responsibility, both as caregiver and breadwinner, doing whatever it took to maintain their stability. Still, Poppy was a motherly figure to Willow. This was especially true after they had lost their parents.

They finished their meal slowly, indulging in every bite. The conversation was a light, infrequent hum between them.

When everything was cleaned up, Willow felt the familiar pull of responsibility calling her back to her computer. She hugged Poppy briefly, offered another soft thank you for the dinner, and made her way back upstairs, the weight of her work already settling back in.

***

Once in her office, Willow breathed out a long sigh, slipping off her cream cardigan in favor of the white racerback tank top beneath. Delicate gold rings gleamed on a few fingers—minimal but striking on her pianist's hands.

She hung the cardigan over the back of her chair, then sank back into the plush leather, the chair offering support where it was needed most. No regrets about spending the extra cash for comfort. Back support was one of the things she'd never skimp on.

Willow let her fingers fly across the keyboard, the mouse darting around the screen in erratic bursts. More emails landed in her inbox by the minute, and she was already overwhelmed. Willow reached under the desk again, flipping open the mini-fridge with another quiet click.

What was a long night without liquid courage?

Willow took a long swig, the cool beer sliding down her throat as she returned to the grind. She lost track of time until the little clock in the corner of her screen read 12:30 a.m. By now, she was ahead of the game. The reports were filed, the spreadsheets meticulously updated, and everything was in its rightful place.

Her desk had become a graveyard of empty beer bottles, and when Willow stood, she felt her knees wobble. She wasn't the best at holding her liquor, and the liquid felt like it was sloshing over the edge of her stomach. *I may have overdone it.*

But it was a perfect opportunity to relax and let the day end on a high note.

She needed it. Pressure still hung heavy on her sagging shoulders.

Willow slipped out the door and crept her way down the hallway to her bedroom. Poppy was a heavy sleeper, but Willow preferred not to risk waking her up.

A few seconds later, she stood in front of her bedroom door. She turned the knob slowly, eased it open, and stepped inside.

Her room was her own personal sanctuary, meticulously curated to offer solace from the daily hustle and bustle. It was a place to help her shoulder the weight of chronic fatigue, that relentless phantom she couldn't seem to shake, no matter how many treatments or remedies were offered. Nothing worked—no pill, no supplement, no "miracle cure."

The cardigan hit the floor as soon as the door shut, followed by her tank top and bra. She shed her jeans and socks with the same slow, unbalanced movements, her feet dragging toward the king-sized bed.

Stumbling sideways a little, she threw back the

covers and hopped up to climb beneath the cotton sheets, the material softly brushing over her legs. With a quiet sigh, she reached for her bedside table, opening the drawer and rummaging until she found what she was looking for—a silver bullet vibrator.

Willow leaned back, pressing the power button until it hummed to life, then let her knees fall apart. In seconds, the toy was positioned at her core, her breath quickening as pleasure began to flood her system.

LORE

Silver isn't deadly to werewolves.
They are, however, far more
susceptible to the effects of
nightshade than humans are.

Nightshade can be used as a
paralytic agent if applied topically.

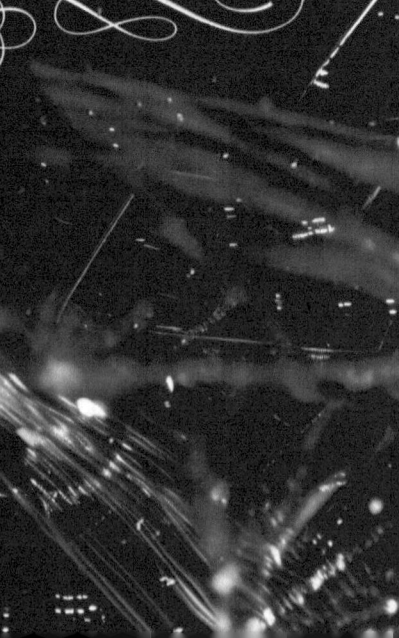

MILO

CHAPTER TWO

The night called to him, rich with promise, both lush and bright; only a wolf would find light in the darkness. To humans, the street was dim, with stretches of gold and blue flickering across the blacktop, spilling from glowing windows and flickering television screens like a net cast over the night.

Milo had only just arrived in town a month or so back. Barely had his feet touched American soil before he found himself tangled in this mess.

He sucked in a sharp breath, pushing it all away, determined not to let his thoughts drag him back to the chaos in his mind. The distraction had to be forgotten for now. That was all it was, a distraction. There were more pressing matters now. Namely, the fantasy of pale thighs wrapped around his head while his tongue lapped greedily at his mate's sweet cunt.

A shiver ran down his spine. Milo shifted, adjusting himself. He'd figured his time in the special forces would be a boon for this mission. It had been, but the real skill in slipping through shadows, unseen and unheard, came from the lupine blood flowing in his veins. He wasn't a gifted soldier just because of human talents.

Nestled high between two oak branches, he scanned the area, noting every subtle noise as his head swiveled slowly. It wasn't likely anybody would find him here, but it was still wise to exercise caution when committing criminal activities.

Milo licked his lips. His attention snapped

back to Willow, who was still blissfully unaware. She was on her back, pleasuring herself, and he had a front-row seat to the show. He couldn't tear his gaze away from the exquisite expressions she made as her orgasm built, eyes squeezed tight, lips parted in a perfect O.

His fingers twitched, aching with the need to act, but he stopped himself. What he wouldn't give to feel her slick mouth around him, to force her to submit with his cock in her throat. The strain in his pants was almost unbearable now.

"What is it, Arlo?" Milo murmured, sensing the presence of his second-in-command behind him. He must have tracked him by scent.

"You need to come home. The McGarvey pack has called a meeting."

He could hear the crisp press of old snow underfoot as Arlo slowly closed the distance between them.

Milo didn't respond, instead throwing a quick, scathing glare over his shoulder. He turned back to Willow, still completely unaware, still putting on a show just for him and his unintended, and unwanted, audience.

"She's not going anywhere, Milo. Leave it."

He wanted to argue, but instead, he spared one last look at the woman who captivated him so wholly, and then he slipped silently from his perch. He landed softly on the ground, moving like a shadow toward Arlo so they could go back to the waiting car.

***

"Are you fucking serious?"

Milo could kill him. He could twist his head clean off.

"Yeah, well, what was I supposed to do, dude?" Titan squeaked, wringing his hands nervously, the whites of his eyes flashing bright even in the dim light.

"You're telling me you found a McGarvey wolf on our territory, so you tied him up and shoved him in your trunk?"

Each word raised his blood pressure. This could spiral out of control fast. If McGarvey was feeling unpleasant, he might see this as a declaration of war. Milo ran his hands down his face and screamed into his palms. Of course, things went to shit as soon as he came back. Of course, this would happen.

"Milo, look, I'm sorry," Titan sputtered, hands spread out in a pleading gesture. "I know I fucked up. But what if he saw some shit he shouldn't have? Shouldn't we, like, question him or something?"

"What we should be questioning is whether or not there'll be backlash over this little stunt."

Arlo's gravelly voice cut through the tension, low but not unkind. The man had the patience of a saint, especially with the youngest member of their pack, who in many ways was still learning the ropes of both being a man and a wolf.

Unfortunately, he was also an idiot.

Milo pinched the bridge of his nose, the weight of the situation landing like a ballistic. After a long pause, he crossed his arms and spoke slowly, choosing his words carefully.

"Fine. What's done is done. Where is he now?"

Titan offered a sheepish smile.

"You're not fucking serious," Milo said flatly.

***

The walk to the car was short, urgency making it impossible for Milo to settle himself. He still couldn't stop thinking about the incredible scene he'd been blessed enough to witness earlier. He could be lying in bed now, watching Willow sleep through the cameras he'd installed in her bedroom. The idea lingered, but he jerked his head toward the car as Titan pressed a button on his keys.

"Well, what do we have here?" Arlo drawled, his gaze fixed on the now-open trunk.

"A punk in a trunk," Milo chuckled in return, as the three crowded around. The man inside was growling and screaming through the gag, kicking viciously, thrashing as if he could tear through the restraints. He wouldn't be able to; they were soaked in a nightshade infusion.

"Sorry, bud," Milo said coolly. "But I don't think you're going anywhere. At least, not anytime soon. Titan tells me you were snooping in places you shouldn't have been. You know what we do to rogue wolves who put their noses where they don't belong?"

Milo reached down, grabbing the man by the throat and pinning him against the polyester lining of the trunk. Their captive went wild, twisting and screeching in rage, but the fear in his eyes was unmistakable.

"Aw, come on, Milo," Titan piped up. "You're really scaring him."

"He should be fucking scared," Milo snapped. "You don't step onto my territory whenever you damn well please. There are consequences."

It was all for the show, of course. He wouldn't hurt him. Not while the fate of the entire city depended on Colin's grace. A war between them would spell disaster for the human inhabitants of the city's underbelly. The casualties would be a problem for them all.

"Are you going to behave if I untie you?" Milo asked flatly, receiving only an angry thrash in return. He couldn't blame the guy. If it were him, he'd be just as eager to lash out once freed.

But that wasn't something Milo wanted to deal with right now.

"I'll leave you in here to think about things.

Just chill for a while, alright?"

With that, the trunk slammed shut, and the three men turned back into the manor, waiting for the McGarvey pack to arrive.

***

The sound of an engine broke the silence. The manor was well-hidden, tucked deep into the suburbs, surrounded by trees and acreage. They owned apartments in the city, but wolves weren't made for concrete and steel. This place would always be home.

Milo, with Arlo and Titan by his side, strode out of the entryway, chest out, chin high. He would bow to no wolf, regardless of circumstance. His boots crunched the gravel, but the tires of the black SUV did the same, louder, as it pulled into the driveway.

The four doors swung open, and out climbed the McGarvey pack. Milo didn't recognize the others, but he knew Colin McGarvey, their alpha, and Jenner, the alpha's personal bitch.

"What a beautiful evening, Mr. Schwarz. Don't you think?" McGarvey said, pleasant but cold. Milo didn't buy it. McGarvey would tear his throat out without hesitation if the opportunity arose.

"I believe we have something of yours."

"I believe you do," McGarvey responded, his voice now cool and dry.

"I apologize for the oversight."

McGarvey twirled his mustache, his eyes narrowing as the silence collected once more. He was thankful that the smell of fear wasn't permeating the air. Milo had been worried that Titan would cower in the presence of McGarvey.

It was good to know the kid had balls. Hopefully, that wouldn't be an issue in the future.

"Well, mistakes do happen. I suppose we could overlook this, couldn't we, gentlemen?"

The two men at McGarvey's side grunted in agreement, Jenner flashing a sly smile.

Little weasel, Milo growled inwardly.

Out loud, he said, "Alright, well, we appreciate your understanding, McGarvey. If you follow Arlo, he'll help you retrieve your man."

It was odd that McGarvey was so controlled. It was in his nature, but even he should be more volatile about one of his pack members being taken in such a way.

"Thomas, Chuck," McGarvey called, snapping his fingers.

Arlo motioned to the two men who followed, leading them toward Titan's car.

McGarvey spoke again.

"So, enjoying being home? You've had quite the adventure."

Milo grunted, narrowing his eyes. It was a sore point for him, his extended absence from the pack.

"It's been great."

Milo wouldn't entertain small talk with a rival alpha. McGarvey had a way of extracting information without you even realizing it, stealing pieces of knowledge from seemingly inconsequential snippets.

"Such a lovely time of year. So many scents in the air. It's... tantalizing."

Milo's ears perked, but he kept his face impassive.

"Sure is. Really love the flowers and the birds."

McGarvey smiled at the lackluster reply. "The birds and the bees, as well." A scuffle caught Milo's attention. Titan dove out of the way as the previously tied-up man lunged after him. Rolling his eyes, Milo glanced back at McGarvey. The man's eyes had never left him. His icy blue gaze sent a chill down Milo's spine.

"Alright, enough. Let's go," McGarvey barked, turning his gaze back to the car.

The kidnapped man stormed past them, throwing open the door to the SUV and slamming himself inside.

"So dramatic, isn't he?" McGarvey murmured, amused.

"I might have been more so, myself," Milo responded dryly.

"I'm sure you would. It's higher stakes when you suddenly have so much to lose."

That caught Milo's attention. He couldn't

possibly be talking about Willow. They shouldn't even know about her. No one outside of his pack did. He declined to respond, however, and raise even higher the guillotine hanging overhead.

"You're absolutely right. Good night, McGarvey. Let's not do this again."

With that, Milo turned sharply, Arlo and Titan following, and the three walked away, not once looking back.

WILLOW

CHAPTER THREE

Sunlight filtered through the windows, stretching across her giant bed, inching closer and closer to her face. Willow shifted restlessly, trying to avoid the early morning. After the third attempt, she sat up with a frustrated huff.

It was Saturday, 6:00 a.m. Why the hell was she up so early on a Saturday? Especially after a night like the one before. She'd barely scraped together five hours of sleep—far too little for her to function properly, usually.

Willow rolled over and felt something hard jab into her side. Her brow furrowed, and she reached beneath herself, letting out a little laugh when she realized what it was.

"Oh, uh, hey. I think it's time to go home now."

She leaned over to slip the sex toy back into the drawer of her bedside table, swinging her legs over the edge of the bed. Standing up, she winced, her head throbbing lightly. It wasn't unbearable. She'd braced herself for a full-blown hangover, but instead, it felt like she could take some ibuprofen and move on. She was feeling oddly optimistic about the day ahead.

After all, there was a farmer's market downtown.

Willow padded over to her dresser, pulling out her clothes for the day. She chose a white tank top embroidered with delicate sky-blue birds, one of her favorite shirts, with blue jean shorts. The forecast had sold her on the promise of warm weather, perfect for getting a little sun.

She and Poppy didn't go into the heart of the city much. It was only a fifteen-minute drive, but Willow's anxiety kept her from getting behind the wheel of a car. Poppy didn't mind the traffic, but her tendency to drive like a rally car racer put Willow off taking trips with her sister.

Today, she decided she'd pop an anti-anxiety pill and just try to get through it. There was ice cream to devour, lattes to sip, and baked goods to acquire.

Willow made her way downstairs. The condo was hers for the moment; Poppy wouldn't be awake for a couple of hours at least. The stillness of the morning was a blessing. She loved lighting candles and sipping coffee in the quiet before the world was awake. As much as she adored Poppy, her rapid-fire chatter wasn't exactly ideal while she was still trying to rub the sleep from her eyes.

Willow slowly began working the drip coffee maker, filling a liner with fresh grounds and then setting it to make a full pot. Her sister insisted they use it instead of a newer machine that used plastic pods. "Terrible for the environment and our bodies! There are microplastics, Willow!" she had said. Once the coffee maker was done brewing, Willow filled a white mug with the ambrosia of dawn.

Swirling steam danced upward, a soft tornado of scent. She liked her coffee sweeter than most, much to Poppy's dismay. Her sister was convinced that sugar before noon would ruin your entire day. It was endearing, her need to protect Willow however she could, even if it ended in rolling eyes and exaggerated sighs.

With her creamy, sweet beverage in hand, Willow sank into a seat at the counter. The ceramic mug warmed her chilled fingers, grounding her.

She closed her eyes for a moment, concentrating on nothing but the warmth of the mug, the taste of the coffee on her lips, and the rich, comforting aroma that surrounded her.

***

"Come on, Willow, it's not that bad!"

Willow was not reassured by her sister's words. She gripped the handle above her seat with one hand, her other clutching the middle console as if it could somehow anchor her. The anxiety was suffocating.

"I knew I should've taken another pill," she groaned, letting her head fall back against the headrest, squeezing her eyes shut.

"Oh, stop it. We're almost there."

By the time they pulled into the parking lot, Willow was just relieved to be in one piece.

She straightened her tank top and grabbed her purse from the floorboard, slipping the white tote bag up her arm and over her shoulder. It was big enough for a few items, and her sister had brought a couple of reusable bags. They both climbed out of the vehicle and started toward the farmer's market.

After a long stroll through a crowded street, they could finally see the tops of the stalls, colorful tents rising above the crowd.

"Oh, I hope that weird art lady is here again!" Poppy exclaimed enthusiastically.

"Do you mean the one with the scary fetus sculpture, or are you talking about yourself in the third person?"

"Hush, you."

They both laughed softly, taking in the symphony of sights, sounds, and smells. In front of them, a vendor sold cheese, milk, yogurt, and even ice cream. Across from them, a woman tended to her plants, speaking with a curious passerby.

Something caught Willow's eye. She felt her breath catch in her throat, her gaze darting back and forth before it finally settled on him.

He was tall, muscular, and devastatingly handsome. Her heart skipped a beat as their eyes met, the moment stretching, heavy with some meaning unknown to her. It felt like a black hole had opened in her chest, beautifully suffocating.

"Willow, are you listening?"

Poppy's voice broke her reverie as she gave Willow a light tap on the shoulder. When Willow looked back, the man was gone. She wondered if she had imagined the whole thing.

"I think I'm going crazy," she muttered to herself.

"Oh, sweetheart, we've been there for a while."

"Oh my God, Poppy. Come on, let's check out the vegetable stands."

Her voice was dismissive, but she couldn't help the agitation stirring in her gut. She hadn't liked being pulled from whatever that was—whatever had just happened. She tried to shake it off, focusing on the market instead.

They stopped at a tent full of plants from one of the local farms. It was like a jungle, overflowing with ivy and foliage, the leaves thick enough to shield everything around you from view. Willow quickly lost sight of Poppy, but she didn't worry about it. Her sister was often wandering off.

Instead of searching for Poppy, she paused in front of a display of orchids, marveling at their odd shapes. Her fingers brushed the soft petals, and she leaned forward to inhale their fragrance.

"Hey, there."

Willow gasped, startled, and whipped around, nearly colliding with the man from before.

"Oh, God, I'm so sorry," she sputtered, her cheeks bright. She could feel the heat in her face, a rush of warmth spreading.

"No, you're fine," he said, his voice smooth

and reassuring. "I shouldn't have startled you. I just really love orchids and wanted to see them."

He seemed pleasant enough, and Willow didn't feel threatened. There was something oddly magnetic about him. Clearing her throat, she offered, "Would you like to look at them with me?" It was an odd question to ask a stranger, and she wasn't sure why it had left her mouth.

His grin made her heart seize in her chest, brilliant white teeth flashing between soft, kissable lips. Willow blinked rapidly.

What the fuck is wrong with me?

"Yeah, absolutely. Which one's your favorite?"

She turned back to the flowers, trying to steady herself. The man shifted slightly, his torso nearly pressing into hers. She could feel the heat radiating from his barrel chest. His presence was overwhelming, and her breath hitched.

With a trembling finger, she pointed to a pink orchid, her voice barely a whisper.

"That one."

"Ah, good choice," he said, his voice low and intimate. "Orchids are fascinating, you know. They're one of the most ancient plants alive."

"Are they?" she breathed, frozen in place as his scent washed over her. Mint and vanilla.

"Yeah." He reached around her, his chest brushing against her arm as he plucked the flower from the plant, leaving a small piece of stem at the end. Willow's pulse quickened as his hand grazed her skin. "They use mimicry to attract insects that pollinate them."

"Oh?" Her voice was strained. She could feel the heat between her legs, a pulsing, insistent need that made her squeeze her thighs together.

"Yes." His voice had dropped to a murmur as he slid the flower behind her ear, his fingers brushing the sensitive skin of her neck. "They're masters of deception."

Willow's breath caught in her throat. The world around them seemed to fade as she turned to face him, bringing them far too close to each other. There was nothing else anymore, only the intensity of his dark gaze.

"You're not supposed to tear up the flowers," she whispered, mesmerized by his gleaming eyes.

"I think you'll find I'm allowed to do anything I want, Willow."

The sound of her name on his lips sent a shiver down her spine. It was as if he had marked her, claimed her with just one word. Something in the back of her mind screamed at her to run, but her body refused to obey. The real question, however, was, *How does he know my name?*

"There you are!"

The spell was broken. Poppy's voice jolted her back to reality, and she took a step back, reeling.

"Sorry about that, toots. I just felt like

following my heart right to the pot plants. Turns out they don't have any! Who's the dude?"

Poppy's eyes narrowed, noticing how close Willow and the stranger were still standing.

"Oh, he's…" She realized she didn't even know his name. But somehow, he knew hers.

"Milo! Nice to meet you," the man said with a grin, offering a small wave.

"Well, Milo, are you coming with us to get ice cream? Because we're getting ice cream."

Willow's stomach churned. She wanted nothing more than to escape, to forget this strange magnetism she felt toward him. It wasn't unlike her sister to do something like this, ever outgoing and willing to make friends with anybody. But did it have to be this man in particular?

What the fuck is going on?

LORE

The mate bond chooses when
to bless an alpha. The general
consensus is that their mate is
revealed at the "right time" in life
for them to settle down and breed
the next generation.

MILO

CHAPTER FOUR

He couldn't believe his luck. Not only was Willow open to his advances, but her sister was clearly equal parts reckless, trusting, and friendly. Normally, these traits would not be positive, but they worked to his advantage in this case.

They were standing in line for ice cream. He'd meant it when he said it sounded great. With all the scents and sounds, it would be nice to have something that flooded his senses for a little while; it would cut the noise.

It was their turn, and he listened carefully to Willow's order, memorizing it. It was simple enough, just a scoop of peanut butter cup in a waffle cone. Her sister went for rum raisin, which he hadn't even thought was still sold, and then it was his turn.

"I'll just have vanilla, thanks." He pulled out his wallet and handed over his card.

"Hey, wait, you don't have to do that! I mean, you totally can. You just don't have to."

Willow rolled her eyes in response to her sister, slapping her arm. "I think what Poppy means to say is that we can pay for our own ice cream."

"Oh, no, it's not a problem. Don't worry about it. Tell you what, you can get it next time, alright?"

The sisters shrugged it off and waited patiently for their order, Poppy engaging Milo in turbulent small talk, hands flying as she jumped from topic to topic. He did his best to follow along, but she flitted along at such a pace that even a wolf couldn't keep up.

His thoughts were wandering, anyway. It was paramount that he secure Willow as soon as possible. With McGarvey making veiled threats…

If she were to fall into McGarvey's hands, his own would run red with blood, innocent or otherwise. He couldn't allow that to happen.

Milo turned his attention back to Poppy. She was detailing the fungal infection in her toenails and how hard she had been trying to get rid of it. Unsuccessfully, she noted. Milo wasn't sure whether to laugh nervously or simply stare in horrified fascination.

"Poppy, knock it off," Willow chided with a soft sigh.

"What? This is important for you to know. What if it happens to you?"

"Then I'll tell a doctor about it and not some stranger who has no choice but to listen to me."

"He has a choice, Willow. He could walk away at any time."

Milo smiled softly. "I could never walk away from Willow."

Both sisters stopped short, eyeing him incredulously. He'd misstepped. It was far too soon for him to be confessing devotion. On the other hand, it was killing him not to bend her over a bench and take her viciously, screaming to the sky that she was his and his alone.

Milo's name was called out, signaling that their order was ready. He walked over to the counter to collect everything, leaving the sisters in their uncomfortable silence.

When he returned a few seconds later, they seemed far more guarded. No longer was Poppy happily babbling on, and Willow had her arms crossed, face drawn. He smiled tentatively, handing over their cones, and then cleared his throat.

"Why don't we sit down?"

His voice carried a vein of authority that most wouldn't argue with, and this proved to be true for the sisters. Willow and Poppy followed him a few feet to a white picnic table with peeling paint and rickety benches.

Somehow, he still managed to spend most of the day with them, even if it ended with him loaded down with their bags. The entire time, he'd felt their bond shift and groan beneath the weight of their nearness. He knew that she felt the pull as well. He had been breathing in the proof of her arousal the entire day. They were walking back to the parking garage when he noticed goosebumps rising along Willow's exposed arms and a little shiver now and then.

"Wait, hold on," he said, putting the bags down and slipping off his jacket. He put it around Willow's shoulders, and she sucked in a breath. He wished at that moment that she was breath*less*, sucking on his cock instead of the air.

"You really don't have to do that," Willow muttered, but she was slipping her arms into the sleeves while she said it. Milo smiled warmly, the primal beast inside of him roaring with pleasure that she would be covered in his scent. The mingling of their pheromones was almost irresistible.

Poppy looked on with concern. Milo smiled at her, too, hoping he could dispel the hesitation. He regretted what he'd said earlier. It was going to make this whole thing much more difficult.

***

When they reached the car, Willow handed him his jacket. He took it slowly, reluctant to let go, wishing he could leave it with her. If he couldn't stay in her arms, at least a piece of him could linger. Something he owned should remain close to her, even if he couldn't.

Poppy had opened the back of the SUV for him to load the bags into. He slipped his jacket into one of the bags, stuffing it down quickly in a single motion. It was a split-second decision, and one he almost regretted. It would have been bliss to breathe in their blended scents while he fucked his hand to the thought of her.

Milo shuddered, mouth watering as the scent of her slick cunt once more took him over. Willow rounded the car, now standing a few feet away, her presence soft but undeniable. He shut the trunk.

"Thanks for hanging out with us, Milo, and for carrying our stuff back." Her voice was polite, but edged with something he hoped wasn't fear.

Milo took a step forward, eyeing her body language and assessing how the gesture was received. She tensed but didn't move from where she was standing.

"Hey, anytime. Thanks for kind of adopting me for the day. We should do this again sometime."

Willow paused before giving him a smile that didn't quite reach the corners of her eyes.

"Yeah, I think I'd like that."

"Would you like my phone number?"

Offering his instead of asking for hers would give her the illusion of control, a sense that she held the power in this situation. In reality, she didn't. She never had—never would. It had always been fate that she would be his.

And besides, he already knew her number. They weren't hard to find.

Willow nodded, pulling out her phone and entering his number. To his surprise, she gave him her own number right afterward. She gave a small wave, a soft "goodbye," and walked back around her sister's car.

Milo made his way back to his own, the need to get home pressing on him.

WILLOW

CHAPTER FIVE

The ride home was the longest fifteen minutes of Willow's life. She was so exhausted that she couldn't summon the energy to worry about Poppy's driving, and Poppy—equally drained—was driving like a normal person for once.

Willow desperately wanted to talk to her sister about Milo; the concerns, the desires, the fears mingling inside her. Unfortunately, they were both too tired to string together any words that would be even remotely insightful.

A wave of guilt washed over Willow as she considered her own exhaustion.

She knew her sister would likely feel the consequences of this tomorrow, a flare-up that always came after pushing too hard. Part of her wished she'd suggested they take things slower, that they leave earlier, give Poppy more time to rest. But the other part of her knew that her sister was aware of her own limits. It wasn't Willow's place to set them, no matter how often she thought Poppy pushed herself too far.

There was something else, too; something in the back of her mind. They had stayed out fairly late due to the additional member of their group...

Her brow furrowed. She didn't want to think about that right now.

When they finally got home, both of them dragged their feet inside, the weight of the groceries adding to the exhaustion that pressed down on them. They placed the bags on the counter, and Willow told

Poppy to go take a bath, one of the few remedies that helped with her joint pain, and promised she'd handle everything. To her surprise, Poppy agreed without protest and made her way upstairs.

It only made Willow feel worse. It had to be worse than she had originally thought.

Willow mulled over the events of the day as she started unpacking the bags. He had known her name. It sent a shiver down her spine, a chill crawling beneath her skin. The implications were far from innocent. She had replayed the day in her head, wondering if she'd let it slip while they were talking next to the plants, or if he'd overheard it when he'd been nearby.

Either way, he now had her number. That realization had gnawed at her during the ride home. She had been impulsive—acting on the wet spot between her legs, and not a lick of logic was factored into the equation. She kicked herself again for it. She desperately wanted to trust him. She needed to... but she couldn't figure out why.

Her hand brushed against something that shouldn't have been in the bag.

Willow peeked in, and her heart warmed as she realized it was his jacket. Without thinking, she pulled it out and pressed it into her face, breathing in his scent.

She threw it to the counter and stood there frozen.

What the hell was that? she thought to herself in a daze. She stuffed the jacket into her tote bag and rushed around to finish up.

It only took a few minutes to put the fruits and vegetables away. When she finished, she left the dry goods on the counter and headed upstairs. Before she left, without thinking, she reached back into the tote bag and pulled out the jacket.

It was only six in the evening, but her body was already heavy with the need for sleep. Tomorrow would likely be one of those lazy Sundays where neither of them moved around much, both sisters too worn out to do anything but rest.

She'd deal with the jacket situation tomorrow. It wasn't worth stressing about tonight, and besides, she didn't have the energy for it. Willow walked directly to her room, closed the door, and then climbed into bed without so much as getting changed. With her, she held his jacket, which she snuggled into in place of a pillow.

***

The next day, she woke up in the afternoon with the light still on. Willow yawned and stretched, taking her time to let her muscles flex into the motion. It felt incredible, and she was feeling once again that it would be a good day.

And then she remembered.

"Oh, shit," she yelped, rummaging around the bed until she found her cell. There weren't any missed calls or texts from him. She had been half-expecting that he would blow up her phone, and all her fears would be confirmed. Instead, nothing. Not a single ping.

She felt hollow in the pit of her stomach. Willow realized after a moment that she was crushed. She had been hoping that he would have at least reached out. She looked next to her, letting herself trail lazy fingers along the arm of the jacket, still bunched up on her bed.

With a frustrated growl, she tossed her phone to the side and flopped backward onto her bed, hands running down her face.

***

After showering and getting dressed, Willow made her way downstairs. The comforting smell of breakfast rose to meet her as she descended, and she spotted Poppy busy at work in their kitchen.

"Hey, why aren't you resting?" Willow asked, eyes narrowing.

Poppy looked up, her face splitting with a smile.

"Well, the food isn't going to make itself. And besides, I don't want to be stuck in bed all day. I've got things to do, toots."

Willow rolled her eyes but let it go. Prodding her sister wouldn't do any good. It would only spark a spat between them. Instead, she decided to focus on making it a peaceful day.

Even if she was still sulking a little.

While Poppy finished up, Willow went about making herself a cup of coffee. She wouldn't have the quiet morning she'd hoped for, but that was okay. She found comfort in her sister's company, and getting over twelve hours of sleep left her feeling at least somewhat refreshed.

They made their plates and ate in silence until Poppy mentioned the elephant in the room.

"So, this Milo guy…" she started, glancing at Willow expectantly.

"Yeah? The one you decided to invite out to ice cream before you even knew his name?"

"Oh, come on. I just like making friends."

"Okay, well, the people you try to make friends with are creepy."

"But you're my friend!"

"Poppy, we are not friends, we're sisters."

"And your sister is your first friend!"

Willow groaned, putting her face in one hand, while Poppy grinned. Once she had regained composure, her sister started in again.

"Anyway, what's up with him? You two seemed like you were getting cozy."

"Nothing is up. I've never met the guy before.

I don't know. Something just feels weird."

"No, I agree. If you want my honest opinion, I don't like him. Something isn't right with *that* one."

Willow mulled that over, taking a sip of her coffee. It was unlike Poppy to dislike a person so strongly, especially so soon. Her sister was the most social person she knew.

"I don't know. I think I want to see him again. I gave him my number."

Poppy gasped, putting a hand over her heart before saying, "Willow Montgomery!"

"What?!"

"You never give a strange man your phone number! What were you thinking?"

"Well, I did, and there's not much I can do about it now," Willow grumbled. It wasn't like she could hack into his phone and delete herself from his memory. The thought of that, of him losing his memory of her, made her stomach flip. Willow tried to ignore it.

"And you shouldn't be drinking all that sugar before noon."

"Okay, Poppy, I get it. Are we done?"

"I love you."

Willow sighed once more in response before getting up and grabbing her plate. She glanced over at the coffee machine longingly. She would love another cup, but it would make her anxiety spike. Decaf was an option, but decaf was also a sin.

Instead, she grabbed a cup of water and went upstairs to her office. She had some work she wanted to get ahead on, and it would only take an hour or two.

***

She couldn't focus. Every few seconds, her eyes darted toward the phone charging on her desk, her fingers twitching, itching to grab it. Not a single text had come through in the last hour, and the silence was starting to eat at her.

Of course, Willow could make the first move. She could break the ice and reach out to him... but that would mean giving in.

It felt foolish to play these games with a man she had met once, and one she still wasn't sure about. And yet, there was something deeper at play. It was like a primal instinct had awoken inside her. She wanted him to chase her. She wanted him to make her feel hunted.

But she also wanted him to stop making her feel like an idiot with a crush.

"No," she muttered to herself, shaking her head as she stood up and grabbed her phone. She began pacing the room, typing and deleting multiple messages, frustration bubbling. Finally, she paused, took a breath, and settled on something simple.

WILLOW: Hey

She cringed as soon as she sent it.

Was it *too* casual? Too nonchalant? Would he think she didn't care?

Well, then, good. Because I don't care.

Her phone pinged. Willow nearly jumped out of her skin, hands shaking as she tried and failed to unlock it. After another attempt, the text popped up.

MILO: What's up, sleepyhead?

Her eyebrow raised. It was an odd way to respond, given that he had no idea when she had gotten up. She decided to ignore it.

WILLOW: Found ur jacket

MILO: Did you like it?

WILLOW: Why would I like it?

She was back to feeling trepidation. He was just so odd. The entire thing was so strange. She had only been guessing that the jacket had been left on purpose. Willow felt herself shiver.

MILO: I'll have you know that's a nice jacket lol

He avoided the real question. She decided that she would let him go for now.

WILLOW: ur never getting it back now
MILO: Guess I'll have to come take what's mine

It struck her like a bolt of lightning. Her core was throbbing at the thought of him, broad shoulders and strong hands, coming into her room, ripping the jacket off her to reveal a vulnerable nakedness beneath…

WILLOW: I'd like to see u try

MILO: Be careful what you wish for

WILLOW: I prefer living dangerously

MILO: Now, Willow
MILO: Don't lie to me, naughty girl

She couldn't help but squeal at the last message, eyes widening. Before she could stop herself, she was shooting off her response.

MILO

CHAPTER SIX

Milo was sprawled out on a sofa in the manor's primary living room. His lips curled into a devilish smile as the next message came in.

WILLOW: I like that

MILO: Lying to me? That's fucked up

WILLOW: No omg
WILLOW: What u called me, I guess

MILO: Naughty girl? You can be my naughty girl anytime you want, Willow

The last text was a gamble. He wasn't sure if it would push her away or draw her in further. But it was a risk he was willing to take. She must feel the same unbearable need that he did.

Soon enough, he wouldn't need to speak to her through a screen. He'd wake up to her beautiful face, resting next to him on her pillow. It would be a pleasure knowing she looked like an angel in the morning when she'd fucked him like a demon the night before.

WILLOW: Slow down lol

MILO: I've got a better idea. How about we hang out tonight?

He couldn't stop himself. He needed to see
her again, face to face, not just through 4K cameras
in her bedroom or the panes of her window. No, Milo
longed for her, flesh and blood, as if she were his form
of communion. He would worship her every night,
kneeling at the altar between her thighs. Religion had
never held any sway over him, but he knew that he'd
find God with his cock inside of her.

The seconds crawled by, each one heavier
than the last, and still, no message came. He began to
worry that he had pushed her too far this time.

And then, his phone lit up.

WILLOW: I'm game
WILLOW: Details?

Milo grinned. This was the perfect moment
to reveal himself completely, if she played her part. It
all depended on how deeply the connection between
them could sway her this early in the game.

MILO: How about a picnic? I hate the city tbh.
Would love to get out for a bit.

WILLOW: Sounds like fun

MILO: Should I pick you up?

WILLOW: Yeah that's fine i'll send my address later

MILO: Sounds good

With a sigh, he set his phone down and ran a hand through his dark hair. It had grown out a bit since he left the service, and he'd let some facial hair grow in as well. His shadow of a beard was neatly trimmed, but it was still his quiet defiance—a subtle middle finger to the military.

But he wasn't going to dwell on it. He never wanted to think about it again, preferably.

He had better things to worry about, like the most important date of his life.

***

The dresser was neatly arranged with only the essentials. Milo preferred to keep things simple and efficient—his daily uniform consisted of jeans, a black t-shirt, and a black windbreaker. He decided to mix it up a little today, adding a ball cap to the ensemble.

He grabbed his car keys and left his bedroom. The hallway was strangely quiet, an unsettling stillness hanging over him. He had finally adjusted to the level of noise that came with living in a house full of bachelors—no matter how big the place, there was always a ruckus somewhere.

Milo flew down the stairs, the anticipation of

the hunt rising within him, a rush of energy building. The other wolves were nowhere in sight, but their scent lingered, faint traces of their presence. They had likely gone for a run, shifting into their wolf form. He'd need to do that soon, too.

Their absence almost irritated him. There was a plan in place, and if they didn't show up on time, he would blow a fuse.

He practically ripped the front door off the hinges in his rush to get outside, eager to reach the waiting SUV. It was his preferred vehicle for a reason—it was spacious, practical, and far easier to disappear people in when the need arose.

Slipping into the seat, he started the engine and began his drive. Budding trees lining the way and the vibrant greenery burgeoning along the road. Spring was heavy in the air. It wasn't his favorite season—too much mud for that—but he couldn't deny the thrill of watching life awaken in the world once again.

The drive felt longer than it should have, but no matter the distance, it would always stretch like an eternity when he was racing toward her. He cranked up the volume when Rammstein came on, tapping the steering wheel in time with the pounding rhythm, the heavy metal syncing with the rapid thud of his heart. Milo couldn't remember the last time he had felt this nervous about meeting up with someone.

The growing tension in his chest soured the

mood, and he hit the button on the wheel, skipping through songs until he found something more upbeat, something he could scream along to and release the tension.

He settled on "Happy Together" by The Turtles. By the time he was pulling off the exit ramp, his pulse was racing again, a nervous excitement thrumming beneath his skin.

Soon, he reminded himself, forcing the wolf inside to calm, its restless claws dragging against the confines of his control.

He sped through the drive, weaving through traffic where necessary. She lived outside the city limits, too, but on the opposite side of the metropolis. That meant he was around an hour's drive away from her, which was entirely too far. But it wouldn't be for long. Soon, she'd take her rightful place by his side.

Finally, Milo pulled up to the condo. She'd sent him her address like she'd promised. He just hadn't needed it. Milo forced himself to steady his breathing, gripping the steering wheel so tightly that his knuckles went white. Just as he parked, his eyes caught sight of her stepping out of the door. He also saw her sister, standing in the kitchen window and watching them disapprovingly.

Before she could even make it down the front steps, Milo was already out of the car so he could open her door. No bitch of his would ever be expected to open her own door. When she accepted their bond, she would be royalty in his world. It was time she was treated like it.

Willow's soft smile hit him like somebody had thrown a fist into his gut. Despite the sweetness of her slightly lifted lips, he could sense the fear and anxiety coiling beneath the surface. It made his chest tighten. He wanted so badly for her to feel the same joy he did.

But it also stirred the wolf inside him, primed for the chase if she decided to run.

"Hey, you," he said, offering a grin that didn't quite reach his eyes. "Ready to see the most beautiful place ever?"

LORE

Werewolves need to shift into their lupine form regularly. Failure to do so can cause everything from mood changes to outright psychosis.

WILLOW

CHAPTER SEVEN

"Yeah, I'd like that," she said, her lips curling into a careful little smile again. She'd listened to Poppy fretting fiercely before she left—well-deserved, to be fair. Willow still wasn't convinced this was a good idea. In fact, she was fairly certain it wasn't. That was why she'd slipped a can of mace into her bag... and a Taser.

She didn't really know how to use them, aside from the panicked crash course she'd gotten from her sister before it was time to leave. She was pretty sure she wasn't even legally allowed to carry either.

Willow climbed into the SUV, settling into the plush seat. She was grateful she'd opted for athletic leggings and a sweater. Even so, he probably got a solid view of her ass as she climbed up. Her cheeks heated as she shifted in her seat, heat building as she pictured him eyeing her hungrily.

As the door closed beside her, Willow folded her hands in her lap, her feet dangling just above the floorboard. She started swinging them out of habit.

She'd noticed was how big Milo was. He had to be at least a foot taller than her, built like somebody who knew how to fight. It was an intoxicating mix of desire and danger—but if their little trip went sideways?

She was well and truly *fucked*.

But now wasn't the time to think about that, because they were backing out of the driveway.

"So, what do you listen to?"

She glanced over at him, chewing her lip.

"Basically everything," she replied. "You?"

"I'm a big rock guy."

"How do you feel about metal?"

"Pretty damn good."

"Lamb of God?"

"Oh, hell yeah."

Milo gave a command to the hands-free system, calling for one of the band's songs. The growling vocals filled the space, and Willow found herself swinging her feet again, caught off guard by how his eyes crinkled at the corners in the fading light. The way the sunbeams hit his skin made it glow golden and warm, nearly holy. She couldn't help staring.

And then it hit her.

They were going hiking, and the sun was going down. Which meant they'd be out there after dark. A pit opened in her chest, heavy and cavernous, and her head was ringing clear like a warning bell. She pulled out her phone to check that location tracking was still on. That was part of the deal with Poppy. She was to keep it on at all times.

"Reception's probably gonna get spotty as we head out," Milo said casually, eyes still on the road. "It's better at the top, though. That's where we're headed."

Her eyes snapped to him. If he meant to finish the hike, they'd be seeing the trail by moonlight.

"Isn't it going to be pretty late by then?" she asked, her voice tighter than she wanted it to be. Her hands were starting to tremble in her lap.

"Yeah," he said. "But you have to see it at night, under the glow of the full moon. It's worth it. If we run into trouble getting down, I'll carry you."

He said it so easily, like hauling her through the dark wilderness on his back wouldn't even register as a challenge. It terrified and thrilled her, a twisted combination of emotion that left her shifting, thighs squeezing.

"What? A fan of the idea?" Milo was laughing now, voice low and rich, one hand steady on the wheel while the other rested on the center console between them. She said nothing, blushing deeply instead.

The music had faded into meaningless background noise, a soft blur against the roar of her pulse. Willow's eyes kept drifting to Milo's forearms— tanned, strong, and out in the open since he had rolled up the sleeves of his black jacket. She felt the urge to run her fingers along his exposed skin.

He turned his palm up, glancing at her again with a half-smile that made her stomach flutter dangerously. "Do you want to hold hands?"

She inhaled sharply, caught between panic and delight. Anxiety and elation. But yes, God, yes, she did. Her trembling fingers reached for his, sliding over his palm. Their hands fit together so perfectly that it made her chest ache. His warmth bled into her skin like a soothing balm, and Willow softened to the touch.

She slouched back into her seat, eyes fixed straight ahead, and let herself feel whatever was flowing through her.

The weight of his hand in hers.

And the quiet hum of the car.

And the faint scream of the stereo.

The silence stretched between them like a promise. For the first time in what felt like forever, Willow believed she could breathe easily, her vitality revived by whatever spell he had cast.

She was enchanted. Utterly and hopelessly. *Bewitched? Bewizarded?*

She softly laughed at how stupid the entire thing made her feel.

"What?" Milo asked, glancing over, his thumb slowly tracing circles across the top of her hand. The casually intimate motion made her breath hitch.

"Oh, nothing. I was just thinking."

"About?"

"No, don't worry, it's nothing."

"Fine, then," he said, feigning offense with a grin. "Keep your secrets. I don't want them anyway."

"Good," she shot back with an edge hovering between sass and suggestion. "Because I'm not telling you anything."

His smile faltered, just slightly, his jaw tightening. The flicker of hunger in his eyes didn't scare her.

It turned her on.

"I think you'll find," he murmured, lower, almost amused, "a man with my background knows how to get information out of people, Willow."

He tapped the blinker, checked over his shoulder, and merged onto the off-ramp, stealing a glance at her while he did so. It was a smooth motion, and she realized she hadn't felt unsafe once during the drive so far. Not from his driving, at least.

"Oh?" she asked, her tone light and curious. "And what kind of background is that?"

"Ex-military, for starters."

She thought about it for a minute. "I could have guessed that. It makes sense."

And it did. Everything about him screamed discipline and danger, from the build to the posture to the sharp, precise way he moved. He reminded Willow of her grandfather, who had once spoken of his service and never again after.

Milo didn't offer anything else. She almost asked, but then thought better of it. Some answers came at a cost, and some doors stayed shut for a reason. She could feel the weight of whatever was locked behind his silence, and she wasn't ignorant enough to rattle the knob. Instead, Willow let the quiet settle over them like a downy blanket, choosing to focus on the warmth of his hand, the welcome comfort it brought. It was likely safer that way, for both of them.

***

The rest of the drive passed in a mutual stillness, a fleeting moment of peace that felt foreign and fragile. Their hands remained locked together. Willow could feel her palm slick with sweat by now from the heat of their contact, but she didn't care. Somehow, she knew he wouldn't mind, either.

Eventually, the SUV turned off the main road and onto a dirt path that looked mostly forgotten, swallowed by overgrowth even when the winter was just now fading into spring. The trail was rough, littered with branches, but the vehicle navigated with ease.

"You okay?"

Her eyes flicked to Milo as he gave her hand a reassuring squeeze. She realized she'd been holding him in a death grip. The further they drove into the dense, encroaching dark, the more the dread built in her stomach, like an approaching stormhead.

When the SUV finally rolled to a stop and he killed the engine, Willow glanced out her window to see a narrow opening carved into the trees beside her, a path winding into the dense forest. Her stomach twisted. It wasn't fear that she was walking into an untimely death, but something almost more daunting—doubt.

Not about him.

About *herself*.

"Ready?" Milo asked, his voice low as he lifted their still-clasped hands and pressed a kiss to her knuckles.

The intimate gesture ignited her entire body. Willow could have thrown herself over the console and ripped his shirt open. Something primal and starved inside her howled for him. The flicker of arousal blew to a roar that engulfed her lower belly, and her breath hitched, shallow and fast.

"Yes," she whispered.

They let go of each other with a brief reluctance, the absence of his touch immediately noticeable. Each climbed out of their side of the SUV, Willow stepping carefully onto the bar before lowering herself to the ground. Her body had always been unreliable, a little too fragile in places where she should have been stable. She treated herself gently, knowing too well how one wrong step would echo into the next day.

She stared at the trail ahead, uneven and dark, the forest blocking out all traces of light. This was her last chance to walk away from this madness. She could still say no.

But she didn't want to. Even if she couldn't explain it, even if Poppy's voice screamed that it was reckless, she trusted Milo.

Trusted the steady way he looked at her like

she was precious to him.

Trusted the way his fingers had curled around hers like a vow.

Trusted the way that, even now, he was gentle in his advances.

Milo brought a heavy backpack from the backseat and came to her side, his hand finding the small of her back like it had always belonged there.

And so she moved forward.

LORE

Mate bonds are instinctive on both
ends, and nearly impossible to
resist. It takes incredible strength of
spirit to hold it at bay.

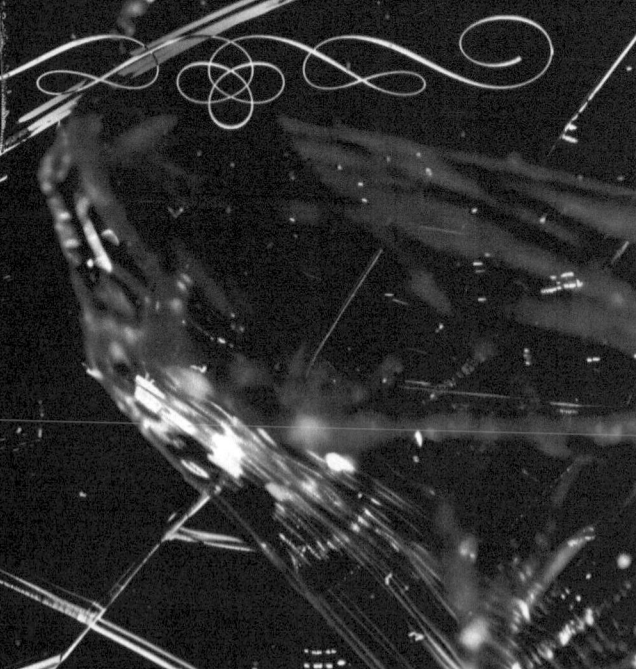

MILO

CHAPTER EIGHT

Willow was playing her part beautifully, slipping into place, unknowingly aligning herself with his plans. Everything was unfolding exactly as he had envisioned. If he could seal the bond tonight, she'd be his in every way that mattered. It all hinged on how she handled the confession.

Milo had never brought a human this close before. Very few were ever trusted with the knowledge that wolves like him walked their streets, passing unnoticed in plain sight.

It wasn't just a secret. It was *sacred*.

Human mates were practically unheard of, though he'd heard stories from other packs, each ending depending on how the human half had received the news.

It was the timing that made things difficult, alongside his fierce need to have her by his side as quickly as possible. The bond could only be sealed beneath the full moon, when the air was thick with magic and their blood would run hot with instinct.

He also had to knot her, which wasn't something you could do without warning.

Milo had one shot a month, and the clock was ticking. The anticipation clawed at his organs. He felt like he was bleeding internally. He couldn't wait to bury his teeth in the soft, gentle curve of her neck, to mark her with something permanent and primal. To make her his—irrevocably, eternally.

Even with his reservations, Milo had no doubt

she would comply. Willow was already halfway there, drawn to him in the way only fate could orchestrate. All he needed was the moon to reach her zenith, Willow's acceptance, and then her sweet surrender. If his gut was right, she'd surrender her aching cunt to him without hesitation, take his knot like she was made for it, and let him ravage her.

Milo had taken the lead, subtly shifting their positions before stepping onto the trail ahead of her. He moved with effortless confidence, glancing back every so often to offer his hand, steadying her as she climbed over moss-slicked logs and the crumbling remains of forgotten stone walls. Each time she stumbled, he was there, promising that they had almost reached their final destination.

He could smell Arlo nearby, waiting, poised to move when Milo was ready. Titan and Lachlan would be in position, too, though their scent hadn't reached him; they were upwind. The air had cooled off, and night had settled over the shadowy landscape. The moon cast silver beams through the thinning trees, blanketing the earth around them in an ethereal glow.

At this point, nothing else mattered but instinct, blood, and breath. The urge to shift thrummed in his bones, wild and unrelenting.

And still, he held the beast back.

The weight of the backpack pressed against Milo's back, but he barely noticed it. Even loaded down with everything he'd packed to win her over, it was nothing against the strength of a wolf. Supernatural power had its perks.

The trail finally spilled them into a clearing, light slicing through the trees like a blade. A narrow waterfall cascaded over a jagged rock face, feeding into a slow-moving river that curved away from them, back into the woods. In the height of summer, this place was breathtaking—lush, blooming, and beautiful. But now, under the cold gaze of the full moon, it looked stripped of life, hollow and pale with a milky glaze.

It didn't feel like a secret paradise.

It felt like a burial ground.

Milo knew he'd misstepped the moment he felt her body go tense behind him. The moon made everything sharper—her emotions echoed around him, each flicker of doubt or fear making him wince.

"Hey," he said, glancing over his shoulder, "I know it looks a little desolate. I didn't think about the time of year. Normally, this place is stunning."

Willow let out a nervous laugh, brittle and tight. Still, she followed. Every step was hesitant, but she came with him all the same.

That willingness was what mattered.

When they were halfway to the waterfall, Milo swung the backpack off his shoulders and crouched beside it. He could feel her eyes on him, cautious, watching every move like he might pull out instruments of torture instead of the promised picnic.

"What?" he said, smiling as he unzipped the bag. "You don't trust me?" His voice was light, teasing, laced with charm. But he was watching her closely. He needed to know the answer.

She didn't respond, and he didn't push. After all, the trust was almost implicit at this point. He didn't require confirmation. Instead, he reached into the bag and pulled out the contents. First, a dark bottle of cherry wine, which he set carefully on the ground, then a folded blanket. He shook the blanket across the cool earth, then slipped off his shoes before stepping onto it.

Willow hesitated for a moment, then mirrored him, socked feet firmly on the fabric, moving like she was trapped somewhere between dream and instinct.

When she sank down onto the blanket beside him, legs stretched out in front of her and arms braced behind her, Milo inhaled deeply, feigning a sigh. Really, he was greedily drinking in her scent. The heady, intoxicating aroma of her arousal clung to the air, thick and sweet, turning his blood molten.

He knew her core was swollen with want by now, her body leading her to where she needed to be even if her mind still hadn't caught up.

He reached for the bottle, pouring them both glasses of wine. Willow took hers without hesitation, downing a long sip. Milo watched with sharp eyes. He reached out, his fingers brushing against her wrist— casual, but electric.

"Hey," he murmured, voice low and edged with disapproval. "Slow down, tiger. It's not going anywhere."

She looked at him with bedroom eyes, hiding behind her thick lashes. Then, with the ghost of a smirk, she lifted the glass again and tilted her head back, draining the rest in defiance of him.

The urge to drag her over his knee for disobedience was almost too much to resist. But he didn't.

Instead, his jaw flexed, the tension in his body barely restrained. He leaned in just enough for his voice to drop like velvet and steel.

"I'd behave myself if I were you, Willow. *Good* girls get nice things."

She met his gaze, steady and intense. "And what do bad girls get?"

Milo didn't answer.

He just let a slow, wicked grin barely split his lips, the tips of his elongated canines resting against the top of his bottom lip. She didn't seem to notice them, instead gazing into his eyes.

"Are you hungry?" Milo asked, his touch feather-light as his fingers grazed her unfortunately clothed arm. Willow gave a slow nod. He reached into the backpack and pulled out an assortment of snacks—some were his favorites, others were the ones he'd seen her eat late at night through the cameras in her room.

"Oh, I love these!" she gasped, lighting up as he handed over a small charcuterie-style snack pack. The neatly divided sections held cheese, dried cranberries, nuts, and chunks of meat. She peeled the packaging with practiced ease, plucking one of each and popping the medley into her mouth.

Milo's pulse jumped.

There was something intimate about watching her enjoy something so simple. Every little thing she did made him feel reverent, like she was art being slowly unveiled.

Milo checked his watch.

22:30.

Right on schedule.

Arlo would be closing in any second. Milo shifted his gaze to Willow, who was blissfully unaware of the world about to crack open at her feet.

He reached out, fingers curling gently around her shoulder. "Do you trust me, Willow?" he asked, serious in a way that sliced through her calm.

Willow's head snapped toward him, eyes wide, body trembling under his touch. "I... I think so," she whispered, the stammer revealing her uncertainty. Milo's thumb traced slow, soothing circles against her shoulder as something massive stirred just beyond the clearing.

Arlo emerged out of the dark, his wolf form silent and hulking, black with streaks of gray around his muzzle and eyes. He looked like death incarnate, and he was staring straight at Willow.

"Don't freak out, baby," Milo murmured, his hand tightening slightly. "Just look behind you."

Willow turned, inch by inch, likely unsure of what she'd find at nearly midnight in the woods.

And once she saw it, she screamed.

WILLOW

CHAPTER NINE

Willow shrieked, falling back in a frenzied scramble to put distance between herself and the animal. It looked like a wolf—except she'd never seen a wolf that big, even in a documentary or at a zoo. It was massive.

She was also pretty damn sure wildlife wasn't supposed to be this bold. Or this close.

Unless it was starving.

Or rabid.

Each horrifying thought sent fresh waves of panic radiating through her chest. They rattled in her ribcage until her diaphragm hurt with her terror. Willow's breaths came sharp and shallow, clouds of vapor curling in the frigid air as she fought off her desire to run. She was fairly certain running was the wrong option.

She squeezed her eyes shut, heart pounding, praying that when she opened them again, it would all be different.

Arms wrapped around her. Strong. Steady. Smelling like peppermint and vanilla. Milo pulled her close, and the moment his warmth pressed against her, the world steadied. In the middle of her chaos, his gravity pulled her slowly down until her feet could rest on solid ground.

"It's okay, Willow. It's just Arlo."

"It has a *name*?" she whispered, high and frantic.

"*He* is actually my best friend."

She'd always heard dogs were man's best friend, and sure, that might track for a guy like Milo. But knowing that did absolutely nothing to calm the fear unfurling inside her chest.

Willow clung to him like he was her lifeline, fingers digging into his forearms with a bruising grip. If it weren't for his jacket, she would be scared of cutting into his skin. Somewhere in the back of her mind, she knew she had to be hurting him.

He gave her a firm squeeze and then let go completely.

She whimpered, instinctively reaching for him again, but Milo was already up, turning away from her and calling to the animal like it wasn't the stuff of nightmares. Her stomach dropped. The giant creature ambled toward them, each heavy pawfall sounding through the clearing with a thump, thump, thump. Willow swore the ground itself recoiled beneath it.

Best friend? she thought to herself with a growing dread. *Maybe if you're the reigning lord of hell.*

"Arlo, roll over for us," Milo said, his voice laced with amusement. It was strange how light he sounded in the presence of a creature that could easily tear them apart, but that ridiculous request made her let out a shaky laugh of her own. And when the massive beast obeyed, getting down and rolling onto its back with a grunt, she felt herself smiling nervously.

The whole thing was absurd.

Then his tone shifted, warmth turning to hesitance. "There's something I haven't told you, Willow," he said quietly. "I'm sorry I haven't been completely honest. But I think you'll understand why."

Before she could ask, two more wolves stepped from the shadows—one with a striking golden coat, the other a bold, burnished red. For a split second, she marveled at their beauty. They exuded the quiet danger of apex predators, their movements elegant and menacing all at once.

She felt a pang when he said, "These aren't wolves, Willow. They're my family."

That word, family, struck a chord. She knew the aching hollowness of losing everyone you loved. For a second, the fear relaxed into something softer.

"Do you have any living relatives?" she asked, her voice quiet, understanding his need to cling to these animals in the face of having nobody else.

"No, Willow," Milo said, looking her dead in the eye. "These are my living relatives. They're not normal wolves."

The smile she'd been wearing went lopsided. She searched his face for some trace of a joke, something that would indicate a thread of sanity still within him, but there was nothing. Just sincerity, raw and unnerving. Her gaze flicked to the wolves, lined up like soldiers, watching her with eerie stillness.

"Maybe it's better if we show you," Milo murmured.

The black one, the largest, began to shimmer. A faint, supernatural glow radiated around him, like the moon itself had shone a spotlight. Her eyes widened as its bones bent and stretched, its spine elongating, its frame morphing. In a few seconds, a fully clothed man stood where the wolf had been.

And for the second time that night, Willow screamed.

She felt the world tilt, her vision narrowing to a pinpoint as the shock overrode everything else in her system. A thick wave of nausea rolled through her—

And then she doubled over and puked onto the blanket beneath her feet. Milo was at her side in an instant, hand firm and comforting on her back, murmuring to her as she gagged and spat, tears stinging her eyes.

There was no way this was real, that any of this was happening.

Her entire body trembled, muscles locking up in the grip of surging adrenaline. Her ears rang, muffling the soothing nonsense Milo tried to feed her. It didn't matter—he was the one who had shattered her world in the first place. Whatever the hell this was, he was the cause. Now nothing would ever be the same again.

"Please, Milo," she whispered hoarsely, turning to him with wide, panicked eyes. "I won't tell anyone. I swear. Just let me go, and we'll pretend like none of this ever happened, okay? I probably... I probably won't even remember in the morning."

Even as the words left her mouth, she knew how pathetic they sounded. She was grasping for straws in a situation that had spun wildly out of control. Willow risked a glance at the man—the wolf—still standing where he'd shifted. His arms were crossed now, posture patient and unbothered. He looked oddly regal in a dark sweater, jeans, and polished oxfords, like he'd stepped out of a country club.

"I told you she'd take it poorly if you did it like this."

The gruff voice cut through the silence—Mr. Country Club. It snapped her back into the moment, and with horrifying clarity, Willow realized this had been planned ahead of time. Not spontaneous. Planned.

But why?

Why *her*?

What kind of lunatic looked at a girl he'd just met and decided that he would reveal that monsters were real and that they wanted to date her?

"She's fine, Arlo. Everything is fine. Right, Willow?" Milo's voice, which had been steady and sure just seconds ago, faltered on her name. It sounded more like a plea than an inquiry, and that alone made her want to scream again. Because no, she was not fine. Nothing about this was fine. It was cosmically, irreparably not fine.

"I think I want to go home," she whispered. Her voice didn't feel like it belonged to her. Everything had slowed down—the sounds, the air, even the way the soft moonlight filtered through the trees swaying all around them—as if the world was sinking underwater, and she was just watching it all happen from the shoreline.

The uncomfortable detachment settled in, constricting her like a serpent coiling tight. But Willow wasn't in her body anymore. She was somewhere else, floating, watching herself freeze up and shut down. Dissociation crept in like an old friend.

"Willow, it's okay. This was always meant to be, sweetheart—"

"Don't fucking call me that," she snapped, voice cracking as she stumbled backward. It felt wrong coming from his mouth.

"Willow, don't run—"

"Don't fucking— I just— I need to go, okay? I have to go."

Then she turned. Bolted. Straight for the treeline like a desperate deer, blind panic guiding her flailing limbs. Behind her, Willow heard a desperate shout. A glance over her shoulder rocked her to her core. The blonde wolf was tearing after her, eating up the terrain between them.

She screamed, desperate and feral. Just as Willow crashed into the forest, the world exploded behind her—fur, fangs, and fury. The red wolf had tackled the blonde, snarling and snapping, pinning him to the ground.

And Milo?

He was running.

Straight for her.

Willow turned and ran again, lungs burning, legs twitching, unprotected feet screaming in pain. She pushed even harder, even with branches biting at her skin as she went, scratching her cheeks and hands. She just knew she had to keep moving away from them. From him. From this nightmare she had been lured so easily into.

Whatever they wanted from her, it couldn't be good.

MILO

CHAPTER TEN

Everything had spiraled out of his control.

This wasn't how it was supposed to happen. Willow was supposed to look at him with trust and understanding in her eyes, not tear-streaked panic as she fled through the forest like prey.

Now he was chasing the woman he was fated to love, crashing through the underbrush as the animal inside him snarled for release.

Milo's breath came in ragged bursts, eyes flashing gold as he struggled to keep himself contained. He was barely holding on to the human. Part of him wanted to wrap her in his arms, soothe the terror from her until she melted into his chest.

But the other?

The other wanted to drag her down into the dirt, tear the fabric from her trembling body, and bury himself inside that dripping heat of hers until the bond sealed and nothing else mattered.

He barely noticed the branches lashing at his face—he was far too focused on the rhythm of Willow's footsteps, the way her scent flooded the air around him, fearful and delicious. He kept his distance, not too far, not too close. Just enough to eventually drive her to exhaustion. It was a hunting tradition passed down since the beginning of time. She *would* tire eventually.

And when she did, that's when he'd have his chance to talk with her. Make her see reason.

Maybe it was easier for him to swallow the

impossible. Being what he was had taught him that reality was elastic; the rules most humans lived by were more like guidelines. Add a stint in the most elite units in the world on top of that, and Milo had learned long ago how to survive the surreal.

It was just under half a mile before she started to slow. Her pace faltered, steps uneven as she tripped over twisted roots and slick leaves. He adjusted his speed, careful not to spook her by closing the distance too quickly.

"Willow," he called out gently, halting as she crumpled, hands braced on her knees, lungs dragging wheezing lungfuls into her heaving chest. "Let's talk, please."

"Get—get away from… me," she gasped, each word strained and shrill with panic.

"I can't do that," he said quietly, the words gentle but firm. "You saw what you saw. There's no going back now."

"Don't say my fucking name," she snapped, bent over the forest floor, hands fisted in the damp leaves. Milo stepped closer, brushing a low-hanging branch aside. She didn't move away from him, but he felt the tension ripple through her like a live wire. Their connection was at its strongest.

Above them, the moon had crowned the sky, full and blinding in her brilliance. He could feel the power only a wolf knew surging through him, panting just beneath his skin. He didn't need a mirror to know what nightmare she was witnessing. His eyes would be glowing now, molten gold in the dark. Milo's frame would loom too large, jaw clenched tight in what could be misconstrued as anger.

Even by daylight, he was something to fear due to his size and presence. God only knew what he looked like bathed in shadows at his primal peak.

"What the fuck are you?" Willow whispered, eyes wide and locked on him, caught between awe and terror. Milo's mouth went dry at the backlit line of her neck—bare, exposed, vulnerable. Her fear was vivid and tangible. And, fuck, it was intoxicating.

"I'm guessing you've heard of werewolves," he said, trying to ignore the scent of her core permeating the air.

She nodded, slow and mechanical, like her brain was still processing, trying to piece together reality from the nonsense he kept piling on. Milo gave her a moment to breathe before he continued, words deliberate and careful.

"That's the human word for us. We just call ourselves wolves. Same concept, minus the campfire horror story bullshit. Well—" he exhaled and dragged a hand through his hair, control hanging on by a thread "—some of it, anyway." This wasn't how he meant for it to go. Not even close.

Milo had heard the horror stories, humans who unraveled the second they realized monsters were real. It shattered their worldview, split their minds wide open. If werewolves existed, what else might be lurking in the dark? It was one thing to observe them in books and movies. It was quite another to stare one down in the flesh. In the real world, people didn't respond with curiosity or fascination; they responded with panic and fear.

But Milo wasn't giving her the luxury of denial. She belonged to him, fated by a force far older and wiser than either of them could comprehend. In time, she'd understand. In time, she'd thank him. Until then, he'd do what was necessary to protect her and to protect the pack.

"Willow, we need to go. It's late, and Poppy's probably losing it." He hoped the mention of her sister would snap her out of it.

"Keep my sister's name out of your fucking mouth. You stay away from her."

Milo exhaled through his nose, jaw flexing. This wasn't like her. She wasn't meant to be this stubborn, this contrary. He knew she was overwhelmed, but this was more than he'd expected. He didn't want to force her home with him. *God*, he really didn't. But the longer she resisted, the more it felt inevitable. He could feel the wolf inside him pacing, preparing.

"Alright, look," he said, voice low and strained. "I'm trying to be the good guy here, Willow. I really am. But you've got to understand—I didn't think it would go like this. I didn't think you would react like this."

"Didn't think—" she snapped, and then wheezed out a laugh that sounded more like a sob, hollow and bitter. "You didn't think I'd be terrified? What did you expect, Milo? For me to thank you?"

She straightened again, chest heaving. "My life was good, Milo. And now I can't go back to it, can I? That's what you're about to tell me, right?"

He let her words hang in the air like a smokescreen between them—acrid, distancing. He didn't interrupt. He let her rage fill the space between until all that was left was silence and the hatred simmering beneath it.

Was that it?

Did she hate him?

The thought pierced like a blade between the ribs, tilted up for the kill. Milo froze. The concept that she might hate him—that the woman he ached for, body and soul, would choose revulsion over fate— was enough to make his blood run cold. He hadn't prepared for this possibility. He'd accounted for fear, shock, even denial... but not outright rejection. Not this bone-deep loathing.

Funny, how the man who predicted enemy movements with the precision of an apex predator had failed to read the one person who mattered most. He laughed bitterly.

"You feel it too, Willow. I know you do," he said, firm and relentless as he moved a few steps closer. "The bond between us—it's real. You don't understand it yet, but you will."

She didn't move. Her eyes were wide and glassy, fixed somewhere past him. Shock had her in a chokehold, and Milo knew he was pushing the limits of what her mind could handle. Still, time was slipping by. They needed to get back to the manor. Willow's new life had already begun, and he intended to help her ease into it…

Even if she came kicking and screaming.

He smelled Arlo before he saw him—earth, pine, and the faint sting of antiseptic. His presence confirmed what Milo already suspected—Titan had been handled. He'd face the consequences soon enough. Threatening an alpha's mate—his mate— was a line no wolf should ever cross, regardless of circumstance. Titan had fucked up royally. There would be blood for that.

With a near-imperceptible nod, Milo gave his consent.

Willow looked puzzled at the movement. She might've asked what it meant, but Arlo was already behind her, one hand sealing her mouth, the other plunging in the needle with a practiced efficiency.

Her body gave two small jerks, then folded in on itself.

Arlo caught her, easing her to the forest floor as if she were made of a material all too breakable. Milo watched, his heart seizing with regret as he stepped closer.

"Road's about a klick east," he said, voice cutting through the quiet. "I'll carry her. Let Lachlan and Titan sort their shit out. I'm done babysitting."

Milo knelt beside Willow's still form, brushing her hair from her face with shaking fingers. She was exquisite like this, silent, his to protect. Soon, she'd be his completely.

He scooped her into his arms and turned toward the trees, Arlo at his side. The woods swallowed them as they made their way to the car.

WILLOW

CHAPTER ELEVEN

Willow woke like she was rising from deep water—slow, heavy, limbs like liquid lead. It wasn't pain she felt. It was more like the blood in her muscles had been replaced with a substance both sluggish and uncooperative. She blinked against the weight of her eyelids, lashes fluttering as the world came into focus by maddeningly slow degrees.

Her fingers twitched. Then curled. Uncurled. *Good.* At least she could move.

And then, she heard it.

Him.

"Willow, baby… can you hear me?"

The words rippled through her, like a disturbance across a pond. They were golden and honeyed, wrapping around her like a promise that things would be alright. Her lips tugged upward as if on their own. The sensations were foreign but somehow comforting. Just hearing him was like being kissed by sunlight in the height of spring, a gentle reminder that the cold was coming to an end. The warmth that bloomed in her chest made her want to weep with elation.

"She's still high as hell, Milo."

"No shit, Titan."

"He's trying to help, Milo."

"Yeah? He can help himself to shutting the fuck up, Arlo."

A laugh burst from her chest, light and breathy. It tumbled from her lips, the sound unfiltered and free. When her eyes finally peeled open, the first thing she saw was him—Milo, crouched beside her.

She smiled.

And then she remembered.

Willow's face crumpled, the fragile threads holding her together snapping. Her heart plummeted, free-falling past her ribs, out of her back, and straight through the earth beneath her. Panic clawed like a wild animal up her throat, and her breathing turned jagged.

When Milo reached for her, she flinched, arms shooting out in a frantic attempt to shove him away. Her eyes brimmed with tears, which spilled over hotly as she fought against his touch—and against herself. Because despite everything, despite the fear of what he was capable of doing, all she wanted was to collapse into him.

To be held.

To be safe.

To be *his*.

The thought made bile rise in her throat, coating her mouth with an acrid tang.

"Willow, it's okay, my love," Milo murmured, his voice soft, hands open like he was praying for her forgiveness, or begging for her surrender.

"Stay… stay the f-fuck away from me," she slurred, whatever drug they gave her still tangling up her tongue. It was also fogging her mind, but not enough to forget who he was.

Or more importantly, what he was.

Her first thought—ridiculously, irrationally—was, Where's my bag? Then, regret hit like a hammer. The Taser. The mace. She hadn't even tried to use them. Not that she thought that they would've made a difference against giant wolf monsters masquerading as men, but still. Maybe it could've bought her a few more seconds. Now, she'd never know.

"Poppy. Oh my God. Poppy," she gasped, the name tumbling out in a panicked exhale as she jolted upright.

The world immediately splintered into a kaleidoscope of pain and shooting stars. Hands caught her, bringing her back to balance. One pressed firmly between her shoulder blades, the other wrapped gently around her arm.

"Easy, baby. Lay back. You need to rest. Your sister's safe. She knows where you are."

"Get off," Willow whimpered, the fight in her voice weakened, but still there. She gave a feeble shake of her head, heart splintering all over again. She didn't understand why it hurt so much. There had been little to nothing between them—just fleeting touches, a handful of flirtatious texts, and that unspoken pull that had tethered them from the start.

It shouldn't have felt like betrayal.

But it did.

"I trusted you, and you lied to me," she breathed, her voice thin and breaking, head bowed as tears slipped down and dripped silently off the bridge of her nose.

"I didn't lie, Willow," Milo said softly, eyes tracking every tremble of her body. "I just didn't tell you everything."

"Same fucking thing," she snapped, her words raw with pain.

Willow's thoughts were clearing, but her body remained weighed down by exhaustion. Despite herself, she relaxed against him, her temple pressing to his chest, as if her body hadn't been able to keep pace with her mind's rage.

"There you go, baby," he whispered, easing her down with careful hands, voice warm and slow like a lullaby, "Just rest."

As his hand started to slip away from hers, she reached out for him, fingertips grazing his skin.

"Don't go," she murmured, already sinking into unconsciousness.

And then she was gone—drifting in the dark, wrapped in the arms of the man who had shattered what she knew of reality.

***

The next time Willow woke, it was to the steady thrum of a heartbeat. She was curled against Milo, tucked into the curvature of his body like she had always belonged there. Not quite face-to-face—he was too tall for that—but close enough to hear his soft, rhythmic breathing.

I hate you, she reminded herself bitterly, even as her fingers decided to disobey, rising to trace the edge of his jaw. His was the kind of jawline artists obsessed over—structured, expressive, the type you sketched in charcoal and then blurred at the edges with the tips of your fingers. Under his thick stubble, she could see the lines beneath, sharp and devastating.

The moment her fingertips made contact, Milo's eyes shot open. At first, there was confusion... then recognition, and then a quiet, soul-deep smile that made her chest ache. His gaze locked with hers, and everything else fell away. Something inside her stirred, reckless and wanting. She needed to lean in and kiss him—to find out what he tasted like.

"Good morning," he murmured, leaning in to nuzzle the crown of her head, his breath warm against her hair.

Willow froze. Her eyes shut tight, as if she could will away the rush of heat blooming low in her belly. Something hard was pressing into her thigh, and just the thought of his cock had her clenching around what was inside her—regrettably, nothing.

"That's not my dick. It's my gun."

"Your fucking what?"

"Ex-military, baby," he said, like that explained everything.

She didn't have the energy to ask why a

werewolf would even need a gun. Instead, she slowly peeled herself away from him, like prying herself off of something sticky, until she'd made it to the other side of the bed. Once there, she sat up, trying to gather herself. Trying not to think about how much her body missed him already.

"Are you hungry?"

Willow glanced back at Milo, who was still curled lazily on his side, looking entirely too comfortable for someone who had just kidnapped her. She didn't answer. Instead, she slipped off the bed, her bare feet sinking into a plush carpet.

She turned slowly, taking in her surroundings with the caution of someone waking up in a stranger's skin. The room was large. Luxuriously so. A grand fireplace dominated the wall across from the bed, and to her left, a wide bay window looked out over a landscape cloaked in darkness. It was beautiful in the way old ruins were, silent and unsettling.

What unsettled her more, though, was the absence of personal effects. No books, no art, no signs of the man who lived within these walls. It was sterile, a holding cell. Wrapping her arms around herself, Willow's eyes swept the space, her heart beating audibly as she began quietly cataloguing possible exits.

If Poppy thought Willow liked things minimal, she'd probably throw a fit after taking a gander at this stark, soulless place.

"My sister will be looking for me," she

announced, squaring her shoulders like she'd just cracked the code to fixing her situation.

Milo didn't even blink. "Your sister knows where you are," he said calmly, "and she knows better than to come looking."

"You don't know my sister," she shot back, chin lifting.

"No," he admitted, his voice like velvet laced with venom, "but I do know how to have footage fabricated, and I know exactly where to cut when I want to get to the heart of something. Or someone."

Her mouth clamped shut, breath catching in her throat. The chill that swept through her veins wasn't from the surroundings—it was the slow realization that she was likely in way over her head.

And she didn't know if, from here, she would sink or swim.

MILO

CHAPTER TWELVE

Milo yawned, stretching the stiffness from his limbs with all the lethargy of a lazy lion. He understood her worry—family ties were hard to sever—but damn, if it wasn't a hassle. If Willow didn't have a sister, everything would've fallen into place with so much less resistance.

Instead, he'd lost a whole man to the Poppy detail, assigning someone full-time to keep eyes on her while Willow acclimated. It wasn't permanent, just a temporary inconvenience until the bond was sealed. After that, the natural order would return.

The only issue was that Poppy could never be allowed to so much as glimpse the truth of what her sister's life would eventually become. She would have to be kept at an arm's distance from now on, and he knew that would prove challenging because of the bond between the sisters.

He watched her with the unblinking focus of a predator tracking prey. Except this wasn't prey. This was his mate, his destiny, and her silence was suffocating him. The storm swirling in her eyes told him everything he needed to know—she was pissed, and maybe rightfully so. But someday, she'd understand.

"Are you hungry?" he asked again, forcing a calm he didn't feel, his tone carefully pitched to be gentle, nonthreatening. Milo had captured and contained prisoners before. He wasn't new to keeping people in captivity. But never like this—never someone meant to rule beside him.

This was her queendom, whether she knew it yet or not. While he may have dragged her thrashing to the throne, he would never presume to command a queen in her own court.

If she didn't want to eat, he couldn't make her.

"No," she whimpered, voice cracking as she turned away from him. The sound of her crying tore through him. It was worse than any wound he'd taken in combat. It sounded so much like a symphony of suffering, and every note drove into him like shrapnel. Milo wanted to go to her, wanted to hold her. Comfort her. Love her.

"Why are you doing this to me?" she choked out, voice strangled and small. Her legs gave way as she pressed her shoulder against the wall and sank down, hands cradling her head. He stood there, helpless, watching the woman fated to be his fall apart because of his actions.

He crawled to the other side of the bed and dropped down into a crouch next to her. She didn't shift away or react. It wasn't acceptance, but it wasn't rejection either, and that was enough. Milo moved slowly, carefully sliding his arms around her and drawing her away from the cold wall, pressing her into the warmth of his chest.

To his surprise, she didn't resist. She collapsed into Milo like she'd been waiting for him to catch her. Her fists clutched his shirt, knuckles white with rage, her face buried in the crook of his neck as sobs racked her small frame.

"Willow," he murmured, voice hoarse, "I'm so sorry, baby…" The words felt thin, useless, such a small fraction of what she deserved to hear. But he held her tighter, kissed the top of her head, and let her fall apart in his arms.

"I fucking hate you," she screamed into his shoulder, raw and broken. "I hate you so fucking much."

But she didn't let go.

That was proof that somewhere beneath all that fury, she still felt it, too. And if she still felt it…

He still had a chance.

When her sobs finally quieted to hitching sniffles and the tension in her body eased, Milo stayed perfectly still. It was only when her breathing settled into a deep, steady rhythm that he realized she'd fallen asleep. He should have known she would crash—he'd read of her chronic fatigue in her medical file, and to say that these past twenty-four hours had been a lot was an understatement.

Milo winced, recognizing how poorly he had actually planned things. He just wanted her with him so badly, wanted her to see the truth and accept him for what he was; what they were.

He lifted her from the floor and laid her gently back on the bed. He pulled the blanket up over her small frame, brushing a few strands of hair from her cheek before pressing a kiss to her temple. For a moment, he just stood there, watching her sleep.

So peaceful

So vulnerable.

His.

He slipped from the room, silent as a shadow. If she woke and tried to run, it wouldn't matter. He'd hear her.

Not that she'd get far. The tracker he'd injected into the nape of her neck saw to that.

***

Milo paused halfway down the stairs, one hand gripping the banister as Titan stepped through the front door. He didn't move—just leaned there, watching the younger wolf with glowing eyes. Titan kept his gaze down, jaw tight, shoulders squared in a half-defensive posture. He knew he was in trouble. He just didn't know when it was coming.

Good. Let him anticipate it.

Milo wasn't going to mete out the consequences just yet. That moment would come when Willow was present to witness it firsthand. She needed to see exactly how far he was willing to go to protect what was his.

"What's the status on Poppy?" he asked, voice deep and clear.

Titan flinched at the sound, but answered

quickly. "She's not happy. Arlo said she's…
cooperating. Kind of? He already caught her trying to
call the cops once."

Milo rolled his eyes. "Let her. I'm not worried
about it." Almost every cop in a ten-mile radius wore
a leash, and he was the one holding it.

The ones that he didn't command knew better.
None of them would risk the kind of fallout that came
with crossing Milo Schwarz. They knew what he was
capable of, and he didn't mind reminding them if
they forgot.

"Good. Report back to Lachlan. See if he's
got anything worth your time," Milo said, waving a
hand dismissively. Then, with a pause, "And get your
homework done. We don't need McGarvey to have
any other reason to pay a visit."

Titan's mouth twitched, irritation surfacing.
Milo saw it, but didn't care.

"What?" he snapped. "You gonna tell me I'm
not your real dad? That you're a big boy in a master's
program now? Get the fuck out of my face, Titan."

Wisely, the wolf turned and disappeared down
the hall, teeth clenched but silent. Milo didn't bother
watching him go. His mind was already turning
toward more important things, like the woman
sleeping in his bed upstairs.

What was he going to do with her?

He continued down the stairs, jaw set and
thoughts tangled. First order of business: beer.

Second? Preparing everything for Willow when she woke. He wanted her wrapped in luxury, surrounded by every comfort he could offer. Whether she loved him or hated him, she would know she was cherished.

His queen would want for nothing.

Rounding the corner into the sleek, cavernous kitchen, Milo headed straight for the fridge and yanked open the door. He grabbed the first long-neck bottle he saw, twisted the cap with a practiced flick, and took a long swig. The bitter fizz rolled over his tongue just as a familiar scent crept in behind him.

"Yes, Lachlan. Can I help you?"

"The shipment's here."

"The semis?"

"Yeah. They're waiting at the docks. Want Titan to oversee it?"

Milo nodded, taking another swig. "Yeah. Make it quick."

Lachlan dipped his head and disappeared just as silently as he'd come. Milo stayed put, staring out the window over the sink.

Running this empire wasn't the same as being in uniform. The military had been brutal, but at least there had been discipline and predictability. Out here, in this shadow world of wolves and weapons, of blood and backdoor deals? It was chaos.

Milo was just trying his damned best to stay ahead of the game.

He downed the last of the beer and reached

for another. One of the more convenient perks of being a wolf was a sky-high tolerance. Alcohol didn't affect them the same way it did humans.

Lachlan had once mentioned that it probably had something to do with their liver function, that they simply metabolized things far more quickly. The doctor was always full of theories, ever the deep thinker, but never was able to go in-depth. He was too busy elbow-deep in surgery or teaching resident doctors.

Out of everyone in the pack, Lachlan was probably the most decent, too smart and too good for this goddamn circus he called a pack.

He always kept his phone close. They all did, like most people, but for Lachlan, it wasn't just a habit. It was a necessity. The man was always on call. It was bizarre to think about the duality of their world—one moment providing cover for a packmate in a warehouse shootout, the next racing to the hospital to save a child's life.

Milo exhaled through his nose, grabbing another beer before heading out of the kitchen. There were calls to make, plans to set in motion, problems to solve. Being alpha meant that he was never off the clock, much like Lachlan.

The city never fucking slept.

So, neither did he.

WILLOW

CHAPTER THIRTEEN

When Willow woke again, it felt like her blood was once again made of cement. Every limb was heavy, her muscles sore from tension and disuse. She blinked against the sunlight filtering through the oversized bay window…

Bay window?

She didn't *have* a bay window.

Reality slammed into her. The memories crashed down in waves—the hike, the wolves, Milo's glowing eyes, the way he'd towered over her while she begged for her life. Willow's breath hitched, heart picking up speed until her pulse pounded in her ears. She had cried in his arms, sobbed like a small child. He probably thought it meant something.

It didn't. How could it?

Milo wasn't just dangerous; he was deranged. And on top of that? Apparently, a supernatural creature. Briefly, she wondered if she had hallucinated all of it. Clearly, however, her surroundings disproved that hopeful theory.

Her hands trembled as she peeled back the blankets, slipping from the bed with slow, cautious movements. She crept toward the window, bracing herself on the frame as she peered outside. The view was deceptively serene—a sprawling garden behind a white picket fence, a gorgeous patio, grill, pool.

Beyond that, endless stretch of trees, standing silent and solemn.

She was well and truly fucked.

There was no way she was anywhere near the city limits. She couldn't see what was on the other side of the house, but something told her that even the driveway wouldn't lead to freedom. More than likely, it led to more of the same—isolation, control, and him. Milo didn't seem like the kind of man who made mistakes. He wouldn't have brought her anywhere she could escape from.

Willow's breath hitched, chest rising and falling with all the force she could muster. Her muscles twitched from holding onto tension for far too long. The only thing keeping her upright now was adrenaline. At least she was still wearing her hiking clothes. That had to mean he hadn't...

She swallowed hard, refusing to finish the thought.

And yet, her cheeks flushed deep red. The traitorous heat crawling up her neck was born from a knee-jerk reaction—from the thought of large hands gripping her waist, calloused fingers sliding lower, one pair of lips parting another. She pressed her palms to her burning face.

This was so *wrong*.

He had kidnapped her. He was keeping her here. She should be thinking about weapons and escape routes, and certainly not what his tongue could do if given the chance.

A sharp knock shattered the quiet, sending Willow's heart into her throat. She barely had time to spin around before the door creaked open and Milo stepped inside like he belonged there.

"Hey, Willow," he said gently, that maddening smile tugging at the corners of his mouth.

She didn't respond. Just leveled him with a glare, jaw clenched tight enough to crack rocks. She wasn't giving him the satisfaction of a hello.

"Would you like a tour of your new home?"

The words hit her like an icy wall of water. Her spine stiffened. "My new home?" she echoed, scoffing softly in disbelief. Her voice was brittle, like it might shatter if she spoke any louder.

He either didn't hear her or ignored her completely—both possibilities were on-brand.

"Come on," he coaxed, gesturing toward the door. "Let's get you out of here. Being locked up in a room like this isn't good for you."

Willow hesitated for only a second too long before stepping forward. Something about his presence pulled at her, like gravity was suddenly a living thing with a name and a pulse. His hand extended, patient and inviting, but she stopped short. Her fingers longed to intertwine with his, and she hated herself for it.

She didn't move to touch him.

Milo seemed to understand. His hand dropped quietly to his side. He turned and walked out of the doorway, motioning for her to follow.

***

The house was breathtaking, massive, and dripping in old-world grandeur. It had the decadent, haunting charm of estates built long before zoning laws and modern taste. Every corner she turned revealed extravagance, oil paintings, gilded frames, and impossibly tall ceilings.

Her fingertips skimmed along the smooth, polished banister as they descended the sweeping staircase.

"That's the front door," Milo said casually, gesturing toward the towering entryway. "So, this is the front of the manor. If you turn here…" he veered right, "you'll find the kitchen."

Willow followed him warily, half expecting the floor to open beneath her, and she stopped short when they stepped into the room. Her breath caught in her throat.

The kitchen was a masterpiece. Sleek, stainless steel met dark wood and marble in perfect harmony. She was no stranger to little luxuries and had the handbags to prove it, but this was next-level. This screamed old money.

Wait, my bag

"My bag," she said, voice sharp and sudden. "And my phone. I want them."

She crossed her arms, squaring her shoulders. She wasn't sure if it made her look intimidating or just pissed off, but she'd take either at this point.

Milo hesitated. His brow twitched. "You can have your bag," he said slowly, each word carefully weighed. "The phone's another story."

Willow scoffed, looking away before he could see her deflate. She hadn't expected it to work, but it would have been nice if it did.

They stood in a loaded silence. Willow kept her arms crossed, brows furrowing as she worked through different avenues of escape. Playing along until she could make a run for it might be the best option on the table.

Before she could make a decision, Milo's voice cut through the still-heavy air. "Lachlan, get in here."

A redhead rounded the corner, looking more ready to scrub in for surgery than take part in a hostage situation. He was wearing green scrubs with yellow rubber ducks on them, a pair of light blue Crocs. His undereyes sagged with exhaustion.

"Hey, Willow, it's so good to see you again," he said, extending a hand like this was a formal meeting and not a waking nightmare.

She blinked, then hesitantly uncrossed her arms long enough to accept his offer. Lachlan's grasp was confident, but gentle, like he knew how to hold fragile things without breaking them.

"I'm Lachlan," he said, his bright smile crooked. "We already met, but uh, let's not worry about that right now. What's up, boss?" Lachlan asked, shifting his attention to Milo, who stood like a force just barely contained.

"Is Willow's room set up?" Milo responded.

"Absolutely. I had Arlo organize the crew, and I oversaw everything until I was called into the hospital. Titan took over from there."

"Great, thanks."

Her room? That must mean he didn't expect her to share his bed… which was almost disappointing, much to her chagrin.

Lachlan gave Willow a brief, polite nod before turning to go, but Milo's voice stopped him mid-step.

"Oh, and Lachlan?"

The redhead paused, glancing back at Milo over his shoulder.

"If you ever touch her again like that, I'll break both your fucking hands."

Lachlan didn't flinch. If anything, his brows lifted with mild amusement, lips twitching like he was fighting a smile.

"Of course, Milo. My apologies."

He slipped out of the room.

"That was absolutely psychotic," Willow snapped, arms wrapping tight around herself. "You can't treat people like that."

Milo watched her in silence, something dangerous flashing in his dark eyes. Then he moved— slow, deliberate, like a predator who knew exactly how close he could get before his prey sensed danger.

He didn't stop until he was in front of her.

With a gentleness that didn't match the tension rolling off his body, Milo raised his hand and took her chin between his fingers, tilting her face up until their eyes locked.

"You're mine, Willow," he said. "And I'll have the hands of any man who forgets that. Understand me, and mind yourself accordingly."

"I don't belong to any man," she whispered, chin held high even as her knees threatened to buckle. Their eyes locked like magnets, her breath hitching as she fought the urge to drop her gaze to his lips.

Milo's smile was slow, a dangerous curve that didn't reach his eyes.

"No," he murmured. "You're right. You don't belong to a man, Willow."

A heartbeat passed.

"After all, I am no man."

The words stole the air from her lungs. She was trembling—not with fear, but with the brutal effort of keeping herself rooted, of not collapsing into the pull of him.

"No," she said again, voice quivering like a string pulled too taut. "You're not a man."

Her lip curled, defiance flaring even as her body betrayed her with heat and need.

"You're a monster."

His expression didn't change, but the flicker in his eyes said everything.

MILO

CHAPTER FOURTEEN

Monster? Yeah, alright..

Milo had to hold back a laugh. A monster? If only she knew the half of it. The things he'd done, the blood on his hands, made the title feel almost quaint. And still, she stood before him, glaring like she had claws of her own.

Her defiance was beautiful—a little flame flickering in the dark, stubbornly refusing to be snuffed out. She reminded him of a kitten, all hiss and spit, trying to act big while her heart was ready to give. She was breathtaking when she was angry.

He could smell her arousal, heady and impossible to ignore. It clung to the air like a challenge, daring him to act. And though he wouldn't take her—not yet—he'd make damn sure she remembered who she belonged to.

"You're trembling," he said, voice low and dark. "Not from fear. So tell me, Willow… if I'm such a monster, why are you so wet?"

Her eyes widened, lips parting in a soft gasp as her body betrayed her. Rage warred with desire across her face, but he didn't give her time to choose.

In a blur of movement, Milo spun her around and pressed her forward, bracing her against the countertop. She was bent in half over the edge, breath knocked from her lungs in a startled sound that teetered between protest and need as her feet kicked against the cabinets.

"Still think I'm a monster?" he growled into

her ear, one hand firm against her back, the other tracing up her inner thigh. Even from that distance, he could feel the heat pulsing from her core.

She made a pathetic little noise, and he stilled. He wouldn't cross the line, as much as he wanted to rip her pants off and bury his face between those beautiful legs. Instead, he hovered, breathing in that soothing, addictive scent.

"If I ever lay a hand on you, Willow…" he whispered, voice rough with restraint, "it'll be only because you begged me to."

***

Aside from their little lovers' spat, the tour went smoothly. He walked her through the library, the game room, the sprawling backyard, and even the garage, where she gazed longingly at the lineup of vehicles. Unfortunately for Willow, he'd already ensured they wouldn't be a possible route of escape for her, even if she had the balls to drive in the first place.

Finally, they reached the last stop.

"I saved something special for last," he said, pausing in front of a heavy door on the third floor with a gleam in his eye.

"Yeah? Is it the exit?" she snapped.

He barked a laugh, turning to look at her over his shoulder. It was genuine, deep and rumbling.

"Something you'll like even better," he shot back, "once you lose the attitude."

She sighed, but he didn't miss the shift of her energy. She was softening. Even if her mouth hadn't caught up yet, the rest of her body was giving her away—the subtle lean toward him, the way her gaze flicked between his eyes and mouth, the unmistakable scent of arousal still soaking her panties.

She could fight it all she wanted. He had already won.

He opened the door without another word, swinging it wide to reveal the room he had painstakingly curated just for her with the help of the rest of the pack.

A king-sized bed dominated the space, dressed in luxury linens designed to stay cool and regulate temperature. The en suite bathroom was fully stocked with her favorite products—every brand, every scent, every detail accounted for.

The colors were soft, neutral, calming. He'd even set up an oil diffuser, its gentle scent winding slowly through the air, and arranged plants along the bay window.

"Am I supposed to thank you?" she whispered, arms wrapped around herself, voice small and broken up with subtle sniffles.

Every tear she shed felt like a thorn twisting deeper into his chest. A slow, steady bleed he couldn't stop. It wasn't just guilt; it was grief. He'd broken something that he desperately needed to fix.

"Willow…" he breathed, stepping closer. "It won't always be like this. There are things you don't know yet. I'm not asking you to thank me. I'm just asking you to trust me, just like I did on the trail."

He couldn't tell her about McGarvey. Not yet. Her worldview was already fractured into splinters. If he added one more fissure, she might lose it completely. And he couldn't bear the thought of watching her come undone.

"No. Don't. Just… go."

The words hit hard—a direct blow strong enough to pierce body armor. But he didn't argue. He didn't plead.

Milo stood there for one heartbeat longer than he should have—long enough to memorize the way she looked when she pushed him away. Then he turned on his heel and walked out, giving her the space she sought.

***

Milo closed the door with precision. Quiet, clean, final. The sound of the latch clicking into place echoed louder in his skull than any explosion he'd ever walked through. He descended the stairs like a predator on the prowl. The house was silent now, all three packmates going about their business as instructed.

Willow's voice still rang in his head: *No. Don't. Just… go.*

He had. Against every instinct, against the very core of what he knew to be right, he'd walked away.

Now he needed to bleed it out.

Milo stalked down the hall and into the gym room. A punching bag hung in the corner, reinforced with Kevlar lining and bolted directly into the ceiling beams. The first hit came fast, a blur of motion. The next three were lethal combinations, jab, cross, elbow, hook. He didn't stop to tape his hands.

He didn't need to.

Pain brought clarity.

He saw her face with every strike. Every strike mirrored a moment he wished he could take back. Not because he regretted it; he'd do it all again. No, because he couldn't stand the look in her eyes when she'd finally realized what he was.

Not a man.

A monster.

She was *right*.

By the time his knuckles split open, leaking thin trails of blood down his wrists, Milo was breathing hard. Not from exhaustion, though. It was from restraint; that was the real workout.

Finally feeling like he was back down on earth, Milo leaned against the wall and stared straight ahead, breathing heavily through his nose.

It was hard, the return to civilian life. He missed the simplicity of being enlisted. In Delta Force, everything had a chain of command. An SOP. A failsafe.

With her?

No protocol. No backup. Just instinct and obsession. He had executed recon missions in deep cover across three continents. He could hold his breath underwater for over two minutes. He had saved, taken, and changed countless lives.

But Willow?

Her moves were the only ones he couldn't predict. She was all soft eyes and gentle hands, the kind of variable they warned you about in selection. *Don't fall for seduction,* they had said. *These women are here to target you specifically.*

He had failed those directives the moment he saw her. How could he not? They were fated. Destined. In some ways, he supposed, even doomed.

He turned toward the table in the corner, where his sidearm sat untouched. Old habits died hard. Every piece was cleaned nightly, every bullet accounted for. He picked up the Glock and checked the chamber, even though he knew it was clear. He always checked. Complacency got people killed.

But there was no target to neutralize. Just the unbearable stillness of losing ground he thought he had secured.

He looked toward the door, listening hard. No footsteps above. No movement. He was alone.

Without her, though, he always would be. He could live with hate. Hate was something. Hate meant he still had space in her head.

But this broken woman who barely had fight left? That was altogether different.

He set the Glock back down, tied off his bleeding hands with gauze and vet tape, and then he stood tall, shoulders squared, spine straight. A soldier again.

This mission wasn't failed.

Just delayed.

WILLOW

CHAPTER FIFTEEN

Willow scanned the room, wide-eyed and silent. She took in the layout, marking exits, trying to suss out weak spots. It wasn't something that was second nature to her. In fact, she was rarely an observant person.

But in this situation, she'd have to be.

There had to be a weak point. A vent, a cracked window latch, a door with a faulty hinge. Something. Milo wasn't sloppy, but no one was perfect.

The room itself was beautiful. Every inch was tailored to her comfort, curated down to the oils in the diffuser and the little bird pattern on the bedding. That just made it feel colder, because it seemed so calculated. He didn't do this just to be kind. He did this to win her over.

Her mind was still spiraling, trying to compute the impossible and find her footing on ground that kept shifting beneath her.

She swayed where she stood, knees aching, limbs heavy with exhaustion. Everything hurt, physically, emotionally, existentially. She didn't want to sleep. She didn't want to let her guard down, but she didn't think she had a choice.

The bed loomed, sorely tempting in its softness, its promise of rest. She hated how badly she wanted to sink into it. Hated more that she knew she would. But it was just for a little while. Just long enough to rest her body.

Willow walked over, climbed in, and pulled the blankets tight around her trembling frame.

She had to rest.

Because war was coming.

And she needed to be ready.

***

Willow woke to dusky light filtering through the bay window's frosted panes, gold and gray painting long, dappled shadows across the floor. Her eyes opened slowly, lashes fluttering as she blinked away the remnants of uneasy dreams of beasts, darkness, terror.

Every part of her begged for more rest. The ache in her bones, the weight behind her eyes, that warm, sleepy urge to roll over, pull the covers high, and let her energy replenish.

But she didn't have time for that.

Willow exhaled hard through her nose and pushed herself up. Her muscles protested with every movement. Even so, she rolled her shoulders, stretched out her legs, and planted her feet on the cool hardwood floor.

Her eyes swept the room again, sharper this time. The shadows were longer now, every corner darker. Every potential exit was still sealed tight. It was perfectly constructed to be a beautiful prison.

And she was the inmate.

Willow stood. Her pulse pounded low in her throat, a steady rhythm that matched her resolve. She didn't care how many men he had. She didn't care how far off the grid he'd taken her, or how hopeless it looked. Where there was a will, there was a way, and hers was engraved in iron. But as her mind worked through every possibility, every crack, every weak point in the house's defenses, one truth rose to the surface with grim finality. This wasn't going to end without blood.

Willow had never been a violent person. Kindness came naturally, and she was an unrepentant people pleaser. Violence had always felt crude by comparison, loud and uncivilized. The last resort of men who didn't know how to regulate themselves.

But this place didn't speak the language of peace. If she was going to survive, it was time to learn the rhythm of war.

She wasn't vicious by nature, but nature could be rewritten. She would peel away her softness like a second skin, let her loving heart harden in the face of his madness.

No, Willow had never been a violent person.

But she could now see that she was perfectly capable of becoming one.

Willow combed the room with the eyes of a captive, not admiring, but simply assessing. She ran her fingers along the window frame, checking for hidden latches or locks. Nothing. Reinforced glass.

The bay window was decorative, but still practical. Naturally. Her attention moved to the walls, the floorboards, even the vent covers—anything that might offer an edge, a crack or an oversight.

She padded into the en suite bathroom next, dazzled by the size of it. Marble countertops, a rainfall shower, a clawfoot tub, a multitude of features far out of her tax bracket.

Willow shook herself from the moment of admiration. Now wasn't the time.

She opened drawers and rifled through cabinets, finding only practical necessities. It was nice to know she would want for nothing, however, and that she wouldn't be forced into conversation just to ask for them.

Until it hit her.

There weren't any tampons.

Willow flushed so hard she could feel the heat in her face. And then another, significantly more horrifying thought dawned on her. Having to ask her captors for tampons or pads was humiliating enough... but what if she didn't even need to ask?

She wanted to vomit.

Would they be able to smell it?

She stood frozen in the middle of the bathroom, trying not to spiral, but the memory slammed into her like a freight train—Milo, casually remarking on her soaked panties with a confidence that hadn't registered until now. At the time, she'd thought it was just a lucky guess.

But, no.

He could smell her getting hot for him.

"Oh my God," she whispered, pressing her hands to her cheeks in horror. That meant all of them could. Every werewolf in the fucking house could likely smell when she was...

She wanted to drop dead.

And then, a knock.

She rushed out of the bathroom and managed to get back to the bed. Before she could say a word, however, the door cracked open, and Milo's voice followed. "Are you decent?"

"Yeah," she croaked, her voice cracking. She cleared her throat, but before she could try again, he was already inside. The door clicked shut behind him with that same careful, calculated precision he always carried.

Oh, right, she thought bitterly. *Super hearing. Of course he heard me.*

His presence filled the room like smoke, spreading out to fill the space, curling inside her lungs until her breath caught in her throat. He looked good. Even dressed in a black shirt and dark jeans, sleeves pushed to the elbows, Milo was mouthwateringly handsome.

Willow's gaze lingered for a second too long on the bulge of his biceps before she forced herself to look away. Her mind had snagged on a detail that she had just remembered—he had knocked.

He'd also asked if she was dressed.

Those were odd choices for a kidnapper who was obsessed with her.

Milo held her gaze lightly, like she was liable to bite. Willow didn't give him the satisfaction. She stayed quiet, arms crossed, flexing her jaw, eyes darting between him and the floor.

He shifted, clearly expecting resistance and not quite knowing what to do with her silence.

Finally, she spoke.

"So, how long do you plan on keeping me here?"

Milo didn't even blink. "As long as I need to."

The answer made her grind her teeth. Pushing back was pointless.

"And what about my sister?" she snapped. "What are you doing with her? She's disabled, Milo. She needs me."

His brow lifted slightly, but his face stayed unreadable, carved from stone. "She's fine. I've assigned Arlo to keep her company."

Willow's lip curled. "Assigned?"

"They're getting along great," he added, with a nonchalance that made her stomach turn. "I promise."

Like they were just playing house. Like none of this was completely insane.

"What if he… changes, or whatever, and eats

her?" she exclaimed, throwing her hands up.

"That's not really how that works."

"Then why did that red one try to kill me?"

He rubbed a hand over his jaw, dark stubble scratching against his palm. "Titan's a pup," Milo said, voice low. "His prey drive was activated."

"But I was in danger," Willow shot back. "And Poppy could be, too."

"I'm not going to hurt your sister," he replied, quieter this time, like he was trying not to snap. "And neither is Arlo. I'd stake my life on that."

She scoffed. "Big promises from someone who kidnapped me."

Milo's eyes flickered gold in the light of the sun's dying throes, but he didn't rise to the bait. "You have every right to hate me right now. But I am trying to keep you both safe."

"Safe from what?" she demanded, stepping closer. "Certainly not from you."

Willow's breath caught. For a moment, neither of them moved. They were just two people on opposite ends of a battlefield that only one of them understood.

Finally, he spoke. "Please, Willow, just come eat."

She stood there for a moment before she began moving toward him. Willow knew she needed to eat, even if such a standard thing would feel so abnormal in these conditions.

***

The entire pack was present, save for Mr. Country Club, and so was enough food to feed a small army. As Willow and Milo stepped into the dining room, Lachlan and Titan were mid-argument, voices low and clipped, clearly discussing something urgent. But the moment they entered, the conversation stopped on a dime. Both men turned toward them, masks slipping into place like soldiers caught off-duty.

"Hey, you two. I hope you're hungry," Lachlan said, offering a crooked smile. His blue-green eyes sparkled with a kind of effortless charm that made her uneasy. Too friendly. Too normal.

The table was overflowing, plated high with dishes she knew and loved. Comfort foods, indulgences, it was all there. Willow shivered, arms wrapping tight around herself. He must have been watching her longer than she realized.

She should've run the second he said her name without her having mentioned it. Instead, she was here, a prisoner served her favorite meal. It felt so much like a death row nicety.

"You have to eat first, Willow," came a Milo's low voice to her left, "It's a sign of respect. The alpha's mate always eats first."

Feeling acutely out of place—and cringing inwardly at being called his mate—Willow moved toward the table, hand trembling as she reached for a plate. The scent of the food was rich and overwhelming, and though her stomach growled traitorously, the rest of her was too tightly wound to feel real hunger. Every bite would taste like ash.

She let her stomach take over. A cautious scoop of shepherd's pie. A spoonful of creamy potatoes au gratin. A slice of bittersweet cranberry sauce. Before she realized it, the plate was nearly full, her body betraying her again by reaching for comfort where her heart felt none.

By the time she made it to an empty seat at the long dining table, she wasn't sure if she was dreading the meal or quietly grateful for the distraction it offered.

Maybe both.

MILO

CHAPTER SIXTEEN

As soon as Willow set her fork down, Milo moved with quiet precision. He waited until Titan and Lachlan had filled their plates, a code ingrained deep in his bones. The alpha ate last. Whether they were crouched over a fresh kill on a ridge in the wilderness or seated at a mahogany table with warmth and civility, the principle stood. Protecting your own was the only objective that truly mattered.

He made his own selections with purpose— grilled chicken, a rare steak, roasted potatoes, and a medley of vegetables. Functional food to fuel him. It was a habit rooted in years of training under a commanding officer who lived and breathed nutrition. The man had been intense, borderline obsessive, but Milo couldn't argue with the results.

Sliding into the seat beside Willow, his gaze flicked briefly to her plate. She hadn't gone for anything overly indulgent, but she'd chosen hearty, nostalgic comfort. He allowed himself the smallest glimmer of pride. Maybe she didn't realize it yet, but she was choosing to find comfort in the situation, however meager. She was surviving.

And survival was the first step toward belonging.

He desperately wanted her to belong. Needed her to. Willow wasn't just some captive in a cage—she was a queen, a leader-in-waiting who had no idea of the weight her presence carried. Milo ached for the moment when she would see it. When she'd stop shrinking and start taking up space. The power she could hold was breathtaking, if she reached for it.

He glanced sideways, watching her closely, cataloging every twitch of her fingers, every breath she took. She didn't know it yet, but this was already hers.

The house, the land, the empire...

She could have it *all*.

While Milo sank deeper into his thoughts, the clatter of forks and knives filled the room. Everyone had begun eating in earnest, the quiet falling naturally, comfortably, and easily. It was Lachlan, of course, who broke it. He had always been a unifying force among a group, even when he and Milo had been kids.

"So, how are classes going, Titan?" Lachlan asked, light but loaded with implication.

The younger wolf groaned dramatically, slumping back in his chair like the weight of academia might kill him. "Can we talk about literally anything else? McGarvey's up my ass on every paper. I haven't seen anything higher than a C in weeks. My GPA's circling the drain."

Lachlan barked out a laugh, shaking his head like an older brother watching a younger sibling flail.

"Have you tried telling McGarvey he can meet you out back?" Milo teased.

"Great plan, Milo," Titan deadpanned, throwing a hand in the air. "Let me just get my GPA and my ass beat to hell."

The two other men laughed, low, comfortable, and familiar. Willow let out something between a scoff and a breathy chuckle, like she couldn't help herself. Milo heard it. It meant the world to him.

"Who's McGarvey?"

The question caught Milo off guard, but hearing her voice soothed him—quiet, cautious, like rainfall on a tin roof. He glanced at Lachlan and Titan, an unspoken exchange passing between the three, before turning his attention back to her.

"He leads the only pack in the city that rivals ours."

Her brows furrowed. "There are more of you?"

That soft note of awe in her voice encouraged him to continue. "Yes," he said carefully. "There are. A few smaller packs here and there, but it's mostly us and the McGarvey pack. Pack names follow the alpha's last name, so if leadership changes, the name does, too."

He hadn't meant to offer so much, but she didn't look scared, just curious. He could work with that. It was better than fear, and certainly better than hate.

So he kept talking, just a little longer.

"It's not often that happens. Usually, somebody has to die."

Willow went still as she absently pushed the

remnants of her food around her plate. It was just scraps now. A few lonely peas, a bit of potato.

Milo watched her closely and couldn't help the small smirk that tugged at his mouth.

"I promise I'm not going to die anytime soon, Willow," he said, locking eyes with her like he was issuing a vow.

She flushed deeply. "I'm not worried about that, actually."

"I think the lady doth protest too much."

She rolled her eyes. "Don't quote Shakespeare at me. You probably don't even know how to read."

"Let grief convert to anger; blunt not the heart, enrage it."

Willow's mouth snapped shut. He wasn't sure what amused him more—her surprise, or the fact that she'd assumed he was some illiterate brute.

He wasn't.

He knew the quote had likely hit home because it meant something. It wasn't just Shakespearean flair, it was a mirror. A sharp-edged truth she wasn't ready to admit aloud, that her sorrow was the heart of the problem, not her rage.

That was why she was acting like this. Milo could see it clear as day. She wasn't being difficult for the sake of it. She was spiraling, trying to hold on to anything that still felt like hers.

"Well, I'm finished," Titan announced suddenly, standing with a clatter and reaching for his plate.

"Sit the fuck down."

Milo's voice hit the air like a gunshot. The growl beneath it echoed.

Titan froze. Eyes wide, he dropped back into his seat. Milo wasn't just the alpha—he was the executioner too, and he still hadn't dealt out the punishment that was to come. Titan was aware that he was biding his time. He was foolish to push his buttons at this point.

"No, I'm finished too," Willow said sharply, pushing back from the table. The scrape of her chair echoed through the room as she stood, and all three men turned to watch her with varying degrees of caution and curiosity.

She picked up her plate with trembling fingers.

"I'll take care of it," Milo murmured, reaching out. His hand grazed her arm—a feather-light touch, but it might as well have been a collar by the way she froze.

"Thank you," she said, and though her voice faltered, she didn't flinch or pull away.

Milo tipped his head and looked at her, like she was some specimen he hadn't finished studying. His gaze softened, warming as he cataloged each curve and crinkle of her face. The way her brows knit when she was uncertain. The tiny twitch in her jaw when she was trying to be brave. The lines near her mouth—not from sorrow, but from joy. From laughter.

From *love*.

She was so many things he was not.

And that was exactly why he needed her.

Not just as his mate, but as the part of him that had been missing all along.

The best part of him, he hoped.

When she walked away, Milo watched every step. The sway of her hips, the line of her spine as it curved down into the delicious swell of her ass— it was all burned into his memory, filed away like classified intel.

There were moments when he wished he'd installed cameras in the room he'd built for her. Not for control. Not even for strategy. Just to see her. To know she was safe. To feel connected. But he hadn't. Because now, it wouldn't be for her safety.

Before, he had only wanted to connect with her on a personal level, had only wanted to keep tabs on her to ensure her safety. He didn't have the same excuse anymore. It would now feel like a violation.

Milo scrubbed a hand over his face, shaking the thought loose like a soldier clearing a jammed weapon. He didn't have time for self-indulgence. Not tonight. Not with everything else in motion.

Pining could wait.

His wolves needed him.

***

"You know, this shit is getting really old."

"Shut up, Titan, and keep digging."

They were deep into nowhere now, miles beyond the last semblance of civilization. Just trees, shadows, and the cold bite of a springtime night. The air clung damp and sharp to their skin, but sweat still beaded down their necks and soaked their collars as they worked.

Above them, the moon hung like a lazy sentinel, just a sliver of silver barely cutting through the dark. It wasn't enough to see by, but they didn't need light to do what they were doing. They'd done it often enough at this point. For Milo, perhaps in a different way entirely, but it was really all the same.

The job was simple. Two dealers had gone off script, started cutting shit into product without permission. Thought they could make a few extra bucks on the side and not pay the cost. Milo didn't tolerate that kind of thinking.

Punishment was swift. Ruthless. Eternal.

And Milo always carried it out himself.

With every shovelful of cold earth, Milo cursed their names under his breath. His movements were sharp and methodical, the kind of effort that came not from anger but from a deep, steady belief in consequence. Justice, after all, didn't have to shout. It just had to bury you deep enough that no one ever found you.

Milo paused, one boot crunching against the torn-up soil as he leaned forward, resting both hands on the shovel's handle. His phone buzzed insistently against his thigh, a signal from the only man with clearance to interrupt him mid-burial.

With a grunt, he yanked the device from his back pocket and pressed it to his ear. "Kind of busy here, Arlo."

"Yeah, I figured. Didn't mean to rain on your little funeral parade," Arlo replied, voice laced with his usual dry edge, "but I thought you'd want to be in the know on this particular piece of intel."

Milo's jaw tightened. His eyes flicked toward Titan, who was still digging like his life depended on it. In fairness, it kind of did.

"I'm listening," he said.

LORE

It is tradition for alphas to be
both judge and executioner.

It is largely seen as cowardly to
have a lower-ranking wolf take care
of the responsibilities you should
be shouldering as their leader.

PART TWO

WILLOW

CHAPTER SEVENTEEN

Willow walked the stairs slowly, her fingers trailing along the smooth banister. Every step echoed, feet dragging just enough to show her reluctance. The house was beautiful, achingly so. Not in the garish way that new money bragged. No, this was generational elegance. Quiet wealth, the type that whispered.

She took her time, letting her gaze linger on the oil paintings that lined the walls and on the antique rugs, woven with intricately detailed stories. Everything here had been chosen with intention, every detail laid out like a visual seduction.

As she walked, she began to see the patterns.

It all involved wolves.

Willow turned sharply, her breath catching as her eyes darted back to the artwork that lined the hall. At first glance, they were just portraits, stoic figures posed with regal posture. But now? Now, she saw it. Every single one featured a wolf. Not center stage, but always present. At a knee. Peeking out from behind trees. Perched just behind a shoulder. All of them, watching.

She looked down, eyes sweeping the length of the runner beneath her feet. Woven vines, floral borders, and wolves. It was subtle but unmistakable. This wasn't just a house. It was a monument, a shrine to a bloodline steeped in the supernatural.

She felt like laughing. Instead, she turned on her heel and walked into the room that Milo had put together for her.

Sleep pulled at her again, thick and relentless. With a sigh, she peeled off her clothing piece by piece, casting each item into the growing pile by the bed until she was down to nothing but her bra and panties.

Even those, she shed, letting the fabric flutter to the floor.

At this point, she didn't care. If Milo had darker intentions, a few scraps of cotton weren't going to stop him. And she sure as hell wasn't going to sleep in something uncomfortable.

Her body still belonged to *her*.

***

She woke with a jolt, mind still fogged from sleep, but heart pounding like a war drum. Something was wrong. Very wrong.

Her wrists tugged against something… fabric? Rope? No, leather. She blinked, disoriented, only to realize she was bound to the bedpost. Panic like fire crawled beneath her skin as she tested the limits of her movement.

She felt someone between her legs.

The man looked up.

Golden, glowing eyes.

A predator's grin.

Willow thrashed—wild, primal, desperate. Her

wrists strained against the binds, body slick with sweat and twitching with adrenaline. Then, just as suddenly, she went still. She could hear her own heartbeat, thudding hard in her ears.

"I told you I wouldn't touch you unless you begged for it," Milo growled, voice like gravel, grin sharp as a sword. "So beg, Willow."

She met his gaze, unflinching, her teeth bared in open defiance.

"Fuck you."

But her body, the traitorous thing, answered differently. Heat bloomed low in her belly; it was an unmistakable sign of her need. Shame made acrid, burning bile rise in her throat. Even now, trembling with fury, she could feel it: the subtle, damning ache of desperation burning its way through her resolve.

She hated him.

But she *wanted* him, and that truth made her want to scream.

His breath ghosted over the sensitive curve of her mound, slow and deliberate, and then his grip tightened possessively around her thighs, fingers digging in just enough to remind her who was in control. Her mouth was parted, breath coming in shallow pulls, eyes fluttering half-shut as her resolve unraveled thread by thread.

"Beg for it, Willow," he rumbled, the glint in his eyes suspended in molten gold—a predator at the edge of the kill.

She screamed in frustration, throwing her head back, shaking it as if the motion alone could loosen the craving taking over her. She didn't want him to keep talking—she wanted his mouth there.

Devouring her.

Her back arched.

Her breath hitched.

Her sanity frayed.

She broke.

"Oh, God. Fuck, fine," she whimpered, voice thick and needy. "Milo, please. Just fucking do it."

She watched the predation in his eyes shift, softening into something far more dangerous. Desire gave way to hunger, to desperation, like a condemned woman about to savor her final meal before meeting the finality of a blade. For a split second, Willow almost regretted the words she'd whispered—until his tongue dragged up her slick seam, and her head snapped back, mouth falling open in a soundless cry.

With gentle fingers, he spread her open, and she felt his tongue flicking along her entrance. A low groan escaped his mouth, and she felt a shudder make its way down her back. He was *moaning into her pussy*.

Milo slid his hands along her thighs with commanding precision, holding her in place like he was claiming territory. Willow's breathing hitched, her body taut with the tension of fear and want colliding inside her.

His gaze flicked to hers—unyielding, waiting.

"Willow," he murmured, his voice low and steady, "you have to tell me that you want this."

Her pride clawed its way to the surface, threatening to choke off the words rising in her throat. But so did the frustration, her desperate, throbbing body pushed too close to the edge. She twisted against his grip, but he didn't budge. Not even a little. The restraint in his hold was infuriating. And thrilling.

"Beg me for it," he growled. "This time, I want you to mean it."

Willow's lip trembled. Not from fear, but from the suffocating vulnerability of knowing he had her. He knew it. She knew it. She could lie to herself, but her silence was already starting to scream.

When she finally spoke, her voice was hoarse, ragged, almost broken.

"Don't you dare leave me like this."

His lips quirked at the corner, and she hated how much it turned her on. "That's not begging."

She snapped. "You're such an ass."

His hand slid up her stomach, anchoring her with his weight. "Say it, and I'll give you everything you want and more."

She hesitated for one more moment, then whispered the words like a curse slipping past her clenched teeth:

"Please, Milo. I want it. I want you to eat my pussy. I need it."

The atmosphere cracked like lightning,

splitting open a quiet sky. He leaned in, slowly, a predator savoring the moment before the kill, and whispered against her skin:

"Good girl."

And then he leaned back in and claimed her.

Milo's mouth moved over her as though he were tasting something sacred. Every pass of his tongue was calculated, slow, like he was committing the shape of her to memory. Willow's body bowed off the bed, her hands jerking against the restraints as his lips closed around her aching center.

He sucked—hard. Deliberate. Dominant.

She screamed.

A string of broken moans spilled from her lips, each one more ragged than the last. His fingers curled inside her with military precision, stroking that one devastating spot over and over until she was writhing beneath him, her breath hitching, her voice gone hoarse.

"Milo, I can't," she gasped. Then again, louder. "Milo, it's too much."

He didn't stop.

She didn't want him to.

Her body chased the edge, trembling, unraveling—all under the command of his expert hands and mouth.

But then, he stopped.

Milo pulled away from her, face shining with her wetness, and stared intensely into her eyes. Willow gaped back at him, fully flushed and wild-eyed.

"It could be so good, you know," he purred, rubbing a thumb against the heated skin of her thigh.

"What are you doing?" she whimpered, pulling desperately against her restraints.

"Giving you a taste of what's to come."

***

Willow jolted awake, sheets twisted around her body, damp with sweat and something more shameful. Her hair clung to her neck and shoulders in sticky strands, skin hot to the touch. Between her thighs, there was a throbbing ache that made her stomach flutter.

No. No fucking way.

Had she just had a wet dream?

Disgusted—mostly with herself—she flung the covers off and staggered to the bathroom. She turned the water to ice-cold and stepped straight into the stream. The shock of it slammed into her chest, forcing a gasp from her lips as her whole body clenched.

She deserved it.

It was absurd. Pathetic, even. That she was having filthy, depraved dreams about the man who had stolen her away. Her captor…

With those hands. That mouth. That voice. Delicious. Decadent. *Dirty.*

She groaned, low in her throat, as the water heated and steam curled around her trembling body. Willow's hand moved almost without thought, fingers slipping between tense thighs to find that aching bundle of nerves. One slow circle, then another. A sigh escaped her lips.

But it wasn't enough. It was never enough.

She needed more. Harder. Deeper. She needed the kind of touch only he had given her—the kind that destroyed her common sense, the kind she hated herself for craving.

Willow scrubbed her skin raw, like she could slough away the sins of the previous night. Like she could peel away the heat, the ache, the way his mouth had ruined her for anyone else. By the time she stepped out, her body was flushed red beneath the fluorescent light, steam billowing in towering pillars.

Still, the pulse between her thighs hadn't quieted. It throbbed, steady and maddening.

She didn't bother drying off. Dripping and flushed, she stalked straight to the bedside drawer, yanking it open with the kind of desperation that made her feel empty.

She groaned aloud. Of course. The man who abducted her, watched her, and obsessed over her hadn't thought to grab her vibrator when he ransacked her room.

Honestly, she wasn't even sure if she wanted the damn thing to be here. The thought of him touching it—handling it—made her skin prickle. That was hers, a secret part of herself. And yet...

Her breath hitched.

He'd already been there.

Willow flushed, trying to shake the memory loose, trying to reframe it as nothing more than a filthy dream conjured by captivity and stress. But her body told another story, one written in slick heat and trembling thighs.

It wasn't real, she told herself. Just a nightmare.

But the worst part?

She knew—deep inside her bones, deep where denial couldn't reach—that it hadn't been a nightmare at all.

MILO

CHAPTER EIGHTEEN

He woke to birdsong.

Not the frantic kind that accompanied early dawn, but something softer and slower. Like the world itself had taken a breath and exhaled just for him. Milo's eyes blinked open, heavy with sleep, and a rare, lazy smile tugged at his lips.

Today felt right.

There was a stillness in the house that eased his nerves. Lachlan was elbow-deep in a surgical shift. Titan had been sent off on a glorified errand with vague instructions and even vaguer directions— mostly because Milo had been in the mood to fuck with him.

The pack was scattered.

Which meant…

It was just him.

And *her*, of course.

He stretched, muscles rolling beneath his skin like shifting earth. Milo wasn't just brute strength— he was power made elegant, violence tempered by discipline. Flexibility was a quiet weapon, one honed as mercilessly as his aim. No wasted motion. No unnecessary bulk. Everything about his body was curated to perfection.

Slipping from beneath the covers, he padded toward the bathroom. The mirror greeted him with the face of a man sculpted by war and trauma, and he met his own gaze with a grim acknowledgement.

Overpriced electric toothbrush in hand, he

ran through the motions with discipline. Grooming wasn't vanity. It was part of the ritual. Another layer of control.

Once finished, he dressed in his uniform of choice—dark jeans, black t-shirt, bare feet on hardwood floors.

Then he made his way to the kitchen.

He had a mate to feed.

***

The kitchen glowed in the early light, golden beams spilling across the counters. The polished granite reflected it back in warm brilliance, casting soft shadows that danced with the promise of a new day. Milo paused at the threshold, hand braced against the doorframe, and let it wash over him.

For just a second, he allowed himself the indulgence of a fantasy.

Willow, standing barefoot by the stove, one of his shirts draped over her. Her hair tousled from sleep, her laughter curling through the room like smoke. A spatula in one hand, a rounded belly cradled by the other—swelling with his child.

The image took his breath.

It was primal, the kind of need that didn't come with logic or restraint. Just the unrelenting drive to claim, to keep, to build. Milo's breath caught as a sharp bolt of arousal struck him low, hunger twisting inside him like a blade. His cock twitched.

Shaking the image from his mind, he crossed the threshold and made a beeline for the fridge. It wasn't just Willow distracting him. Wolves weren't made to be alone. Without his second at his side, Milo felt the shift in his center of gravity. Arlo was his anchor, his closest friend, his tether to reason when everything else tilted off-axis.

Watching his best friend from afar, Milo realized just how much of his own stability was tied up in the man. Distraction was necessary—productive distraction.

He knew her preferences down to the last detail. Sweet coffee. Sweeter breakfast. Pancakes drenched in maple syrup, buried under a mountain of whipped cream. Milo pulled the ingredients for pancakes and got to work with practiced ease. Eggs cracked, flour measured, butter melted. By the time he was folding in chocolate chips, the iron hot and hissing, he sensed her.

If he'd been shifted, his ears would have swiveled backward. Even in his human form, he didn't need to look. His senses told him everything.

Bare feet on the stairs.

Tentative footsteps.

And the scent, God, the scent hit him like a freight train. Hot, sweet arousal thick in the morning air. His jaw clenched, fists tightening around the bowl. He had to force himself to loosen his grip before the glass broke.

He heard her creeping across the kitchen floor, each step cautious but far from silent to his attentive ears. The gentle scrape of metal against cotton made his grin bloom slow and wicked. A flying pan was his guess.

Adorable.

Milo didn't even pause.

In one fluid motion, he turned, caught her wrist in his calloused palm, and spun her into his arms. His other arm coiled tight around her waist, anchoring her to his chest where she belonged.

She gasped, but didn't resist.

He leaned in, breath brushing her lips, their foreheads nearly touching. His voice was a low, rumbling whisper that hung like a noose in the space between them.

"Planning to help me get some more beauty rest before breakfast, sweetheart?" he murmured, amusement and hunger braided thick in his tone. "That's one way to keep a man interested."

For a breathless moment, time stilled.

They hovered there, suspended in dangerous electricity, her chest rising and falling against his. Willow's breath came in shallow pulls, her thighs clenching as desire seemed to war with obstinacy. Her eyes were barely open, dark lashes fluttering, and a flush crawled its way up the column of her exposed neck like a secret she couldn't hide.

Metal clattered to the floor.

The pan slipped from her fingers.

He released her wrist, only to slide his hand up the back of her neck. His fingers wove into the hair at her nape, grounding her, guiding her.

When their lips met, it was a ghost of a kiss—soft, searching, careful.

But that caution couldn't survive the spark between them roaring into something all-consuming. The moment she melted into him, Milo devoured her. The kiss turned hungry, greedy, punishing. He deepened it, his tongue brushing past her lips to dance with hers in a slow, claiming rhythm. A quiet growl of satisfaction rumbled in his chest—she was still fighting for control, even now. It made him want her more.

The hand that cradled her neck stayed gentle, but his other one slid down, resting at the curve of her thigh. Willow's breath hitched, a soft whimper escaping as she shifted closer, her body pressing into his like she couldn't help it.

He knew what she was asking for without words. Still, he wasn't one to give in so easily.

But she was being good. For once.

His palm slid gently over her heat, holding her there, and he murmured against her lips, voice husky and low, "This what you're after?"

Willow's reply was breathless, her voice trembling with need. *"Yes…"*

He smiled again, dark and knowing, and he

kissed her again.

"Too fucking bad."

She stared at him, wide-eyed and breathless, stunned by the sudden loss of contact. As Milo withdrew his hand, her jaw tightened, disbelief curdling into fury. Her expression twisted into ferocity—eyes blazing, lips curled, a snarl spreading on a face far too delicate for such anger.

The fire in her eyes only sharpened his hunger. It thrilled him, the idea of dragging her to the floor, of earning her surrender the only way his wolf understood—through dominance, through possession, through force she'd come to crave. He could already picture it.

But it wasn't time. Not yet.

"I hate you."

Milo's grin was all teeth. He couldn't hold back a laugh as she spun on her heel and stormed toward the dining room, the scent of her dripping pussy trailing in her wake like perfume. But she didn't leave. Despite her rage, the promise of her favorite foods had been enough to keep her close.

Or maybe, just maybe, it was something else that made her stay.

Milo turned back to the stove, laser-focused, resuming his quiet mission of feeding his mate. Not just because she needed strength, but because he wanted her whole—body, mind, and spirit. Today would require all three.

The last pancake landed on the top of a stack when he heard the sharp clip of her footsteps. She stomped to the fridge like a woman on a warpath, grabbing a bounty—maple syrup, butter, whipped cream—and stormed back to the dining room.

Even when she was spoiling for a fight, she still took initiative. Still made herself useful.

She was infuriated, no doubt.

But she was also, at heart, endlessly good in a way that he was endlessly not.

WILLOW

CHAPTER NINETEEN

He had to be joking.

One minute, he was touching her with abandon—palming her heat, dragging her toward the brink.

The next, he was whistling under his breath while flipping pancakes like none of it had happened. Like she wasn't still burning from the inside out.

Willow's skin prickled. This version of him— the domestic, apronless house-husband—made her stomach twist. Not from fear, but from a far more dangerous attraction. She knew better than to let her guard down. Humanizing your captor was the first step toward losing yourself. And yet…

Those lips.

Those hands.

That voice in her ear, rough with hunger.

She clenched her jaw, biting back the heat that pooled low in her belly. Willow set the containers down with enough force to lightly rattle the table. Her fingers were locked around the syrup bottle like it might anchor her to reality. When she heard the thud echo back at her, she closed her eyes and inhaled slowly through her nose. No. He wasn't worth the explosion simmering just beneath her skin.

She could survive this without falling apart.

A moment later, he entered like he hadn't just pulled her apart in the kitchen—carrying a plate stacked with pancakes and a smug sense of satisfaction. He added two place settings to the table, as though it were a brunch date and not a meal with a woman he'd kidnapped.

Willow sank into the nearest chair, arms crossed tight over her chest. She didn't bother looking at him. Not even when he cleared his throat like a host waiting for her thanks.

Fuck you, buddy, she thought.

Instead of pushing, he simply placed a plate in front of her and began stacking three fluffy pancakes onto it. Willow sighed through her nose, snatching the tub of butter with a little more force than necessary. She hated that he was getting his way. Again. Every moment with him felt like a silent victory on his part, whether he said it or not.

Still, she knew better than to let spite win. Starving herself wouldn't weaken him. It would only make her vulnerable, and she couldn't afford that.

She needed her strength.

If she wanted even a chance at getting out of here, she'd need his trust first. That was going to be the tricky part.

"So," Willow began, jaw tight, eyes fixed on her plate, "what do you actually do for work?"

She shifted in her seat, trying not to wince. Her body still pulsed from earlier, every nerve ending raw and agitated. Small talk was almost laughable under the circumstances, but she forced it out anyway. She could feel her swollen heat pressing into the seat beneath her.

Milo didn't miss a beat. "You're looking at it," he said simply, slicing into his own stack. "My job is making sure the pack is cared for. That the business runs nice and smooth."

"Business?" She looked up at him, her brows knitting. Something in the way he said it gave her pause.

He met her gaze evenly. "That's right, sweetheart. We're the pipeline. Anything coming into this city—guns, drugs, product of any kind—passes through us first. We make sure it gets where it needs to go."

Willow's stomach twisted, her appetite evaporating.

"So you're the reason half the people in this city are suffering and addicted," she said, voice sharp enough to draw blood. Her knife scraped across the plate as she cut into her food like it had personally wronged her.

"That's one way to look at it," Milo replied, utterly unfazed. "Or you could look at the fact that we ensure shit is clean to keep overdose rates down."

She glared at her pancakes like they might turn into a weapon. "It's fucking disgusting. Nothing you do to smooth it over is going to make it less so."

Milo's fork paused midair. He didn't argue. Didn't apologize. Just changed the topic.

"I have a surprise for you today. I think you're going to like it."

She glanced up at him, suspicious and guarded. She wasn't sure where he was going with this, and she also wasn't excited. She hated surprises as a rule, and especially when they came from a madman who was holding her against her will.

"Just trust me."

Somewhere, deep down, she desperately wished she could.

***

Willow had swapped her pajamas for something better suited to the heat, a white racerback and jean shorts. The days were growing warmer as spring faded slowly into summer, and the sunlight filtering through the windows only made her crave freedom more. She longed for beach days—salt in the air, toes buried in warm sand, a drink sweating in her hand as she and her sister clinked glasses and drifted into their usual rhythm of easy laughter and deep conversation.

Poppy.

Her heart twisted. Just the thought of her sister sent a pulse of anxiety racing through her chest. Was she safe? Had Arlo hurt her? Was he kind? The not knowing was worse than being held captive.

Still, a small smile ghosted across her lips. Poppy wasn't the type to go down easy. If anyone could give a werewolf hell, it was her sister.

He'd told her to be ready to leave as soon as possible, his voice crackling with barely contained excitement. That, more than anything, made her stomach twist into knots. Whatever had him this worked up couldn't possibly end well for her.

Willow descended the stairs slowly, each step a silent protest. And then she paused, her breath caught halfway in her chest.

There he was.

Milo stood at the bottom, tall and broad and cut from shadow and sun, the light slashing across his cheekbones like an artist had sketched him into being. It wasn't fair. He looked like a god dressed in plain clothing.

He glanced up, catching her stare. Her breath hitched. He smirked.

She huffed, turning her face away with a scowl. *It's not my fault he looks like that,* she thought bitterly, willing her pulse to slow.

Willow all but ran down the rest of the steps, stopping at the bottom with crossed arms.

"Well?" she said expectantly,

"Come on. It's a short car ride."

***

Willow's foot tapped against the floorboard, almost involuntarily, in time with the music thrumming from the speakers. Something aggressive, industrial—Hatebreed, maybe. She didn't know the song, but the guttural vocals steadied her frayed nerves.

She was still skeptical of wherever they were heading and whatever he had planned once they arrived.

Milo gifted her silence, eyes trained on the blacktop, hands loose but assured on the wheel. He didn't press for conversation. Didn't try to fill the space. She was grateful. She had nothing to say to him, and the ache between her thighs was still a low, persistent throb that made thinking difficult.

The SUV shot down the highway like it owned the road. Milo wove through traffic with smooth, assertive movements, passing slower cars with a twitch of impatience. She watched him—the way he commanded the vehicle like it was an extension of himself—and couldn't help but feel a faint flicker of envy.

Things would be so much easier if she could drive like this.

"Y'know, people are going to do drugs whether you like it or not," Milo said, voice infuriatingly casual.

Willow's brows lifted, her mouth parting. He couldn't be serious.

Apparently, he was.

She didn't answer right away—didn't trust herself to. Instead, she let out a low, unimpressed hum, her gaze fixed on the road ahead. The restraint it took not to glance at him was monumental, but she wasn't about to give him the satisfaction of her full attention.

"We should really be focusing on decriminalization and programs to help people who get addicted. There's a market for it, Willow, and if we weren't on top, there would be a lot more death. Trust me."

His voice was quiet, but steady.

Willow kept her expression neutral, eyes still trained on the red sedan in front of them. It would be so easy to believe him, to let the silk-soft cadence of his voice chip away at her resolve and soften her heart. But she didn't know if it was truth or manipulation, and that made all the difference.

And yet, beneath the mire of suspicion, she wanted to believe that this was the real him. Willow wasn't going to tell him that, though. Let him wonder.

Let him work for her forgiveness.

The rest of the ride passed in loaded silence, tension hovering thick between them like a fog that wouldn't lift. Willow's pulse thumped harder with every mile, quickening even more as Milo flicked the blinker and took the off-ramp with that same unnerving calm. He didn't say a word, but she could feel the anticipation rolling off him, steady and sure.

He navigated the winding roads of a quiet neighborhood, the kind where the trees stood tall and the sidewalks were cracked and buckling. Eventually, the narrow street ended in the entrance to a park— lush and sprawling, with winding trails that snaked through the green like veins.

And then she saw them.

Willow's breath hitched, her chest tightening so suddenly she had to put a hand over her heart.

Of course.

Of fucking course.

LORE

There are many laws to learn in
the world of wolves.

They are governed by laws as old
as time, and adhere to them almost
compulsively. Those who stray
from them are dealt with.

MILO

CHAPTER TWENTY

Milo's grin was instant, sharp and boyish, when he saw her expression shift. She lit up like a struck match the second she saw her sister. The giddy spark in her voice was so unlike the woman who'd been cursing his name just hours ago, it nearly knocked the wind from his lungs.

She reached for the handle without hesitation.

He had, of course, locked the doors.

"Unlock the fucking door," she whined, yanking at it like sheer willpower might make it budge.

"Hold on." He held up a hand. "There are ground rules."

She let out a groan and pressed her face to the window, eyes locked on the pair not far off. Her breath fogged the glass, clouding her vision, as she listened to him. Or at least, he was hoping she was listening.

"Don't try to run. Don't make a scene. When I say it's time to go, we leave."

She snapped her head toward him, eyes flashing like light glinting off ice.

"Fine. If we're running on your schedule, I'd like to get out there and see her, since we're losing time."

Milo pressed the unlock button without another word, and Willow was out of the SUV before he turned back around. She nearly stumbled in her rush, but caught herself, legs flying beneath her.

He watched her go—his girl, sweet and gentle and radiant—tearing through the open green toward the one person who mattered most to her.

Willow collided with her sister in a tight hug. Poppy wrapped her arms around her younger sister with a softness that made Milo's throat tighten. Arlo stood nearby at a respectful distance, his expression unreadable.

Milo felt his chest ache differently now.

It wasn't just about Willow seeing Poppy.

It was Arlo's absence, too.

Milo killed the engine and stepped out, the door closing behind him with a hollow thunk. He locked it with a quiet chirp of confirmation and strode toward the reunion unfolding before him.

Poppy had her hands on Willow's face, cradling it like she was trying to memorize every feature—or maybe confirm they hadn't been altered. Her fingers pressed in hard enough that Willow winced, but she didn't pull away.

He gave them space, or an illusion of it.

Every word between them drifted to him on the breeze. He could've recited the conversation word for word if pressed. But he didn't linger on it and tried his best to put it out of his mind. Instead of eavesdropping, Milo turned toward Arlo, whose mouth twitched up into a half-smile as they closed the distance between them.

The two clasped each other in a firm,

brotherly hug. Arlo thudded a hand against his back, the sound solid and grounding. Milo squeezed once before letting go, the gesture quiet but deeply felt.

"How's she doing?" Arlo asked, nodding toward the sisters with a lift of his chin.

"She's a handful," Milo replied, arms folding across his chest as he watched Willow hug Poppy. "But we're making progress. Turns out that intel you dropped on me was dead-on."

Arlo let out a barking laugh. "But I'm guessing you didn't knot her."

Milo's head whipped toward him. "How the fuck would you know that?"

"She can walk straight."

They both chuckled, the kind of laughter that only came from understanding what Willow soon would. The tension that had strung Milo tight over the past few days began to bleed off in the warmth of their shared humor.

Arlo clapped him on the back. "The bond runs deep. You're in her head now. It's only a matter of time."

Milo grunted softly, but his focus was elsewhere. Willow's tone had shifted, drawing his attention like a magnet. He tilted his head just slightly, tuning in to the conversation he wasn't supposed to be eavesdropping on.

"Has he… hurt you?" Poppy's voice was barely audible, strained and trembling.

"No," Willow replied without hesitation. "None of them have."

"Do you promise me?"

"Yes."

That was enough to make the corner of Milo's mouth curl, smug and quiet.

She could've said anything, especially after what happened in the kitchen. But she didn't. She hadn't twisted the truth. She told her sister he hadn't hurt her.

Because he hadn't.

Because she wanted it. Whether she was ready to admit that out loud or not.

Arlo followed Milo's gaze, eyes narrowing slightly with understanding.

"She's sharp," he said, keeping his voice low. "Bit of a smartass, but sweet under the surface. Asked a lot of questions, but she's playing nice—for now."

Milo nodded, barely absorbing the words. His attention was locked on Willow like he was watching prey, except there was no intent to harm; just to possess. She was all sunshine bound by tension, laughing with her sister, her body language betraying the war waging inside her.

He'd seen it.

And he recognized it now.

"She's softening," Milo muttered, more to himself than anyone else.

"Dangerous thing, underestimating your

target," Arlo offered carefully.

"I'm not underestimating her," Milo said, eyes dark. "Trust me. I have a game plan."

He shifted slightly, adjusting the discomfort growing beneath his jeans.

He was just waiting for nightfall.

***

They didn't leave for hours, Milo allowing the sisters as much time as he could. The ride back was tense, marked by a fragile silence, occasionally broken by sniffles. Willow had turned her face to the window, cheek pressed to the glass, trying to disappear into the passing landscape. Milo didn't need to look to know she was crying—he could smell it. Salt laced with sorrow, sharp in his nose.

They were leaving behind the only tether she had to normalcy, and she was unraveling at the seams.

"You know," he said, voice low and raw, "I feel the same when Arlo's not with me."

Willow's breath hitched, a soft, wet sound. "Like hell you do," she whispered, swiping at her face with the back of her hand. Milo didn't argue. Just adjusted his grip on the wheel, knuckles white, and kept driving into the quickly fading daylight.

As soon as the tires crunched against the gravel drive, Willow was out of the SUV like a shot, her figure blurring past the hood before the engine had even gone quiet.

Milo sat frozen behind the wheel, hands slack in his lap, heart twisting painfully in his chest. Watching her cry felt like watching glass shatter in slow motion.

It would be easy for him to follow. To close the space between them, gather her trembling form in his arms, and hold her until her sobs subsided.

Still, he knew she'd reject him.

For now, there were business matters to tend to. With a rough sigh, Milo shifted into reverse, cutting the wheel. His hands gripped the wheel tighter than necessary, every fiber of him resisting the act of leaving her behind. What he wanted was to charge back through that door, wrap her up in his arms, and shield her from everything that weighed on her mind.

But she wasn't ready for that.

Not yet.

LORE

The mate bond has benefits beyond
finding your fated other half.

It's possible to feel the emotions of
the other through the bond, and
this can translate to feeling things
you've never felt before.

There's an old saying among
wolves: "The bond is enough to
make a sociopath feel love."

WILLOW

CHAPTER TWENTY-ONE

She curled into herself, arms wrapped tight around the pillow that had come to stand in for everything she'd lost. Fat, silent tears slipped down her pink cheeks, soaking into the fabric without ceremony. It wasn't late, but her body had surrendered to the bone-deep exhaustion of repeated heartbreak. Every limb felt weighted. Every breath was a quiet surrender.

Sleep took her again, as it had so often lately. There was nothing else to do. No job to tend to. No emails to check. No life to return to.

Maybe he did me a favor by deciding to keep me here, she thought bitterly.

She let go, falling fast and hard into the quiet chasm of sleep.

***

Willow woke with a start, disoriented and too warm, her cheek sticking uncomfortably to the pillow where a line of drool had dried. Her limbs felt heavy, her body sluggish, like she'd been pulled from the wreckage of a bad dream. The sheets were tangled around her legs, and her skin was damp with sweat.

She stretched gingerly, letting each group of muscles loosen their knots, joints popping in protest. As her arms reached overhead, her wrists brushed against the headboard—no restraints, not this time, but her body remembered. She'd dreamed that he had been here. Between her legs. Moaning. Tongue twisting inside her like he had all the time in the world and a calling to answer.

She clenched her thighs reflexively, heat blooming in her core and rising to her cheeks.

And then the guilt crept in.

The reminder that she was still a prisoner here. Still in his territory, under his roof, surrounded by men who could tear her apart without breaking a sweat. Her breath caught in her chest. She needed to stay sharp. She couldn't afford to forget what this was.

Even if her body did.

She willed away the imagery, the desire, the feelings associated with them.

Willow finally slipped out of bed, desperate for distraction, the cool air brushing her bare legs and arms as she padded toward the door. The floor was cold under her feet. She opened the door slowly, half-expecting someone to be standing on the other side. No one was.

The hallway beyond was dim, moonlight filtering through narrow windows and catching on the sheen of polished floors. As she walked, she admired the ornate tapestries that hung from the walls.

Until she remembered the wolves.

Willow shuddered.

She walked softly, her fingertips trailing along the carved wood of the banister as she descended the grand staircase. The space opened wide below her, the silence of the manor somehow louder at night, every creak and shift in the house echoing like a threat. The scent of the kitchen called to her—coffee grounds, and something meaty.

At the bottom of the stairs, she turned left, passing through the archway and into the kitchen.

It was still stunning, in that cold, magazine-spread kind of way. High ceilings, marble countertops, stainless steel appliances polished to a mirror shine. Willow glanced around cautiously. No signs of life. No Milo. Just the low hum of the fridge and the tick of an antique clock mounted above the doorframe.

For a moment, she simply stood there, letting the quiet settle around her. The freedom to move—even just through this house—felt like a fragile gift. She stepped farther in, eyeing the cabinets, unsure of where to go to get what she needed. All she wanted was a cup of coffee.

"Hey there, Willow."

She startled, hand flying to her chest as her heart jerked painfully. Lachlan stood just a few feet away, leaning casually against the doorframe like he'd been there all along. He was dressed in scrubs again—this pair light blue, patterned with little teddy bears clutching stethoscopes. His smile was warm, easy, the kind that made you feel like you weren't intruding. But the circles under his eyes told a different story. They were as dark as she'd ever seen on a person.

"Didn't mean to sneak up on you," he said,

lifting his hands in surrender. "Comes with the territory, the wolf thing and all that. It freaks the nurses out, too."

There was a softness in his tone, a gentle kindness that contrasted sharply with everything else in this house. He didn't look at her like she was prey. Just like she was in need of a cup of tea and some good conversation.

"You're fine. I startle easily," she murmured, arms folding across her chest. Her voice was nearly inaudible—but of course, that didn't matter here. Stupid fucking wolf powers, she grumbled internally, jaw tightening.

Lachlan didn't comment on her shift in mood. Instead, he offered her another smile, this one softer, more deliberate. "Would you like a cup of coffee? I was just about to make one myself."

Willow hesitated, then glanced at him. His presence was disarming, like he'd been built to ease tension, not create it. Despite everything, she wanted to like Lachlan. It would be easier to have at least one lifeline in this mess.

"Yeah," she said, barely above a whisper. She cleared her throat. "That would be great."

Lachlan gave a simple nod and moved around her, keeping a respectful distance as he stepped to the counter. Willow trailed after him, careful not to get too close, leaning her weight onto the edge of the counter as she watched him move with practiced ease.

It was quiet, oddly domestic. Just a moment, she let herself breathe.

He moved quietly, asking what she liked in her coffee as he went. His tone was easy, unhurried, like this wasn't the middle of a hostage situation but an ordinary morning between acquaintances. She answered with short, clipped phrases.

When the coffee was ready, they settled into a quiet rhythm, sitting across from each other at the kitchen island. Willow wasn't entirely sure why she'd agreed to linger. Maybe it was foolish. But the truth was, she ached for anything that resembled normal. A conversation without barbed edges. A moment without Milo.

Something human in all this madness.

"So, how are you settling in?"

Willow lifted the mug to her lips and took her time sipping, letting the silence hang uncomfortably thick between them. She didn't owe him any answers, but his gaze pressed the words from her anyway.

"Well, all things considered," she said, voice dry as bone, "I guess just fine."

Her expression sharpened as she set the mug down, eyes cold and unreadable. Lachlan's easy smile faltered, a flicker of regret tightening the space between his brows.

"I really am sorry about all this," he murmured. "If it were up to me, things would've gone a lot differently."

"So, what's with the whole mate thing, anyway? Can't he just, like, find somebody else? Somebody more willing?"

She hit the last word hard, her voice tight as she dropped her gaze. It wasn't a real question; more of a desperate hope, clinging to the edge of reason.

Lachlan exhaled through his nose, his smile soft and sad. "I wish I could tell you otherwise, but... no. It doesn't work like that. A mate bond is not something we choose. It's instinct. It's written in the stars, so to speak."

His voice dipped, gentling further. "It's mutual, too, Willow. That pull you feel? That's the bond."

Willow's thumb skimmed along the rim of her mug, her brow furrowed in thought. She didn't want to say it, didn't want to give it air, but the truth pressed up against her ribs.

"Yeah," she admitted, barely above a whisper. "I do feel it."

Her voice cracked, and she set the mug down with a soft clink before burying her face in her hands. "I don't know. None of this makes sense."

Lachlan, mercifully, let her sit in the not-knowing. After a few moments of collecting herself, she spoke up again.

"So what are you guys, anyway? The werewolf mafia?"

Lachlan blinked, startled. His brow ticked up

slowly, and for a second, he just stared at her like he wasn't sure if she was joking.

"I'm sorry?"

She shrugged, tone sharp. "I was talking to Milo, and he said that you sold drugs and guns."

The corner of his mouth twitched, not quite a smile, not quite a frown.

"If we're being blunt, yes, I suppose that's the bare bones of it."

Willow's eyes narrowed.

He sighed, resting his forearms on the counter, fingers drumming lightly. "Werewolf history is steeped in blood, Willow. You have to understand that we didn't exactly have a seat at the table in society. For a long time, we survived in the shadows. That legacy carries down. The cycle continues."

He was silent for a moment, allowing his words to sink in before continuing.

"Even now, with all the wealth and power we've built, it's almost impossible to separate from the underbelly we were born into. It's what we know."

She leaned back slightly, arms crossed, gaze sharp as a blade. "Okay, but you're a doctor. Can't you just pay the bills? Why would you choose to engage with shit like that? You took an oath."

Lachlan nodded once, slow and thoughtful.

"Technically speaking, yes. I could. I make more than enough to live a clean life. As for the oath, I'm not in charge of executions."

His voice was calm, but there was a heaviness behind it.

"The reality is that it's not that simple. There are more moving parts than you know. If we pulled out—if Milo stepped away from the table—it wouldn't just end. It would simply change hands."

Willow blinked, her frown deepening.

"There'd be a massive power vacuum," he continued steadily. "People would die. Innocents, mostly. And the wolves who'd take over?" He looked her dead in the eye, not a hint of apology in his tone. "You'd much rather it be us. I promise you that."

Her attention was caught. "Why are the other guys so bad?"

Lachlan suddenly looked uncomfortable, shifting in his chair.

"It's nothing you need to worry about. Milo will make sure of that."

Willow wanted to dig deeper, press harder, ask the dozens of questions filling her mind. But the subtle shift in Lachlan's posture told her everything; he was retreating behind his walls. Instead, she changed the subject.

"I always thought werewolves were monsters."

That earned a barking laugh from Lachlan, bright and unguarded. His teeth flashed in the warm kitchen light, the sound startling in its sincerity.

"Well," he said, still grinning, "there's some truth to that lore, I'm afraid. Though it's not pretty."

Willow's brow arched. "Oh?"

His smile dimmed just slightly, replaced with something more serious. "If you're born a wolf, your body's built for it. But if you're bitten…" He shook his head. "There's a risk. Some people don't make it through the first shift. They get caught in between, trapped in a living hell. The pain, the instinct... it drives them mad."

She felt her breath hitch, icy fingers of fear wrapping around her spine as a shiver rolled down her back.

Lachlan caught the change. "Hey, it's okay," he said quickly, voice gentle. "Milo would never risk that with you. And it doesn't just happen from a bite. To pass on the gift, it has to be intentional. You have to be intending to pass it on. Accidental turnings aren't really a thing."

Willow exhaled, slow and shaky.

Well, she thought, gnawing nervously at her thumbnail, *that's a relief… I guess.*

Lachlan's pocket lit up, a sharp flash of green glowing through the thin fabric. A second later, a shrill series of beeps erupted, followed by frantic vibration. He reached in and pulled out a small pager—plastic, scratched at the corners, and clearly well-worn.

"Oh, shit," he muttered, eyes scanning the message before flashing Willow an apologetic smile. "Work's calling."

Before she could say a word, he was gone,

pushing off the counter and darting out of the room in a blur of motion that reminded her he wasn't quite human.

The silence returned.

Willow sat still, the quiet pressing in on her like a weight. It was suffocating. The hum of the refrigerator and the distant ticking of a clock were the only sounds left to keep her company. For one absurd moment, she almost wished Milo would come stalking in just to break the stillness. At least his presence filled the room and gave her something to focus on.

With a long, heavy sigh, she drained the rest of her coffee and rose reluctantly. She rinsed both mugs and left them in the sink before turning back toward the entryway. There was nothing to do now. No one to talk to.

Sleep, then.

She could always go back to sleep.

LORE

It is frowned upon to turn a human
unless specific conditions arise.

For example, when a werewolf
finds their mate bond is with a
human, they may decide to turn
them, mutually or otherwise.

MILO

CHAPTER TWENTY-TWO

The sharp crack of gunfire rang through the private shooting range, echoing off concrete and steel, although he barely heard it through his ear protection. Milo adjusted his grip on the Glock and squeezed the trigger again. Headshot. Center mass. Headshot.

He didn't miss. He never did.

An acrid scent clung to the air, sharp and comforting. It reminded him of long nights in hostile territory, fingers wrapped around steel, blood in his mouth, and a mission clock ticking down like a bomb.

Delta doesn't feel, he reminded himself.

But he wasn't Delta anymore.

Milo holstered the weapon, breathing out slowly and steadily, watching the target sway at the end of the lane. He didn't want to think about those days. Not the sounds. Not the faces.

Not the goddamn *children*.

Instead, he thought of Willow.

That defiant little chin tilted up at him. Her eyes, blue and blazing. The way her voice cracked when she cursed his name, like it tasted too sweet to spit out so viciously.

He could smell her, even now. Her scent clung to his clothes, to his thoughts; he was undeniably hers.

Milo pulled the slide back and reloaded. Every click and snap of metal was a balm against the ache clawing at his chest.

She's not ready yet, he reminded himself. *But soon.*

He raised the gun again and centered the next

target.

Soon, she'll understand.

Then, he fired.

Too many variables. Too much silence. In the world of wolves, silence never meant peace. A storm was coming. He could feel it in his bones, in the way the air tasted; too still, too clean.

McGarvey had gone quiet, and he never stayed quiet for long.

Milo didn't trust it. It wasn't like him to lie low unless he was planning something that would hit like a sniper's bullet—silent, sudden, deadly. Every instinct Milo had, sharpened by years in the field, told him that the calm was about to fracture. Something was moving beneath the surface, and he hadn't clocked it yet. That alone was enough to put him on edge.

He'd been considering relocating Willow. Somewhere more secure. Somewhere farther from reach. But the idea left a bitter taste in his mouth. He didn't want to be without her unless he had no other choice. But choices were thinning out.

And he knew better than anyone, the worst kind of war was the one you couldn't see coming.

With a sigh, Milo flicked on the safety and holstered his weapon. It was time to go.

***

The engine rumbled low beneath him, a

steady growl that mirrored the growing tension in Milo's gut. The city lights blurred past the windshield as he drove, jaw tight, one hand on the wheel, the other drumming restlessly against his thigh. The meeting with McGarvey had been a long time coming, but he didn't trust the timing of the man reaching out.

Not for a second.

The air inside the SUV felt too hot, even with the AC blasting. He rolled his neck, trying to loosen the knot at the base of his spine, but it only cinched tighter. Every instinct he had, every scrap of training drilled into him during his special forces days, told him this was a setup of some sort. McGarvey never came to the table without something sharp hidden behind his back.

And Milo couldn't afford to bleed.

Not now. Not with Willow under his roof. Not with the bond half-complete and her scent lingering on his skin as a signal to every other wolf that she existed, and she was his.

His fingers curled tighter on the wheel. He was walking into the lion's den without a plan.

Milo rolled onto the dock road with the slow precision of a man expecting an ambush. The headlights washed over the row of rust-stained warehouses and shipping containers stacked sky-high. The SUV crunched over gravel as he pulled into the shadow of one of the larger structures, Building 12. It was a good choice. Isolated. Close to water. Easy exits in every direction.

He cut the engine.

Titan was already there, leaning against the side of a black Charger with his arms crossed and a scowl that likely hadn't budged since puberty. The younger wolf straightened as Milo stepped out, heavy boots landing on the concrete like punctuation marks.

"You made good time," Titan muttered, falling in step as Milo passed.

"I wasn't stopping for red lights," Milo replied, scanning the building with sharp eyes. "You see any movement?"

"Just the usual rats. No signs of McGarvey's wolves yet."

"Then they're already inside."

Milo led the way toward the warehouse's side door, every step echoing beneath the high steel roof. He could smell the river, rust, and something else underneath it all—something wrong.

The quickly mounting tension sharpened as they reached the threshold.

The metal door groaned on rusted hinges as Milo pushed, the sound bouncing down the darkened corridor like a warning shot. Cold air met them first, sea-drenched and metallic, followed by the faint flicker of fluorescent lights, one of them stuttering overhead like a faulty nerve. Milo moved first.

He swept the space with his eyes, mentally

marking the exits, counting shadows, cataloging angles. It was muscle memory now. Doorways. Blind spots. Cracks in the concrete that could trip a man running for cover. Every sense dialed in, heightened by the wolf inside him.

Titan followed a step behind, too loud. Too tense. Milo could hear his heartbeat, the fluttering of uncertainty bleeding out through his pores.

"Breathe through it, pup," Milo murmured under his breath. Titan didn't answer, but his pace steadied.

They turned a corner into a massive, open room where the ceiling rose in a cavernous arc overhead. It had once housed freight. Now, it held something far heavier.

McGarvey stood at the center of it all, arms crossed, jaw tight, his pack flanking him like obedient dogs. Five men. No visible weapons.

That didn't mean they weren't armed.

Milo stepped forward.

"McGarvey."

McGarvey's smile slithered across his face.

"Milo," he drawled, voice smooth as aged bourbon and just as full-bodied. "Always a pleasure. And Titan, of course. I do hope you're hard at work on the essay I assigned."

Milo didn't return the smile, ignoring his pointed words.

He stopped ten paces away, feet planted like

concrete and arms loose at his sides, relaxed but ready. "Let's skip the formalities. You called this meeting. What do you want?"

McGarvey let out a low chuckle, brushing imaginary lint off the shoulder of his charcoal blazer. "So direct. It's charming, in a beastly sort of way." He took a slow step forward, his pack staying firmly behind him.

"I want peace, Milo," McGarvey said, lifting his palms in what reeked of mock sincerity. "At least for now. The city's bleeding. Our men are restless. Tensions are rising, and if we don't ease the pressure, we'll be wiping blood off our floors for months."

"You're not wrong," Milo said flatly. "But you don't usually care about the chaos or the cleanup."

"True." McGarvey's grin widened. "But I do care about optics. And business. War is so… messy."

He let the pause linger.

"I propose a truce. Temporary, of course. We give the city time to breathe. You and I keep our wolves in line."

Milo narrowed his eyes.

"And what's in it for you?"

McGarvey's grin didn't falter. If anything, it grew wider.

"Oh, Milo. Must everything be transactional with you?" He took another measured step forward, the heel of his Italian leather loafer clicking against the concrete floor. "Fine. I'll humor you."

He folded his hands behind his back, posture unnervingly elegant for someone who'd likely gutted a man in the last week.

"What I want," McGarvey said smoothly, "is time. Time to let things settle. Time to get my people and territory in order again." He arched an eyebrow. "Frankly, I think you could use the same."

Milo didn't respond, his expression unreadable.

McGarvey continued, voice low and persuasive. "You've been sloppy lately. Distracted. And it's showing. Not very alpha of you."

Titan tensed beside him, and Milo's fists clenched.

"I'm warning you, McGarvey..." he growled.

"Alright, alright," McGarvey chuckled, tone light, amused. "But you do need to tread carefully."

His smile dropped.

"Take the deal, Milo, or we all bleed."

Milo stared McGarvey down, jaw tight, muscles coiling beneath his shirt like a trigger primed. Every instinct in his body screamed to reject the offer, to bare his teeth and show that no one—especially not McGarvey—could dictate his next move.

But instinct didn't build empires. Strategy did.

He gave a slow, curt nod. "Fine. We'll stick to our parts of town. You do the same. No skirmishes. No overreaching."

McGarvey's grin returned like a mask being

slid back into place. "Smart man."

Milo turned on his heel without another word, Titan falling into step beside him. They moved with purpose, each footfall echoing through the cavernous building. The silence between them was thick until they pushed through the front doors and stepped into the cold air, the city lights glittering against the black water in the distance.

Only then did Titan speak, rubbing the back of his neck and exhaling hard.

"That guy is such a dick," he muttered. "Worst homework I've ever had in my life. And it's not even subtle. He gave me a twenty-page paper on power struggles in hierarchical systems—like he's not talking about the packs."

Milo snorted, unlocking his car and tossing Titan a look over the roof.

"Don't flunk."

"I'd rather get shot."

LORE

While highly territorial, packs do
interact regularly with each other
due to the tight-knit familial bond.

Higher-ranking packs tend to be
far more sensitive about their turf.

WILLOW

CHAPTER TWENTY-THREE

Sleep hadn't come easily. By the time morning rolled around, Willow had climbed out of bed with a new mission, determined to salvage whatever control she could. If she couldn't escape yet, she could at least stop wallowing and start thinking clearly.

She decided she needed sunlight on her skin, needed proof the world still existed beyond the walls of Milo's carefully constructed kingdom.

She ended up barefoot on the back patio, the light warming her arms as she settled into one of the Adirondack chairs with a tired sigh and a book she had snagged from a shelf she'd come across.

The late afternoon sun slanted across the back porch, washing the boards in smearing golden puddles. Her knees were drawn to her chest, arms wrapped around her shins, a book held against her leg. Her eyes drifted across the sprawling backyard— first to the neat little garden surrounded by a low, white fence, then to the still blue surface of the pool. The place was so peaceful that it was offensive.

It didn't feel like a prison right now.

And yet, she was still a captive.

The soft breeze teased at the hem of her white sundress, pulling a few strands of hair across her cheek. She didn't brush them away. She didn't move at all. Stillness had become a sort of armor lately—if she stayed quiet long enough, maybe her thoughts would too.

But no such luck.

Milo lived in her head like a ghost, lingering in the darkest parts of her mind, whispering things she didn't want to hear. The shape of his mouth, the strength in his hands, the tenderness behind the violence—it all sat heavy in her memory. Worse than any one moment was the confusion it left behind. She didn't want to want him. She didn't want to like him.

And yet…

Her stomach turned.

Lachlan's words echoed. A mate bond is instinctual… on both parts.

She had felt it—that pull, the unrelenting heat in her blood when Milo was near. It was like gravity had changed its rules and chosen him as her new center. Every time she tried to push it away, it came back stronger. She hated it. Hated how her body and heart refused to fall in line with her brain.

Werewolves. Crime lords. Mate bonds.

None of this was normal. And yet, here she was—sitting on a sun-drenched porch like a princess in a tower, trapped in what she was sure was someone else's fairytale.

Titan appeared, snapping her from her thoughts with his muddy boots thudding against the wooden boards as he shoved the back door open with his hip. He was juggling a stack of burger patties in one hand and a large bag of chips in the other. Behind him, Lachlan followed with a tray of marinated chicken and a six-pack dangling from his fingers.

"Hope you're hungry, Willow," Titan called out, flashing her a boyish grin as he made a beeline for the grill tucked beside the porch railing. "We're doing barbecue tonight."

Willow blinked up at him, squinting against the sun. "Didn't realize you took dinner requests."

"Oh, for you? Always," Lachlan said with a wink, already setting the tray down on the side table beside the grill. "But for now, our dear alpha decided it was a good night for grilling, which usually means we get to do the work and he gets to stand around and supervise."

"Lies and slander," came Milo's voice from the open slider.

Willow's heart gave an unhelpful lurch.

He stepped through the open door, dressed in dark jeans and a navy t-shirt that clung to his chest and arms in maddening ways. His eyes found hers, that familiar heat sparking to life in their depths.

Willow turned away before he could say anything, fixing her gaze on the garden as if it were the most fascinating thing she'd ever seen.

Unbothered, Milo strolled to the railing and leaned on it beside her, letting the breeze lift a few strands of his hair. "Even prisoners deserve good meals," he said quietly, eyes still on her.

She didn't answer.

But she didn't move away either.

Willow's voice cut through the air, cool and sharp. "Strange sentiment coming from you. You don't exactly strike me as a fan of rehabilitation over punishment."

Milo didn't respond at first. He stayed where he was, eyes fixed on the tree line like he could see through the pines and straight into whatever future he was dreaming up.

Finally, his voice came low and even. "You might be surprised who I am, Willow, and what I believe. But you'd have to bother to get to know me."

Then, without waiting for her reply, he pushed off the railing and walked to where Lachlan was setting out utensils. Wordlessly, he picked up the tongs and began helping.

The grill hissed as the first pieces of steak hit the grate, smoke curling upward in thin tendrils. Milo moved with practiced ease. Lachlan stood beside him, sleeves rolled, fussing over the marinade bowl with surgical precision.

Titan was leaned against the porch rail with a cold beer in hand, watching the whole thing unfold like it was the most effort he planned to exert all day.

"Do you think McGarvey will give me an extension on—" Titan began.

Milo didn't look up, cutting him off. "No, and I think it would be a mistake to ask him for one."

Willow heard them vaguely, their voices drifting across the yard. She didn't so much as lift her head. The book in her lap was open again, her thumb idly holding the page.

After some blessedly quiet time, the sun began its descent behind the trees, casting long, amber shadows across the yard. The scent of grilled meat clung to the air, rich and decadent. Lachlan was plating ribs and skewers with careful hands, humming to himself as he arranged everything on the outdoor table. Milo stood by the grill, arms crossed, his expression unreadable.

Titan had just cracked open another beer when Milo turned.

"Alright," Milo said, voice low, "dinner's ready... but first, Titan, we have some unfinished business regarding the night Willow met you."

The younger wolf froze, bottle half-raised to his lips. "What'd'ya mean?"

Milo didn't answer.

Titan's eyes widened, and in the next heartbeat, he was gone—feet pounding across the lawn, beer bottle shattering against the deck. Willow startled, her head jerking up in time to see a blur of movement shoot toward the pool. She stood halfway, uncertain, heart suddenly racing.

Milo moved just as fast, a silent predator cutting across the yard with ease. He didn't shift. He didn't need to. Within seconds, he was gaining ground, his long strides eating the distance.

Titan rounded the pool, breath ragged,

skidding in the grass.

But it was too late.

Milo caught him by the collar and yanked him back just before he reached the concrete.

She was out of her chair.

Willow launched herself across the yard, her bare feet pounding, fury bubbling in her chest. Within seconds, she was between them, slipping into the narrow space.

Milo's fist hovered midair, frozen. Titan flinched, face turned, breath held.

"Absolutely the fuck not," she howled, voice sharp. She jumped to meet Milo's eyes and shoved her book into his chest.

"Willow—"

Something inside her snapped. Every ounce of anger, every inch of exhaustion, every second of being caged; it all detonated at once.

She started barking.

Loud, sharp, hysterical barks, one after the other, exploding from her lungs in rapid bursts.

Milo blinked, stunned. He stumbled back, caught off guard as she advanced on him, still barking.

"Bark, bark, bark. That's what you sound like," she snarled. "*You* need to cool the fuck off."

She shoved him.

Hard.

Milo had nowhere to go but backwards.

The water engulfed his form.

The book went flying after him.

Willow stood at the edge, chest heaving, heart pounding.

Milo surfaced in a smooth glide, water cascading down his broad shoulders as the ripples fanned out around him. He ran a hand over his face, slicking his darkened hair back, then turned to glance at the floating casualty of her wrath—her book.

Reaching out, he plucked it from the surface with two fingers on the spine, shaking it gently like a wet kitten, then turned it in his hands. His expression shifted from curiosity to something close to delight.

"You like Shakespeare?" he called out, a grin spreading.

Willow's eye twitched. She had forgotten that he was familiar with Shakespeare.

She let out one final scream—this one less rage, more resignation—before spinning on her heel and storming away from the pool and toward the deck, fists clenched and shoulders tight. She didn't care that everyone was watching.

The exhaustion was back, creeping in behind her fury like a tide rolling in after the storm. Her limbs felt heavy, her chest hollow. All she wanted now was the dark solitude of her room, the comfort of silence, and the soft embrace of blankets.

Fuck him and his stupid fucking Shakespeare bullshit, she thought bitterly as she slipped in through the sliding door and headed upstairs.

MILO

CHAPTER TWENTY FOUR

Lachlan peered down at Milo, a brow raised as he scooped a bite of potato salad into his mouth. "You good down there?"

"Yeah, great. Why do you ask?"

Lachlan hummed, chewing thoughtfully. "You just seem a little wet, is all."

Milo grinned, sharp and wolfish, even as his chest ached. "If that's what's worrying you, I'd be terrified for Willow tonight."

"You're gross, you know that?" Lachlan said, sighing. "Willow's right. You need to settle down."

Milo didn't argue. He let the water cradle him, cooling his skin even as his clothes fought to drag him down, and his thoughts turned back to Willow. She was somehow so soft even in her fury.

Lachlan finished the last bite of his potato salad, crumpled the paper plate, and tossed it into the nearby trash can with a clean shot. Then, he offered a hand down to Milo.

"You ready to fill me in with what happened at that meeting?"

Milo sighed, letting his legs drop until he was upright in the water. "Not a whole lot."

"But something did happen?"

With a practiced heave, Lachlan pulled him from the water, Milo landing on the stone pool deck with barely a splash. His shirt clung to his body like a second skin, water cascading from his jeans as he ran a hand through his dripping hair.

Once he was up, the two of them walked toward the back porch in silence for a beat, until Milo spoke, voice low and taut.

"He wants some sort of ceasefire between us."

Lachlan's head snapped toward him, eyes narrowing. "And?"

"I agreed to it, but I'm questioning what it entails. It feels almost like he wants to make a grab for territory and for us to roll over while he does it."

Lachlan hissed softly. "He's been after a few pockets for a while."

"Regardless of the reason, it feels wrong," Milo muttered, wiping water from his brow. "I know he's up to something."

Lachlan stopped just inside the doorway, folding his arms. "And Willow?"

"He'll never so much as set eyes on her if I can help it," Milo growled. "She's not a piece on this board. She's off-limits."

Lachlan nodded. "I don't even think McGarvey would go that far, honestly. It would go against the very nature of our laws."

"Yeah. But everything is different now." Milo looked toward the stairs, where Willow had vanished minutes before. "I can't take chances, Lachlan. Not with her life riding on the outcomes."

***

Milo moved through the quiet house, his bare feet silent against the cool floor. The night had finally wound down, the last threads of sunlight long since faded, and the manor had settled into a stillness that felt like pressure building behind his eyes.

He walked into his room, shrugging off his shirt and tossing it into the hamper. The distant chirp of crickets filtered through the open window, but the sound was drowned out by his thoughts.

Of Willow, naturally.

He went about his routine, brushing his teeth with slow, methodical strokes, washing his face like he was preparing for a date instead of bed. He towel-dried, staring at himself in the mirror for a long moment. There were lines in his face that hadn't been there before. New ones, carved not from time, but from stress.

He could still hear the way she had said his name. The memory of her breathless voice from that night was a constant companion now, echoing in his mind like a song on repeat. He'd replayed the moment a hundred times—her softness, her surrender, the tremble in her voice as she begged.

He swallowed hard, dragging a hand down his face. She was unraveling for him, thread by thread, and soon, there'd be nothing left between them but truth and skin.

Milo pulled on a pair of worn sweatpants and padded over to the bed. He sank onto the mattress with a low exhale, staring at the empty space beside him.

Soon, he thought.

***

The fire crackled softly, throwing amber light across the room that flickered and flitted. Shadows stretched long over the antique furniture. The velvet drapes had been pulled back just enough to reveal the snow-covered mountains beyond the tall, arched windows. It was the kind of room that belonged to a place older than memory.

And there, in front of the fireplace, lay the only person who had ever really mattered.

Willow was curled atop the thick fur rug, her bare skin gilded by firelight. Milo watched her from the doorway, barely breathing. Her chest rose and fell in a slow, steady rhythm, and one arm was tucked beneath her head while the other lay loosely over her belly. She was completely at ease, and so fully, beautifully bare.

She hadn't dressed for bed.

Milo stepped forward silently, the weight of his gaze trailing over every inch of her. Her hip curved in the firelight like the edge of a blade. Her back was exposed, spine soft against the fur. He memorized every detail. And though he ached to reach for her, to wake her with his mouth and hands, he didn't. He simply watched, spellbound and still, letting the heat in his chest match the fire that roared behind her. Milo stood in the glow of the fireplace, arms crossed loosely over his chest as he watched her stir. The fur rug shifted with her breathing. The flames played over her skin like they worshipped her as much as he did.

She was waking.

He didn't move.

Didn't *breathe*.

Then she blinked, lashes fluttering open, and her sleepy eyes found him across the room.

"Milo," she rasped, voice soft and thick with sleep. The sound of his name on her lips was enough to anchor him, even when everything else in his world felt untethered.

He stepped closer, slow and careful, like she was prey and yet a forbidden hunt all at once.

"Couldn't sleep," he murmured, keeping his voice low. "Didn't want to wake you."

"You're staring," she said, barely above a whisper. Her tone wasn't accusing. Just tired. Curious.

"You make it hard not to."

Lying there like some kind of dream, flushed with warmth and alive with things he didn't deserve—softness, stillness, light.

When she looked at him again, it was different. Like she was trying to read him, decode something written between the lines of who he was and who he wanted to be.

Perhaps somebody worthy of her.

"You always look at me like you've already decided how the story ends," she said, her voice steady this time.

He dropped into a crouch, careful to keep space between them. His hands curled into loose fists on his thighs.

"That's because it's already been told," he said. "Ours is a story as old as time, sweetheart."

She looked at him for a long time, and in that silence, he could hear every heartbeat. Hers. His. The bond humming like a live wire between them.

"You scare me," she whispered.

"I scare myself," he admitted.

But he didn't back away.

And she didn't ask him to.

Her face was so unguarded that it almost made him ache. The fire behind her cast shadows that dipped into the delicate hollows of her collarbones and the curve of her spine.

And she was still nude.

His pulse ticked upward—not out of lust, though it simmered beneath the surface—but out of awe. She was art. Alive and breathing, wrapped in a halo of firelight and fur.

She stared steadily, slowly dragging her body forward across the rug. She wasn't doing it to tease—

she didn't even seem fully aware of the effect she was having—but every movement was a distraction. His brain fogged, pulse thudding in his ears.

"Where are we?" she whispered.

"My childhood bedroom," he responded.

She didn't respond right away, just stared at him. Her expression shifted, uncertain—torn between instinct and logic, between fear and desire.

He could smell the change in her, the heat between her legs, the spark of something unspoken.

But she didn't close the distance.

And neither did he.

Instead, Milo crouched and waited—for her to speak, for her to move toward him, for anything she was willing to give.

Willow shifted closer, slow and deliberate, until there was no space left between them. Her eyes found his—wide, ocean-blue, glinting with something unreadable in the flicker of firelight. Milo held still, barely breathing.

She tilted her chin up, gaze unwavering, an invitation wrapped with uncertainty.

Carefully, he lifted a hand to her face, brushing his knuckles along her cheek before letting his palm settle there. To his shock, she leaned into it. A soft, barely-there sound slipped from her throat, and it hit him like a strike to the sternum.

God, she was going to *ruin* him.

Her eyes held his, challenging and curious.

Milo's heart thudded against his ribs. He wondered what it would be like to have her devotion—to earn it. To taste the sweetness of her trust.

He wanted her.

But he wanted her to choose him more.

So he curled his fingers gently around her jaw, grounding them both, and said nothing. Because this time, she was in control.

And that was exactly how it had to be.

LORE

If children are orphaned for any reason, the pack will always care for them. Community and family are the foundation of every pack.

WILLOW

CHAPTER TWENTY-FIVE

Willow pulled away—not with force, but with hesitancy—her skin still tingling where he'd touched her. That warmth lingered like a healing wound, curling low in her belly, but she refused to let it settle too deeply.

She turned from him, crossing the room with bare feet pressing silently against the worn wood. The glow of the fire outlined her as she walked, illuminating the soft curves of her form. She didn't bother covering herself. If he looked, let him. He'd already seen her. It was no longer about modesty.

It was about control.

The space around her was vast and drenched in understated opulence. She ran her fingers across the edge of a heavy mahogany desk, its surface worn only in the places that hinted at long hours of use.

Her gaze drifted to the shelves lining the far wall, crammed with books that she was sure smelled of leather and dust. There was a globe in the corner, antique and faded, next to a tufted armchair that looked like it had swallowed generations of secrets.

"This doesn't feel like a room for a child," she said, turning her head just enough to catch his profile in the firelight.

She paused at the edge of the dresser, one hand resting on the carved backing. "It feels like it belongs to some history professor in his late fifties."

Her voice had softened. Not accusatory. Just observant, with a hint of humor.

She wondered again just how many versions of Milo existed, and which ones she was meant to love or fear.

Willow drifted away from the dresser and back toward the fireplace, slow and deliberate in every step, as though retracing her path through some dream. The warmth licked at her bare skin, casting her in flickering gold and shadow, and as she lowered herself to the rug, she felt the softness of it cushion her limbs like a lover's hands.

She sat with her back pressed against the couch, drawing her knees up slightly, arms draped loosely around them. Her head tilted to the side, catching him in her periphery. Willow extended a hand and patted the rug beside her twice.

Still watching him, she raised a brow, just slightly.

"Well?" she murmured.

There was no heat in her voice. Just a quiet challenge, daring him to come closer and see what happened when fire met flint. He braved the threat of flame and came to rest beside her, mirroring Willow's position.

"Why are we here?"

She was curious—truly, deeply curious—and it was unsettling in a way she hadn't expected. The edges of her vision felt blurred, dreamlike. The world around her had gone soft, like it had slipped underwater, and now she floated inside it, untethered and disoriented.

"I thought maybe you'd want to know more about me," Milo said quietly, his voice coming in through the haze. "At least, I hope you do. I'm not keeping you here because I want to hurt you, Willow. I'm doing it to protect you. If you knew more, maybe you'd see that."

She didn't answer. Couldn't, really. Her body was too heavy, her thoughts too light.

He was watching her with his head tilted slightly to the side, studying her the way a farmer studies a storm. Not fearful, but aware that it could break him if he wasn't careful. And he should be. She didn't know what she was capable of anymore.

Not with him, at least.

One thing was certain—Milo's heart was not safe in her hands. Willow felt the distance between them like an impassable chasm. The bond tugged at her, but she refused to be pulled. Still, the sting of that resistance hurt more than she wanted to admit.

And yet, she cared. Not in the way he wanted. Not in the way that made sense. But it was there, a quiet ache in her chest every time she saw the storm in his eyes soften for her. That alone made it harder to write him off completely.

She could use that. She could twist the thread of their bond around her finger, sleep in his bed and whisper promises into the dark—all for the sake of an escape. The idea had festered in her mind more than once.

But when the moment came, when she imagined looking into those mournful eyes and lying straight through her teeth, something inside her recoiled.

"Milo, I'm scared."

The words slipped out before she could stop them, barely more than a whisper. They hovered in the space between them, fragile and uncertain. Willow's gaze dropped to the floor. She didn't know who she was anymore. Her life had been gutted and rearranged, and she was stuck somewhere in the ruins, unsure of where to go from there.

"I know, Willow," he said, quiet but steady. "Can I hold you?"

She didn't answer right away. She couldn't. Her body was caught in a strange push and pull— instinct screaming to run, to retreat, while something deeper, something older, begged her to stay.

After a breath, she nodded.

Milo reached out, warm fingers closing gently around her hand. He guided her to the middle of the rug, where the heat licked at her skin almost too softly to feel real. He laid down, rolling onto his side. Willow followed, hesitant, then let herself curl into him.

Her face turned into his chest.

The steady thrum of his heartbeat echoed against her cheek, grounding her in a way nothing else ever had.

Willow lifted her head. For a long moment, she just looked at him; let herself take in the softness around his eyes, the gentle lift of his brow, the way his lips were parted ever so slightly, waiting.

Her hand came up to his chest first, pressing lightly. And then, quietly, without ceremony, she leaned in and brushed her lips against his.

It was slow. Gentle. *Measured.*

When she pulled back, her breath caught at the expression on his face—equal parts stunned and hopeful, like she'd given him something to hold on to. She pressed her body to his, curling against the warmth of him, letting the fire chase away the rest of her fear.

She wasn't sure what this was yet, wasn't ready to give it a name, but she was starting to feel it settle under her skin, making itself at home.

His hands skimmed over her skin like ghosts, pulling every jagged piece of her fractured heart up to the surface. Part of her, the part still bitter with its wounds, wished he'd bleed for it. That he'd press his palm too hard to her chest and feel the sharpness of everything she wasn't ready to give.

But Milo was careful.

He tilted closer, brushing the bridge of his nose up along her throat, his breath warm against the shell of her ear. She shivered, but not from cold. She wanted his mouth, wanted to feel the fire of it marking her skin. But instead of claiming her in the way she knew he wanted to, he offered something softer.

He nudged his nose against hers, sweet and unexpected.

"I want you."

The confession fell from her lips before she could stop it. Maybe it was the ache pooling low in her tender cunt, or the quiet yearning of her heart for something it recognized in him. Maybe it was both. Some wild, instinctual part of her whispered that safety lived somewhere beneath him—beneath his mouth, his worship.

Milo didn't answer right away. Instead, he pressed his face to her cheek, inhaling her scent.

For a moment, she feared he hadn't heard her at all. Then his voice came, low and gravel-rough.

"You're dream-drunk, sweetheart."

The words cut through the haze. She blinked, her breath catching in her throat. Her mouth parted, ready to defend, to say that she meant it, but nothing came.

What does that mean? Willow wondered, the words still echoing in her skull.

As if he'd read her mind, Milo leaned back just enough to see her face. He was cast in shadows, outlined with a halo of light that made him seem otherworldly. His eyes were wild, glowing gold and ancient and full of something ready to strike. But he didn't pounce. He didn't lose himself.

"We're in a dream, Willow," he said softly, voice low in the space between them. "It's part of the bond between us. If the intention is there, we can meet here. It takes practice to control it… But it's useful for a number of reasons."

She blinked at him, trying to make sense of what that meant. Dream. Bond. Intention.

It felt so real—the heat between them, the weight of the fur rug beneath her, the fire crackling behind Milo. But it explained everything—the way the world seemed softer around the edges, the warmth flooding her chest that wasn't entirely her own.

Willow froze.

The haze peeled back in layers, thin at first, like mist dissolving beneath the sun, then ripping apart in sheets that exposed every raw nerve. She remembered in flashes. The abduction. The conversation with Lachlan. The attempted violence by the pool. Each one slid into place like the cocking of a loaded gun.

Her breath hitched. Her jaw tightened.

Rage wasn't the right word. But it was close, so close it scorched her from the inside out.

"You *motherfucker*," she spat, the words slipping through gritted teeth. She bolted upright. "You've been doing this on purpose."

Milo didn't flinch. He lay stretched out beside the fire, half-shadowed and still, like some predator lounging in the sun after a kill.

"You've been toying with me," she snapped, her voice trembling now with disbelief more than fear. "You're such a jackass."

Still, he didn't move. He looked at her the way you peer out the window at a blizzard—like her fury wasn't something to fear, just a storm to wait out.

"You're not wrong," he said finally, sounding vaguely amused. "But I didn't bring you here tonight. I might have chosen the place, but *you* came to *me*."

LORE

The mate bond is weakened by distance. For example, mates are only able to visit each other in their dreams if they're relatively close by.

MILO

CHAPTER TWENTY-SIX

Milo's eyes opened slowly to the gray wash of dawn light stretching through the heavy curtains. His body felt unusually still, his limbs weighted with a phantom of sleep that didn't quite want to let go. But his mind was already moving, pulling him back through the veil of the night before.

Willow.

He could still feel the burn of her anger, sharp and sudden. The way her voice had cracked with betrayal, the fire in her eyes when she realized the dreamscape wasn't just a coincidence.

But that wasn't what lingered.

What lingered was the way she had crawled toward him. The softness in her voice before the storm arrived. The tentative press of her body against his chest. The quiet ache in her kiss.

She came to me.

It hadn't been his doing this time. He hadn't reached for her—hadn't pulled her through the bond. She'd called to him, even if she didn't understand it yet. Something inside her had reached out in the dark, and that meant more to him than anything she could've said.

He laid a forearm over his eyes and exhaled slowly, a smile tugging at the edge of his mouth.

There was hope.

She was still softening.

Milo sat up, the sheets falling away from his chest as he planted his feet on the cold wood floor.

Now that he was awake, the quiet of the morning wasn't comforting—it was loaded. Too quiet, like the hush that came before a firefight. He rolled his shoulders, muscles tight from tension he hadn't worked out in days. Maybe he'd take it out on the bag later. Maybe the range.

As he stood, he moved through the motions of his morning routine with militant efficiency. Brushed teeth, cold water to the face, a clean black shirt pulled over his frame, jeans slung low on his hips. He strapped on his watch last.

But his mind wasn't on the day ahead.

It was on McGarvey.

Milo didn't trust a single fucking thing that came out of his mouth, and ever since their meeting at the docks, he'd felt something rolling in over the horizon. Something was coming, and Milo wasn't going to be caught off-guard when it did.

He could feel it in his gut. McGarvey had his eyes on Willow.

And that terrified him.

His jaw clenched as he stared into the mirror, the lines of his face hard and shadowed. He had taken oaths in his life—some for his country, some for his brothers—but this one was more personal.

If McGarvey so much as breathed in Willow's direction, Milo would wipe his pack off the map.

War was coming, whatever it looked like.

He *would* be ready.

***

Milo stalked downstairs, each step deliberate, soundless. His senses stretched wide, testing the air like antennae. No trace of her yet—his nose told him that much. Willow hadn't come down. Her scent was still faint, dormant. Still upstairs.

But Titan?

Oh, he had been here.

There was the distinct tinge of unease in his scent. Not panic, not dread—just raw, simmering fear. Good. Milo wanted that. He needed Titan to be scared of him. It was a necessary step in his development. Fear created obedience. Obedience ensured survival.

In combat, hesitation got people killed. The quicker Titan internalized that truth, the longer he'd live. Milo knew the formula firsthand.

He had been scared, too.

Back when he was in basic, green and burning with adrenaline, he remembered the internal terror when his commanding officer barked orders. But that fear had sharpened him. Molded him into something leaner, faster, smarter. Eventually, it became understanding.

His commanding officers hadn't been cruel. They'd just known the cost of failure.

Milo didn't need Titan to like him. He needed

him alive. If fear was the bridge that got them there, so be it. At the end of the day, Milo cared deeply for Titan. That was what made him tough on the kid. Even if he *was* a fucking idiot.

He turned into the kitchen and caught Lachlan's scent before he saw him. Lachlan. That ever-present mix of antiseptic and exhaustion clung to the man like a second skin. Milo rounded the corner and found him exactly where he expected—hunched slightly, one hand wrapped around a chipped mug, the other bracing himself on the counter. His bright pink scrubs were wrinkled, the dark circles beneath his eyes bordering on bruises.

"Long night?" Milo asked, coming to stand beside him. He leaned casually against the counter, arms crossed.

Lachlan exhaled through his nose, then took a slow sip before answering.

"Five-hour surgery on a toddler. Defect in her heart. We got her through just fine, but…" He trailed off, shoulders sinking. "It always hits harder when they're that small."

Milo inclined his head, the tight line of his mouth softening slightly. He didn't speak right away. There was nothing to say that would fix what Lachlan carried. He respected his friend's strength, especially in the face of the heartache he so often faced in his practice.

They stood in silence, letting the weight of

unspoken things settle between them. Lachlan nursed the last of his coffee, eyes distant, until finally he broke the stillness with a quiet observation.

"Don't you think it's strange that Jenner wasn't at the meeting?"

Milo's head snapped to the side, eyes narrowing. "How the hell did you know that?"

Lachlan just raised an eyebrow and gave a tired smirk. "Because if he had been, you would've bitched about him by now."

Milo snorted, short and humorless. He exhaled through his nose and shifted his weight, running a hand through his hair. It was only because Jenner was a fucking weasel and deserved it.

"He's McGarvey's little bitch," Milo then muttered, more to himself than to Lachlan. "Always behind him, waiting for his orders."

"Exactly," Lachlan said, voice low. "And he wasn't present at a meeting with you?"

Milo's brow furrowed. The thought itched in the back of his mind. Jenner was a predator, a knife that McGarvey wielded without a sound. If Jenner was missing, he wasn't absent from the playing field. No, he was just up to something.

"You still in touch with that hacker?" Milo asked, his voice low, intent sharpening behind his eyes. An idea was burgeoning.

Lachlan glanced over. "The one that lives in the shipping container?"

"That's the one."

"I am. Why?"

"I want him to scrape every camera feed he can get access to—traffic cams, building security, anything with eyes. Have him scan for Jenner. I want to know what he's been up to."

Lachlan's brow lifted, a flicker of caution passing through his eyes. "You want surveillance inside McGarvey's territory? That's risky business, my friend, after brokering peace."

Milo pushed off the counter, sliding his hands into the back pockets of his jeans. His jaw flexed as he stared ahead, eyes hard with purpose.

"We don't have a choice. Something's coming, and if we don't get ahead of it, she's going to be the one who pays the price. I can't let that happen. She doesn't need to know the details—that'll just scare her. We need to shield her from this entirely."

He turned slightly, locking eyes with Lachlan.

"Whatever it takes, we lock this down. You hear me?"

Lachlan nodded once, quiet but resolute. "Yeah. I hear you."

A voice cut through the tension like a blade— quiet, cool, edged with suspicion.

"Shield me from what?"

Milo stiffened, head snapping toward the entryway where Willow stood. He hadn't heard her approach. Neither had Lachlan, judging by the jolt of his shoulders.

Milo's mouth parted, but no sound came. For the first time in a long while, he was caught flat-footed—no plan, no deflection. Just a wide-eyed stare and a gut-deep realization that he'd been overheard at the worst possible moment.

Willow's arms were crossed, her expression unreadable. But her stance was steel. She'd heard enough to know something was being kept from her. She wasn't going to walk away quietly.

Milo exhaled as he prepped to face the fallout.

Of course she wouldn't back down.

Not *his* mate.

WILLOW

CHAPTER TWENTY-SEVEN

Willow took a step forward, her socks silent against the cool tile, though the heat rising in her chest was anything but quiet. She could feel it, thick and bitter, crawling up her throat. Her eyes bounced between Milo and Lachlan, locking on the former.

"You don't get to keep me in the dark," she said, voice trembling at first, but growing steadier with every word. "If there's danger, if something's happening, I deserve to know."

Milo's jaw flexed. His arms crossed over his chest, his whole posture shifting into something immovable. "The less you know, the safer you are."

"That's bullshit and you know it." Willow stalked closer, planting herself in front of him, eyes blazing. "I'm not a child. I've been kidnapped, locked away, and dragged into your world without a choice. I have a right to know why you're doing this to me."

Lachlan cleared his throat awkwardly. "Well, this is a whole lot of tension I don't need before noon," he mumbled, edging toward the door. "I'm gonna… give you two some space."

He slipped out, disappearing into the house, leaving Willow and Milo locked in a standoff.

"I won't lie to you," Milo said quietly, but the finality in his voice was unmistakable. "But I won't tell you everything, either. Not yet."

Willow shook her head, lips parted in disbelief. "Why not?"

"Because it'll just scare you, Willow. There's

nothing you can do except stay here and make the best of it." He stepped in closer, lowering his voice. "I won't let *anything* happen to you. I *need* you to trust me, baby. I promise."

"*Trust* you?" she echoed, her voice cracking under the weight of disbelief. "That's rich, Milo. Really." Her arms crossed over her chest like armor, trembling as she held herself together by sheer force of will. "You ripped me out of my life, kept me in the dark, and now you want trust from me?"

She took a shaky breath, but didn't give him time to respond.

"I might—might—be able to forgive you for all of it. The kidnapping. The secrets. The manipulation. But only if you start talking to me like I matter. Like I'm a person, not some fragile thing you want to protect." Her voice thickened, tinged with desperation now. "I don't need you to shield me. I need answers. I deserve that much."

Dread was clawing its way up her spine, cold and relentless. The kind of dread that whispered worst-case scenarios into her thoughts until they took root and grew thorns.

If Milo didn't give her something soon, she was going to spiral.

"Is someone after me? Is Poppy in danger?" Willow's voice was sharp, each word laced with rising panic.

Poppy.

The thought of her sister hit like a gut punch, her chest tightening with guilt. She hadn't been thinking about her enough. Not like she should've. But how could she, trapped in this nightmare with her emotions twisted up in knots and her sense of reality fraying at the edges? Still, it didn't excuse it.

Milo just stood there, silent.

He looked like a kicked dog—eyes soft, brow tight, the weight of the world painted across his face. That expression only made her angrier. She didn't want pity. She wanted the truth. Her lips parted to unleash another wave of demands, but he cut her off before she could even inhale.

"Look, Willow. There are some people, some very bad people, who might want to get their hands on you. But we've got it handled. Poppy is fine. Arlo will move her to a secure location if necessary." Willow stared at him, pulse thudding in her ears.

Some very bad people.

The words settled like lead in her stomach, coiling tighter with each passing second. He'd said it so casually, like he was begging her to stay calm. Like he hadn't just confirmed her worst fear in a tone better suited for weather reports.

Her arms wrapped tighter around herself. She didn't know whether to laugh or scream. If the head of the fucking werewolf mafia thought they were bad, then what kind of monsters were they really?

This was a man who could break someone in

half without blinking. A man who had served in the military and who now ran a criminal empire. And he was afraid?

Her knees felt weak.

She wanted to believe him—wanted to cling to the idea that Poppy was safe. That Arlo would protect her. But Willow's trust had been scraped raw, and every new truth felt like a lemon being pressed into the wound.

Still, the look in Milo's eyes… It begged her to believe that he'd keep her safe. And she wanted so desperately to give him that faith.

Willow swallowed the lump in her throat, the tension pressing hard against her ribcage. Her voice came out low, barely more than a whisper.

"Who's after me, Milo?"

He hesitated, jaw tightening just enough for her to notice.

"It's a long story," he said quietly. "Go to the dining room. It'll be more comfortable. Give me a minute and I'll be there. I'll tell you everything I can."

Her body moved before her mind could object, and she walked across the kitchen and into the dining room as though in a trance.

Once there, she sat down, hands in her lap, fingers twisting together anxiously.

A few quiet minutes passed before Milo stepped into the dining room, a plate held in one hand. He set it in front of her without a word—slices of white cheese, thin rounds of salami, a neat stack of crackers, and a small bunch of grapes. Willow arched a brow, staring at the spread like it had personally offended her.

"Really?" she muttered. "A snack plate? Is this one last-ditch effort to distract me?"

"You didn't eat dinner last night," Milo replied, unbothered. "You need something in your stomach."

She rolled her eyes, but her fingers twitched toward the food anyway. "Well, maybe dinner would've gone smoother if a certain someone hadn't tried to pick on somebody half his size."

His mouth twitched, just enough for her to know he was fighting a laugh.

Still, she plucked a grape from the plate, popped it into her mouth, and chewed. Sweet. Cold. Perfect. Her stomach gave a grumble, and she scowled at the sound. He didn't gloat. He didn't have to.

Swallowing, she leaned back in the chair and narrowed her eyes.

"Alright. Let's hear it."

Milo cleared his throat and leaned forward. His fingers threaded together, forearms braced on the table as if grounding himself before dropping a weight between them.

"We're not the only..." His jaw flexed. "Uh, 'werewolf mafia' in the city."

Willow gave a noncommittal, "Mm-hmm,"

before saying, "I'm aware." Her tone invited him to keep talking, even if she wasn't sure she wanted to hear the rest.

"The city's split into two territories. Ours, and the other run by a man named Colin McGarvey. He's Alpha of his pack, and they deal in…" Milo's gaze slid away, his mouth twisting uncomfortably. "A different currency than we do."

She bit into a cracker topped with cheese, the crunch loud in the silence. Her brows drew together, a faint unease prickling in her chest. "What do you mean by a different currency?"

"They deal in people."

Her chewing stopped. The taste in her mouth turned to ash.

"Like… prostitution?" The word came out as a whisper. "Or what?"

"And more." His voice was steady, but there was venom in it. "The organ trade. Black market. They feed on the shit we won't, and they've grown fatter than we should've let them on our scraps."

Willow's blood iced over. Forced sex work. Organs taken from a body that still breathed. They were the kind of nightmares you kept at arm's length, horrors that lived behind a television screen—never something she had looked in the eye.

"And they want me?" Her voice was barely there. "Why?"

"Because you matter to me," Milo said

grimly, "and they want more ground. Their leader, McGarvey, has got some stupid fucking fantasy that he's going to take this city and crown himself king."

She stared down at the plate. The food blurred, her stomach churning, but she'd at least managed to choke down half.

"What happens if they get me?" The question slipped out, brittle with dread.

"You won't ever have to find out." His eyes locked on hers, hard and unyielding. "I will never let that happen, Willow."

She wanted to believe him. Part of her ached to step into his arms, to let his strength wrap around her like armor, to never leave that fortress once she was inside it. But the other part, the part that remembered she'd been kidnapped, was ice and dread. A gang of ruthless sociopathic werewolves was planning a hostage situation with her as the bargaining chip, and she didn't know how to carry that. The entire thing felt absurd.

A sigh escaped her as she leaned back, slipping her hand from under his, folding both in her lap. The exhaustion came all at once, bone-deep.

"I think I need a nap," she murmured with a humorless laugh.

"I think that's smart," he said. "But afterwards, I was thinking we could get you out of the house for a little while."

One brow lifted, but she didn't bother asking

where. The only thing she wanted now was the oblivion of sleep. She'd gotten the answers she'd chased so desperately, but—like a dog finally catching a car—she had no idea what to do with them.

LORE

While most adhere to the laws
compulsively, there are those who
would see them done away with.

MILO

CHAPTER TWENTY EIGHT

Milo stood at the far end of the kitchen, one hand braced on the counter, the other holding his phone to his ear. The low hum of the fridge was the only sound between his clipped words.

"Status on Poppy?"

"She's good," Arlo said. His tone was level, all business. "She's settled in."

Milo's brow ticked, but he didn't press. "She aware of the situation?"

"She's got the broad strokes. I'm keeping it need-to-know, per SOP."

"Copy." Milo shifted his weight, eyes narrowing on the grain of the wood beneath his hand. "I briefed Willow on McGarvey. She took it about how I expected."

"Panic?"

"No. More like... Shock. She knows McGarvey's pack is targeting her for leverage.."

"Good," Arlo said. The faint rustle on the other end told Milo he was moving—pacing, maybe. "What's her status?"

"Fragile. I'm giving her downtime. Figure I'll get her out of the house tonight."

"Make sure you have coverage. You know how I feel about you compromising OpSec," Arlo lectured.

"Roger," Milo glanced toward the hallway where Willow had disappeared hours ago. "We'll bring Titan."

"Roger that," Arlo responded in kind. "I'll

maintain overwatch." There was a faint shift in his tone again, something that sounded almost like a smile. "Poppy's in good hands. Make sure Willow knows that."

"Keep her there, keep her safe. I'll call in once we have better intel."

"Stay frosty, brother."

"Always."

The line clicked dead, leaving Milo with the fridge's hum and the creeping shadow of the night ahead. He slid the phone into his pocket and crossed the kitchen. He cut through the main hall, the afternoon light spilling in from the tall windows, and stepped into the library.

The scent of old paper and leather hung in the air. He moved toward the far wall, eyes skimming the shelves until they found the right book—a thick, worn field manual wedged between two classics. He pulled it halfway out, heard the soft click, and pushed the shelf to the left. The entire bookcase shifted on hidden hinges, revealing a panel inset with a keypad.

He keyed in the sequence from memory. Eight digits, no hesitation. The lock disengaged with a dull clunk, and the panel slid aside to reveal the entrance.

The air inside was cooler, drier. The walls were lined floor to ceiling with matte-black racks, each one holding an arsenal that could outfit a small army. Carbines, sniper rifles, sidearms, all spotless, all maintained to military standard. Rows of magazines sat neatly stacked, each one labeled and organized by caliber. Ammunition crates were stenciled in sharp black lettering, their lids secured with fresh seals.

On the far side, a workbench was spread with field knives, suppressors, optics, and gear pouches, each one laid out with surgical order. A row of tactical vests hung beside them, MOLLE webbing stripped bare, ready to be loaded. Above it all, a wall-mounted map of the city was marked in red grease pencil—two territories, one line bisecting them like a scar.

Milo stepped inside and let the bookcase slide quietly shut behind him. The room's isolation wrapped around him, muting the rest of the house. Here, there were no burning questions that needed immediate answers. Just gear, preparation, and the quiet hum of the dehumidifier in the corner.

His hand skimmed along the racks until it found the one he wanted—an HK416, Delta's workhorse. Short-stroke piston system, 5.56 NATO, sixteen-inch barrel. It had been his go-to long before the military contracts started pushing them into every elite unit. Reliable in mud, sand, snow—didn't matter what you threw at it, it ran clean.

He took it down with the care a man had for a weapon that had never failed him. The weight was perfect, familiar. Muscle memory filled in the blanks, his fingers moving over the charging handle, the forward assist, checking the chamber before locking it back into place.

Marksmanship had been an edge of his back in training—he didn't just pass, he outperformed by an incredible margin, hitting tight groupings at distances that made instructors double-take. It wasn't luck. It was hours on the range until the rifle felt like an extension of his body, until every breath, every squeeze of the trigger was calculated. That discipline had carried him through Delta selection, through the grueling months where every man in the selection process was ready to break.

He slid the rifle into a soft case, grabbed a loaded mag from the stack, and zipped it shut. No need to bring a full kit for tonight. He already had his Glock holstered on his hip, out of sight but ready at a short notice. That was more than enough firepower.

Crossing the room, he tapped the keypad to seal the armory. The bookcase slid silently back into place, leaving no sign of what was hidden behind it. Milo adjusted the strap of the rifle case on his shoulder and walked out, already running tonight's plan through his head.

***

"Is that... a gun?"

Her disbelief was so pure, Milo laughed.

"Are you telling me it's strange for the head of the 'werewolf mafia' to be armed?"

Willow's lips pressed together, a flicker of

awareness passing through her eyes. She knew she'd walked into that one. Instead of answering, she folded her arms and gave a noncommittal little hum.

"Yes, it's a gun," he said, unzipping the case with deliberate care. "And not just any gun. It's the one you're going to learn to shoot with."

She went pale, the shock plain on her face. Milo knew she wasn't violent by nature—hell, she was likely the gentlest person he knew. But this wasn't about nature; it was about survival. And in the wake of McGarvey's moves, survival meant knowing how to put a round exactly where it needed to go.

He zipped the case shut after letting her see the rifle's black, predatory lines. It would ride in the backseat with Titan, close enough to grab if the trouble they were imagining decided to show its face. Some problems couldn't be solved with a handgun.

"Where are we going?" Willow asked as they stepped out into the glare of late-day sunlight. She lifted a hand to shield her eyes, the heat painting her skin in gold.

She wore a sundress the same shade as her eyes, impossibly blue. The cut was simple, nothing meant to tempt, but on her it was earth-shattering. Milo's gaze lingered, tracing the way the fabric shifted with her every step. He could never get his fill, no matter what she had on… though he'd always admit, he liked her best when there was nothing between his hands and her skin.

"That's a surprise." His smile was small, warm. For a moment, it felt like the early days— before the McGarvey problem, before the threat, before he tore her world apart. She'd been different since he'd given her the truth.

He hoped it stayed that way.

Titan lounged against the back door of Milo's SUV, watching them approach. He was dressed in that polished, city-slick style Milo would've mocked on anyone else. But, on Titan, it fit like it had been made for him, which it had been. The guy had expensive taste and a tailor on speed dial.

The air still held the faint bite of fear. Titan hadn't forgotten the last time Milo's temper had come out to play. But Willow had made it clear that wouldn't be happening again, and Milo wasn't foolish enough to test her on it. For all he knew, next time she'd be just as quick to bite as she was to bark.

They climbed in, the thud of three doors shutting in near-perfect unison, and Milo started the car. The SUV was quiet as Milo eased it down the long drive, gravel popping under the tires. Then Willow shifted in her seat, turning to pin Titan with a look.

"Where are we going, Titan?" Her tone was all sweetness, but there was something sinister coiled beneath it.

Titan blinked, caught between two bad options, displeasing her or displeasing Milo.

Milo spared him the decision. "Stop trying to make him get himself in trouble. It's mean."

Willow's laugh burst out, bright and sudden, before she faced forward again. "Yeah, well, you'd know all about being mean."

His smile was slow, deliberate. "Sweetheart, you haven't seen mean yet. But keep being a naughty girl, and I'll be happy to educate you later tonight. How do you feel about knees? Being bent over them?"

The shift in scent was instant, sharp, and undeniable, her body betraying exactly where her mind had gone. In the back seat, Titan groaned, thunking his head against the window.

"Can we not be gross, guys? Please?"

Willow smacked Milo's arm in mock protest, echoing Titan's sentiment. He only smiled wider, watching her lean forward to play with the radio, fingers twirling the dial.

He had a good feeling about tonight.

WILLOW

CHAPTER TWENTY-NINE

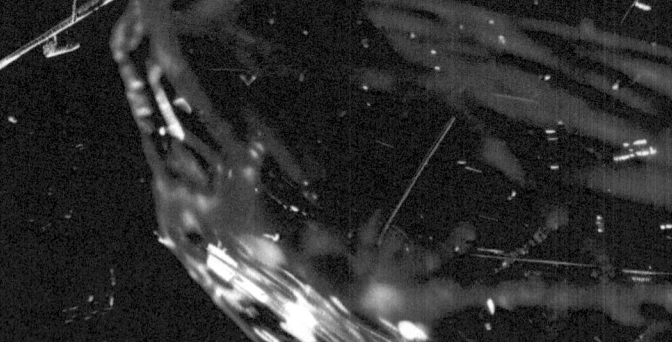

The ride was… pleasant, in a way that felt almost wrong. Willow sat back in her seat, eyes drifting over the blur of trees and sunlit front yards passing beyond the window, and tried not to think about how strange it was to feel even a sliver of peace with everything that was hanging over her head.

On the surface, she kept her shoulders relaxed, her breathing steady. But beneath all the bravado, she was screaming.

McGarvey's name pulsed in her thoughts like a warning bell. Every detail Milo had given her replayed in sharp, ugly fragments—men who dealt in flesh, in organs, in nightmares. She tried to picture what it would mean if they got their hands on her, but her mind shied away from the image. The unknown was bad enough; imagining specifics made her stomach turn.

Her gaze flicked to Milo at the wheel, his profile calm and controlled. The same man who had taken her against her will now positioned himself between her and another predator. Her captor, now her protector. The paradox made her skin prickle.

Logic said she shouldn't trust him—not entirely, or maybe not at all. But the truth was, if McGarvey's people came for her right now, she'd want him there to save her.

That thought twisted in her chest, leaving her unsettled. Every time she thought she had her emotions in order, something else blindsided her, and everything inside her knotted back up again.

She turned back to the window, willing the road ahead to hold no surprises. But deep down, she knew that with Milo, surprises were inevitable.

It was the very nature of the beast.

Of *his* beast.

Willow's feet swung lazily in time with the music; some heavy metal track she didn't recognize. The riffs crawled over her skin in a way that made her shudder with delight.

"You like that, huh?" Milo's voice cut through, casual, his sunglasses catching the last blaze of the setting sun.

"I'm a fan," she said, forcing a small smile when he glanced at her.

"Nice."

The rest of the drive slipped into a comfortable quiet, the kind that almost let her drift off. Her eyelids were heavy when Milo eased the SUV into a right turn and rolled into a parking lot. She blinked, straightening, and scanned their surroundings.

A plant nursery.

Willow arched a brow at him, unsure what to make of it. He was drumming a finger against the steering wheel, watching her with a look that suggested she was supposed to react.

"Uh… thanks?" she offered, her mouth curving into a crooked smile. It wasn't that she minded—plants were fine—but it wasn't exactly what she'd expected when leaving the safety of the manor. Whatever reason he had for bringing her here, she decided not to question it.

Titan yawned, then leaned forward between the front seats. Milo turned and shoved his head back with a flat palm, forcing him into the rear again.

"Aw, fuck you, Milo," Titan muttered, raking a hand through his mussed hair.

"Fuck yourself." Milo reached into the console and held out a small case. "Here. Earbuds. You know the drill."

Titan took them, sliding them in before making a move for the door.

"Oh, and Titan?"

He paused, glancing back.

"Don't fuck it up, or it'll be the last thing you ever fuck up. Tracking?"

Titan's smile was tight, the kind that knew better than to push back. "Tracking," he confirmed, before slipping out fast.

Willow crossed her arms, watching him disappear. "Do you *really* need to be such a dick to him?" She didn't see the point in grinding down the youngest member of the pack. She'd never been a fan of hazing.

Milo hummed low in his throat, one arm stretched out on the wheel, the other resting loosely in his lap.

"Yeah," he said at last, a playful grin tugging at his mouth. "I do, actually."

She huffed, not satisfied with the answer. "What are we waiting for, anyway?"

"Titan's sweeping the place before we step inside. Cameras already say it's clean, but I want boots on the ground before we arrive."

The nerves she tried to bury flickering in her eyes. Her fingers worked restlessly in her lap, twisting until her knuckles turned pink. Milo still spoke like a soldier—clipped, precise—and she found herself wondering if that would ever fade.

Milo plucked another earbud from a separate case, fitting it snugly in place before pressing a finger to its side. "Titan, do you copy?"

A brief pause. Then, "I copy. Over and out."

He turned to her, his voice low, almost gentle. "Are you ready, sweetheart?"

For once, she didn't bristle at the endearment. A faint, weary smile tugged at her mouth as she nodded. Together, they stepped out of the SUV, the air outside cooler, sharper, and carrying the weight of whatever waited in their future.

***

"Are you fucking joking?" Willow's voice pitched up in surprise as she clutched his arm, her face breaking into a grin so wide it almost startled her.

Her eyes lit, sparkling as she took in the scene ahead.

A little animal shelter.

"They do this every week," Milo said, as if it were nothing. "Figured you might like to play with some puppies."

His tone was casual, but she could feel the tension coiled beneath it, the way he was watching her too closely. He was waiting for something—for the other shoe to drop, maybe. And it hit her then that after everything, he might not fully trust this version of her. The one smiling, excited. The one who, for the moment, had forgotten to fight him.

"I've heard of these. They do it for adoption events or whatever, right?" She asked.

"Yeah, exactly."

Willow's hand rested lightly on his arm as they walked in step. His scent wrapped around her— clean and sharp, with something darker and muskier beneath. Where they touched, heat seemed to pool under her skin, spreading until she felt luminous. Milo adjusted his arm, crooking it to give her a more secure hold, and the small gesture sent warmth through her.

She was... happy. If this were another life— her life, the one she'd had before—she could have sworn this was the kind of man she might marry. The kind she'd come home giddy over, curling up on the couch to gush to Poppy about how he'd swept her off her feet with a thoughtful surprise.

But this wasn't that life.

And Milo wasn't just some man.

In fact, he wasn't merely a man at all.

The reality pressed in like a cold draft, reminding her of the jagged edges beneath the moment. She was still caught in a web of shifting danger and emotional whiplash, and the sweetness of it all deflated under the weight of that truth.

"Hey. You good?"

She glanced over to find Milo watching her, his gaze lit with concern.

Willow brushed her hair out of her face and looked straight ahead. "Yeah. Fine. Just… a little all over the place. It's a lot to process."

Silence stretched for a beat before his free hand came over to cover hers, still hooked in the crook of his arm.

"It's going to be alright," he said, voice low, steady. "Whatever comes, we were always meant to be with each other. You feel it too. I know you do."

She tensed. Her mouth opened, ready to tell him to tone it down, but he kept going.

"We don't have to talk about it right now, okay? Let's just… enjoy tonight. Pretend it's all fine. Just for a little while."

Willow let the words settle. He wasn't wrong— dragging herself through the weight of it now would ruin the one moment of lightness she'd had in what felt like years. With a small nod, she decided to let herself breathe.

Just like Milo had said.
Just for a little while.

MILO

CHAPTER THIRTY

"Absolutely not."

Milo pinched the bridge of his nose, elbow braced in the palm of his other hand. When he finally looked up, his fingers slid to cup his cheek, and he found Willow staring at him with the most pitiful expression he'd ever seen.

His chest gave an uncomfortable squeeze.

She was cradling two kittens, both tucked against her chest like they already belonged to her. And to be fair, they were adorable. But they didn't have a pet-friendly household. It wasn't about the werewolf thing; animals that tolerated dogs usually handled his kind just fine.

No, his reasons were far simpler. He didn't want creatures in his home that pissed, shit, and shredded furniture for fun.

Still, with her looking at him like that, the hard line he'd drawn started to blur.

She'd started with the guinea pigs, crouching low to offer them a handful of greens the staff had given her. The little creatures squeaked and shuffled closer, and he caught a quiet smile curving her mouth.

From there, she moved to the birds—colorful flashes of feathers behind bars. She tilted her head, listening as one cocked its own head back at her, the two of them locked in some silent conversation that made her eyes glimmer.

The dogs were next. Big ones, small ones, all pressing to the gate for her touch. She crouched again, letting eager noses bump her palms, laughing when one licked her fingers.

Her joy made his stomach flip.

And then, of course, the cats. She melted for them instantly, scooping one into her arms and letting it curl into her chest for a cuddle it was delighted to have. Watching her like that—open, unguarded, the walls down—it did something to him.

Now he was in a situation he hadn't prepared for, and he hated being unprepared.

"But they love me," she whimpered, lifting the kittens until only her eyes peeked over their backs, pressing her face into their soft fur.

"Yes, and I'm sure they'll learn to love whatever family actually takes them home, Willow."

She lowered them slowly, and he caught the tremble in her bottom lip.

Oh, no. Please. Not that.

Her eyes glossed over, filling with tears, and she sniffled.

"But they'll make me happy. And I don't have anything else that makes me happy because you took it all away from me."

The words hit like a sucker punch.

She's not serious. She did not just go there.

He groaned inwardly, but before he could respond—

"Uhm, hi!"

Both their heads turned toward a shelter

worker approaching, waving brightly.

"Sorry, couldn't help overhearing. Just thought I'd mention that we've got a special today. Two kittens for the adoption fee of one!"

Milo's jaw tightened. He could have murdered her on the spot.

"Perfect! It's settled, then." Willow, who had been crouching on the floor, stood with careful grace, both kittens secure in her arms.

"I'll just go get the paperwork"

With that, the worker strode off.

Milo shot her a look of pure, simmering frustration.

"Y'know," he said, voice low and flat, "I'm starting to think you actually do want to end up over my knee. I did warn you earlier."

He hadn't even considered what her reaction to those words might be. Hadn't even thought about whether it might push her too far.

But she only rolled her eyes, slow and exaggerated, before a small smile tugged at her lips as she looked away.

The worker returned quickly with a clipboard in hand, cheerfully announcing she'd "box them up" while they handled the paperwork. Willow practically bounced in place, the kind of giddiness that made Milo's eye twitch as he began filling in the forms.

"So," he asked gruffly without looking up, "if you like animals this much, why don't you already have some?"

"Well, I wouldn't have had time to take care of them." Her arms crossed, her tone dry but not sharp. "But now I don't have a job, so… y'know. I think I can manage it."

She didn't sound genuinely upset. Which, somehow, irritated him more.

Milo exhaled hard as he scrawled the last signature and handed the clipboard back to the woman. Willow cradled the cardboard carrier like it was the most precious thing in the world, his card sliding into the reader, the beep of approval, and then the two of them stepping out into the evening air.

Titan was exactly where Milo had told him to be, posted by the SUV.

"Oh—Wow, I forgot you were even here," Willow said, blinking at him in genuine surprise.

"Uh… thanks?" Titan frowned, leaning to get a look. "What's in the box?"

Milo groaned, pulling open Willow's door. She set the kittens down on the seat first, then climbed in and put the box in her lap.

"They're kittens!" Willow announced to Titan as he slid into the back seat.

"You let her get kittens?" Titan said in pure disbelief, like Milo had just gone off the deep end.

Milo felt the urge to put his head through the steering wheel.

"So does this mean I can finally get a dog?"

Titan leaned forward between the seats, all hope and no sense.

Milo shoved him back the same way he had earlier. "Absolutely the fuck not."

"Come on, Milo. That's so unfair, dude!"

"She doesn't know it yet," Milo said, eyes on the rearview, "but I'm making her take them back tomorrow."

Willow's head snapped toward him in horror and outrage. He couldn't help it—he laughed, shaking his head as he eased the SUV out of the parking spot.

"Okay, but seriously, why can't we get a dog?"

"Because we have you. Close enough."

"Oh, fuck you, man."

"Right back at you, punk."

***

They stopped at a pet store for the essentials, against Milo's better judgment. The idea of walking into an unsecured location without eyes or ears already inside made his skin prickle.

But Willow had begged him, insisting the kittens couldn't go without for even one night. And when she looked at him like that, there wasn't a damn thing he could do but give in.

He grumbled the whole way in, pushing the cart with the boxed-up kittens riding in the seat. Willow moved ahead of him, plucking toys and treats from the shelves, comparing food brands like she was making a call that might decide the fate of the entire world.

She wore the quiet act of caring like it had always belonged to her. It likely had. His chest tightened as he watched her crouch to read the side of a bag, her hair falling forward, her lip caught lightly between her teeth.

She had no idea what she did to him. No idea how deep it went.

In his head, it was too easy to picture her like this in his home—barefoot, glowing, the swell of his child under her shirt as she moved around the kitchen, or leaned over a laundry basket. That vision hit low and hard, heat curling through him, possessive and dangerous. The beast was coming back to the surface, and it wanted to breed its bitch.

He dragged his eyes back to the cart, forcing himself to focus on the here and now. But the image stayed with him, stubborn as his thudding heartbeat.

"Are you okay?" Willow asked, brows knitting as she studied him.

"Yeah, fine. Just thinking." His tone was easy, the smile that followed enough to put her at ease. She turned back to the row of litter boxes without pressing.

"Get the self-cleaning one," he said, a yawn wrapping around the words.

"It's like five hundred dollars, Milo."

"I don't care."

She hesitated, searching his face for a beat before sliding the box off the shelf and dropping it into the cart. The basket was filling fast—food, toys, beds, that overpriced litter box—and Milo was already doing the math. This was going to be an expensive trip.

But he didn't care. Not even a little. Nothing was too much for her. She was his queen, and he'd see to it she never wanted for a single thing.

And apparently, neither would her cats.

They checked out at the register, Milo taking the bags while Willow carried the boxed-up kittens. Outside, he opened her door, making sure she was settled before Titan appeared to help load the haul into the back.

When the trunk finally clicked shut, Milo stood there for a moment, shaking his head.

God, *what* this woman was doing to him.

WILLOW

CHAPTER THIRTY-ONE

Willow woke to the soft, steady purr of a kitten on either side of her head, their tiny bodies warm against her ears. At the far end of the bed, Milo was stretched, passed out.

She blinked against the haze of sleep, turning her head to press a drowsy kiss to the fur of the kitten nearest her. Both were boys, barely twelve weeks old, and so new to this world. Two small, fragile lives, and they were hers now.

Her gaze slid to Milo, her lips quirking despite herself. She thought about last night—his massive hands cupping those delicate little bodies, the way he'd been careful not to startle them, speaking low and steady as he tucked them into their box while he and Willow set everything up.

Those hands could break a man with little effort, but with the kittens, he'd been patient and controlled. The memory settled in her chest with a warmth she didn't want to examine too closely.

The mate bond was there, a quiet hum beneath her skin, pulling her toward him whether she wanted it or not.

With a grin she couldn't quite help, she kicked out, nudging his calf. He grumbled in his sleep, so she tried rocking him with her foot, though moving a man built like a bull was an exercise in futility.

Still, she kept trying.

"Yes? May I help you, queen of our castle?" he drawled, his voice thick with sleep, edged in amusement.

"I want pancakes."

His head turned toward her, one brow arched, eyes bright with mischief despite the grogginess still clinging to him.

"What's in it for me?"

Heat crept into her cheeks at the low, suggestive note in his tone. She caught it instantly, but refused to take the bait.

Instead, she gave him another shove with her foot. "I'll stop kicking you."

Milo scoffed, the sound rough but fond. "Alright, fine. Pancakes it is."

Willow eased back into the pillow with a contented sigh, the kittens curling close again, their tiny bodies warm against her cheeks. For the moment, everything felt simple.

She wished it could just stay like this.

***

Willow joined Titan and Lachlan already at the table. It struck her how often she found them all in one place, despite their schedules. They always seemed to make time for each other, something that had struck her in the short time she'd been there.

That little blip in time was all it had taken for her life to implode. For her to be kidnapped. For all of this to have happened. It felt absurd, like someone had handed the pen to a teenage girl with a fever and told her to write the next chapters of Willow's life. Not that the teenage girl buried inside her was complaining. She was busy swooning over the handsome, dangerous werewolf who had taken her hostage and…

Willow started shifting in her seat as her pussy began to pulse. She knew without question that both men could scent the change in the air, and the knowledge made her cheeks burn.

They were polite enough not to mention it. But that didn't mean they hadn't noticed.

"So, Willow. How are the kittens?" Lachlan asked, breaking the silence with a steady, measured tone that she welcomed.

"They're adorable." Her voice softened, but there was a rasp to it. "I really wish I could show my sister. She's always loved cats."

The words scraped her throat. Every now and then, the truth of her circumstances crashed back down like a sheet of ice water. She knew she was adapting, making the best of it because that was what people did when their sanity depended on it. But admitting that didn't make the absence of her sister sting less.

"Well, I'm sure she'll love them when she gets to meet them." Lachlan's eyes stayed on her, unreadable. "Do they have names yet?"

"I've got a name picked out for the dog Milo

won't let me get," Titan cut in, leaning back in his chair.

"Shut up, Titan." Lachlan didn't even glance at him, still fixed on Willow.

She tilted her head, narrowing her eyes at the youngest of them. "Why is your name Titan?"

Titan blinked. "I—what?"

Heat crept into her cheeks, the realization that she might have been rude landing late. "I just mean, it's an odd name, I guess."

"She's not wrong," Lachlan chimed in. "It is pretty odd."

"It's traditional!" Titan whined, feigning offense as he pressed a hand to his chest.

"What tradition?" Lachlan countered without missing a beat. "My name is traditional. Your name is a god complex waiting to happen."

A laugh bubbled out of Willow before she could stop it, light and unguarded. For just a moment, the tension at the table thinned, replaced by something dangerously close to normalcy.

"Alright, seriously, what are the kittens' names?" Lachlan asked, inclining his head toward Willow again.

"They don't have names yet."

"Titan, go grab the rest of the shit from the kitchen." Milo cut into the conversation, carrying a plate of pancakes piled high in one hand and a jug of maple syrup in the other.

Titan didn't argue. He pushed back from the table and went without a word.

As soon as he was out of earshot, Willow turned to Milo, who had just settled in beside her. "You don't have to be such a dick to him. He's a kid."

"First of all, Willow, he's a full-grown man," Milo said, rolling his eyes.

"A full-grown man who's killed people," Lachlan added evenly, as if he were reminding her of the weather.

Willow blinked, the weight of the words landing heavy. They were right—Titan wasn't innocent. He wasn't some boy she had to shield from Milo's corruption. He'd taken lives, just the same as the rest of them.

And yet, something in her still wanted to protect him.

"Also, word to the wise," Lachlan said, tapping his ear, "he can hear you patronizing him."

She blushed, a hand rising to cover her mouth.

Fucking werewolf bullshit superpowers. She didn't think she'd ever get used to it.

***

After breakfast, Lachlan headed out for a multi-day shift, and Titan was sent off on some urgent errand. The previously upbeat atmosphere disappeared quickly after that, leaving Willow to retreat back to her room.

The kittens were waiting.

One was a storm gray with bright orange eyes that seemed too sharp for a creature so slight. The other, an orange tabby with startling blue eyes, had white across his belly and on the tips of his paws. Willow stroked their fur absently, admiring them as she considered her situation.

She still wasn't sure she trusted Milo.

Pieces were missing; incidents that didn't line up, shadows she couldn't shine a light on, no matter how she tried. How long had he been watching her before the farmer's market? How had he known her name when she hadn't even seen his face? What else did he know? Those questions gnawed at her.

Willow was certain of one thing only—Milo still had his secrets.

And she wasn't sure she wanted to dig them up. Some truths, once unearthed, couldn't be put back in the ground. Maybe ignorance really was a kind of bliss. Maybe pretending was easier than the alternative when things were already so complicated.

Her gaze drifted to the kittens nestled against her side, their small bodies breathing in perfect rhythm. For a moment, she let herself sink into the simple comfort of watching them. But her thoughts soon slid elsewhere—back to the dream that had haunted her a few nights ago.

Milo's childhood bedroom. The rug beneath

them. He stretched out beside her, close but not pressing, his presence wrapping around her entirely. She remembered the way the light had come through in amber waves, and the strange ache in her chest when she'd felt his lips ghost over her body.

It had felt so real at the time.

And, somehow, she had gone to him.

She shook her head, brushing her fingers over the kittens' fur, as if their warmth could chase the thoughts away. But they lingered—his secrets, her doubts, and the bond between them that pulsed stubbornly beneath it all, demanding to be acknowledged.

Regardless, she was here. And the truth was, there were far worse things in this world than Milo with his watchful eyes and unsettling devotion.

Her mind flickered to McGarvey, the name alone enough to send unease rippling through her. She didn't even know his face, had never heard his voice, but Milo's descriptions had painted him as monstrous, ruthless and predatory. A man who dealt in *human flesh*.

Willow shuddered, pulling the blanket a little tighter around herself. She hoped she would never have to see that man for herself.

For all her doubts, she had one certainty—if McGarvey ever came knocking, she would rather be standing behind her stalker-turned-captor-turned-protector than face the darkness alone.

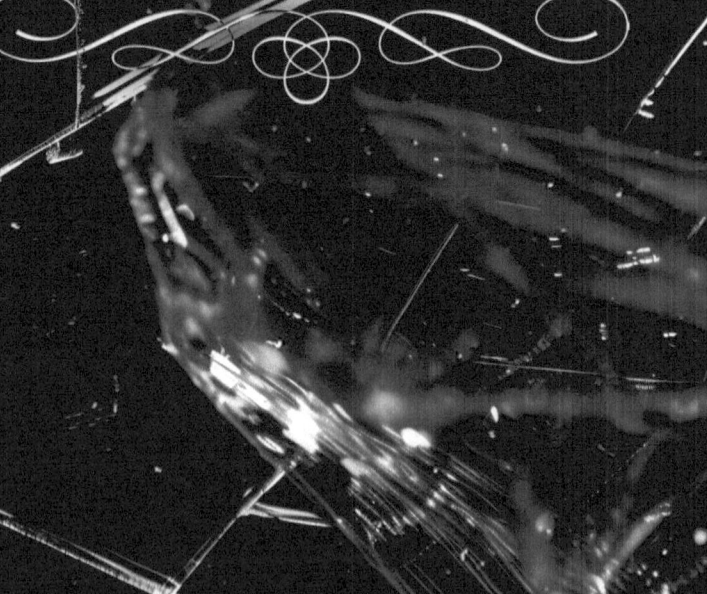

MILO

CHAPTER THIRTY-TWO

"Think she'll put two and two together?"

Milo arched a brow, glancing over at Titan. The younger wolf was hunched over a laptop, a textbook spread open beside it, the glow of the screen brightening his face. The van around them was kitted out like a command post—rows of monitors, wires, gear—and looked entirely nondescript from the outside.

"What?" Milo asked, voice flat.

"That the McGarvey I've been talking about is the same McGarvey who wants to fuck our shit up."

Milo snorted, turning back to the wall of camera feeds flickering in front of him. "Maybe when it's pointed out to her in a very obvious way."

If there was one thing he'd learned about Willow, it was that she wasn't exactly the observant type. And maybe that was for the best. Ignorance could be bliss. He was willing to let her live in it as long as he could, if only to protect her for longer.

It had been a week since the kittens came home, and their care had somehow become part of a mutual rhythm between himself and Willow. Every night since, he and Willow had found each other in their dreams—always the same delicate tether, as if fate itself kept drawing them back together.

There, it was all light touches and the ghost of lips brushing, moments stretched thin with anticipation. Never more than that. Willow wasn't ready. He could feel it in the way she leaned into him and then pulled back, warmth tempered by caution.

And he took what she offered, no matter how little it was compared to what he wanted. He held her close when she allowed it, memorizing the weight of her against him, the scent of her hair, the small sighs she let slip when her guard faltered.

She was warmer with him now. The ice had cracked, melting in places, but the wall was still there—stubborn, unyielding. She gave him pieces, never the whole. And Milo accepted it, even as a part of him ached with the certainty that she was his.

He could wait. He'd take the warmth she offered and bide his time, holding her in dreams until she finally let him hold her in truth.

It had also been a week of chasing his own tail, trying to pin down Jenner. They'd caught glimpses of him here and there, but his presence was always fleeting, a mirage swaying above hot pavement. By the time Milo had boots on the ground, the little weasel had already slipped away, vanishing as though the city itself had conspired to protect him, swallowing him whole.

Now Milo was on the ground himself, hunting Jenner the old-fashioned way. Sometimes that was what it took. You couldn't delegate instinct, couldn't catch a scent through a screen. And being the one in charge meant leading by example, never asking his men to get their hands dirty in ways he wouldn't.

Not that they could match him in training

anyway. Except Arlo.

That absence gnawed at him. It was a gap in the unit that couldn't be patched no matter how tightly he pulled the rest together. Without him, every move felt just a little less sharp, every plan slower to lock into place. It was proving harder to ignore by the day. Even so, Milo understood that Arlo was needed elsewhere. The show had to go on. War would wait for no one.

Something flickered on the feed, familiar enough to snag Milo's attention. His eyes cut to the right-most screen, chair swiveling as he locked onto the image.

There he was.

"A cannoli? Yo, is he serious?" Titan scoffed from behind him, abandoning whatever half-assed work he'd been pretending to do in favor of crowding Milo's shoulder.

Sure enough, Jenner strolled out of a bakery—one owned by the weasels' grandmother's cousin's great-granddaughter, or something equally convoluted. Unlike Milo, Jenner had fairly humble origins, and had clawed his way to the top of the city.

Their circles were small. Everyone knew everyone, and the bloodlines twisted tight. At the top, things stayed stable enough, but the lower rungs were always gnawing at each other, packs snapping at each other for territory and rank.

They'd all grown up in that same mess, which

made tracking Jenner easier in theory. In practice, it just meant the bastard knew how to slip through the cracks better than most.

"Should we make a move? Bag him?" Titan's voice buzzed with eagerness, the kind of reckless energy only inexperience bred.

Milo didn't take his eyes off the feed. "No. We're here for intel, nothing more. We lay low, we watch, we collect. The end."

One wrong move now and it would end in blood on all sides.

He dragged a hand down his face, exhaling slow. It was going to be a long night, made longer with Titan vibrating in his seat, itching for action he wasn't ready for. Milo's patience was stretched thin.

And beneath it, another sense pulled at him.

His mate.

She'd be at home, slipping into bed by now, drawing the blankets over her body. The image hit him hard, clawing at his composure.

He ground his teeth, jaw tight. The month was only half-spent, the moon climbing toward her peak, and already he could feel the beast pacing inside him. Hungry. Restless. Possessive. He had high hopes that she'd let him knot her this time, that their union would be completed and she'd belong to him entirely.

It amazed him sometimes, that everything he felt for her now, all this burning, unrelenting need, was only a shadow of what it would be once they were fully mated. If this was only the fraction, he couldn't imagine the intensity waiting for him on the other side. Milo couldn't fathom how far he'd be willing to go, how much blood he'd spill in her name, once their bond was sealed tight.

But it wasn't just the bond. It wasn't just instinct, or the beast clawing in his chest.

It was her.

Willow, with her stubbornness and wary eyes. The way she softened when she thought no one was looking, how she pressed kisses into the kittens' fur with a tenderness that made his heart ache. He remembered crouching on the floor beside her, both of them laughing as one of the little terrors tried to climb his arm like a tree. She'd looked up at him then, cheeks flushed from laughing too hard, and something inside him had shifted permanently.

He loved her because she was fire and steel, because she was stubborn enough to stand toe-to-toe with him, because she still carried gentleness in a world that had done its best to strip it from her.

And he knew once she was his in truth, there would be nothing in this world or the next that could take her from him.

***

The house was quiet when they returned, Titan peeling off to his own quarters with a muttered good night. The mission had yielded little in the way of results, but Milo didn't care anymore. Not once he crossed the threshold of his room.

Willow was there.

In his bed.

She was curled on her side, the blankets tangled around her legs, hair spilling across his pillow. The kittens were tucked into the crook of her knees, their small bodies rising and falling with the rhythm of her sleep.

For a long moment, he just stood in the doorway, silent. His chest clenched so hard it almost hurt. He'd envisioned this, dreamed of it, craved it, but he hadn't expected it to hit him like this.

Not lust, though that was always there, simmering under his skin whenever she was near. This was something heavier. The sight of her in his space, on his sheets, her scent already woven into the air...

It undid him.

He stepped inside quietly, every movement controlled. His boots were silent as he set them aside, his hands deliberate as he shrugged out of his jacket. Willow's presence pulled at him like a magnet, drawing him closer until he stood beside the bed, looking down at her.

Her lips were parted slightly, lashes brushing her cheeks. She looked peaceful, unguarded in a way she never was awake. He could almost imagine this was normal. That she was his fully bonded mate, asleep after waiting up for him, the bed warm from her body as he slid in beside her.

Milo dragged a hand down his face, exhaling slowly. The beast inside him stirred at the thought, whispering, "Mate." His mate.

Careful, he sat on the edge of the bed, the mattress dipping under his weight. One of the kittens stirred, stretching before tucking itself back against Willow's legs. She shifted, just barely, her hand brushing over the empty side of the bed as if searching for him even in sleep.

His throat tightened.

Milo let himself feel it all—the want, the devotion, the bone-deep certainty that she belonged to him. And he promised himself, silently, that one day she'd wake up in this bed and know it too.

WILLOW

CHAPTER THIRTY THREE

Willow surfaced slowly from sleep, the warmth of the kittens curled against her legs anchoring her in the cocoon of blankets. She stretched, blinking against the sleep still thick in her eyes—then froze.

Milo was there.

Sitting on the edge of the bed, broad shoulders hunched slightly forward, eyes fixed on her. Watching. Eyes glowing.

Her breath caught. She pushed herself up on her elbows, the sheet sliding down her chest. "How long have you been sitting there?"

"Definitely not long enough to be weird."

Willow almost laughed. Her heart thudded. She searched his face, trying to read the expression there, but it was too much all at once—concern, exhaustion, that unreadable intensity that always seemed to sharpen when his gaze was on her.

And then, there was the state of his eyes.

"Do your eyes just do that, or are you doing it on purpose?" she asked, brows scrunched.

He raised an eyebrow. "I can make them not do it, but it's a subconscious reaction." His hand flexed against his thigh, restless. "Anyway, I didn't mean to wake you."

She sat up fully, tugging the blanket into her lap. "So you just decided to watch me sleep instead?"

"Yeah." The corner of his mouth curved, not quite a smile. "I like seeing you peaceful. You fight me too hard when you're awake."

Heat flared in her cheeks. She dropped her eyes to the kittens, who were blinking sleepily up at her as though they, too, were curious about the tension between their humans.

"You make that sound like I'm a constant battle."

"You are." His tone softened, but it still held weight. "And I wouldn't trade it. But seeing you like this…" He trailed off, shaking his head. "It makes me think there's a chance."

Willow's throat went dry. She wanted to argue, to remind him that she hadn't chosen this, that she was still here against her will. But the words tangled with what she felt in the pit of her stomach every time his voice dipped like that.

So instead, she asked, "Did the mission go well?"

His jaw worked. "Not as well as I wanted." Then his eyes found hers again, steady, unflinching. "But I came home. To you. In my bed."

Her chest tightened, breath catching. She had come in here to get the kittens, and fallen asleep while playing with them. She hadn't done it purposefully. Probably.

Her thoughts were running circles until she almost felt dizzy. He was her captor. He was supposed to be the enemy. The reason her entire world had been torn apart.

And yet, he had come home to her. He had sat

there, silent and steady, just to watch her at peace for a little while.

Willow swallowed hard, fingers clutching the blanket in her lap as she sat up, fighting herself. She should push him away, keep that wall between them, remind herself that none of this was safe. But when she looked at him—at the exhaustion in his eyes, at the way he seemed to be holding himself together just by sheer willpower—her resistance fractured.

Before she could second-guess it, she leaned forward.

Her lips brushed his. Soft, tentative. A question.

Milo went still for a heartbeat, and then he answered, his mouth pressing back with quiet certainty. The kiss deepened slowly, like he was afraid she'd spook if he moved too fast. But she didn't pull away. She leaned into it, heat blooming low in her belly.

When one of the kittens gave a disgruntled little mewl, they broke off just long enough for Milo to scoop the pair of them gently from the bed and set them on the floor.

And then his mouth was on hers again, no hesitation this time.

The kiss was hungrier now, her hands fisting in his shirt as he pulled her closer, closer, until she felt like she was being melded into him. Willow gasped into his mouth, her heart hammering as his hand slid along her jaw, tilting her head to take more of him. She knew she should stop. She knew this was spiraling quickly. But the truth was, she didn't want to stop. Not when every nerve in her body was alight, not when the bond between them glowed so brilliantly, it felt like her body had become luminous under his hands.

Milo's mouth claimed hers again after a short break to breathe—deeper this time, his hand anchoring her jaw as though he could keep her from slipping away. She yielded, fingers curling into his shirt, pulling him closer again until their chests brushed, until the air between them was filled with their heat.

He shifted, the mattress dipping as he braced a hand beside her head. With careful, deliberate movement, he guided her back against the pillows. The world seemed to narrow to the heat of his body pressing over hers, his weight caging her in without crushing.

Willow's pulse stuttered. She should have felt trapped. Pinned. And she did…

But she liked it. Every inch of her ached with a longing she didn't know how to fight.

Milo hovered just above her, their lips still brushing, their breath mingling. His eyes searched hers—dark, *burning*, yet holding that thread of restraint, as though he was daring her to tell him no.

She didn't.

Instead, she arched up so she could grind into

him, closing the distance, her mouth finding his again with a hunger that startled even her. He groaned low in his chest, the sound vibrating through her as his hand slid from her jaw to cradle the side of her throat, his thumb stroking once across her skin.

Slow. Controlled. Every movement a battle between what they both wanted and the fragile line they teetered on. Her pussy was pounding with desire at his nearness. She didn't care anymore. She needed him.

Willow's hands roamed higher, slipping over his shoulders, feeling the strength coiled beneath the fabric of his shirt. She clung to him, anchoring herself as if letting go would undo her completely.

He broke the kiss just long enough to rest his forehead against hers, his breath unsteady. "We don't have to do anything you don't want to, Willow."
Her chest rose and fell against his, her lips swollen from his kisses, her voice barely more than a whisper. "Milo, please. Don't stop."

His weight hovered over her, lips coaxing hers open, drawing out every soft sound she was willing to give him. His hand slid down, skimming the side of her body, pausing at her hip, asking for permission. Willow's breath hitched, and instead of pulling back, she lifted her arms, fingers tangling in his hair, wordlessly giving him her answer.

He moved slowly, deliberately, as if each motion was sacred. His mouth broke from hers, trailing down. Heat followed everywhere he touched, each kiss branding her until she felt fevered.

The air was cool against her bare skin with his hot breath wafting across it, her chest rising and falling too fast. Milo's gaze darkened, reverent as it swept over her, but he didn't rush. He leaned down, flicking his tongue against the pebbled peak of her breast, pleasure spreading warm and solid across her chest, anchoring her against the maelstrom inside.

Willow arched into him, a small, desperate sound catching in her throat. His mouth continued its assault, and she shivered at the tenderness in his licking, sucking, nibbling. There was no cruelty here, no dominance wielded like a weapon. Just him, stripped down to the bone, showing her what it meant to be claimed without force.

Her hands clung to him, nails dragging over his back, urging him closer. The bond was undeniable now, pulling her under, telling her this was where she belonged.

With him.

Under him.

Always.

When his hand finally slid lower, settling over the heat between her tensing thighs, she gasped, anticipation knitting tight in her belly. He kissed her again, slow and consuming, as though he could steady her with his mouth alone.

And Willow let herself fall into it, into him—

into the dangerous, undeniable truth that she wanted him, too.

He broke from her mouth only to trail kisses lower, down her throat, over the hollow of her collarbone, each one setting her nerves alight. By the time he pulled the last of her clothes away, Willow was trembling beneath him, her body bare and flushed, her breath coming too fast.

For a moment, he just looked at her. His expression was dark, awestruck, like she was something of impossible value he wasn't sure he deserved. "You're perfect," he whispered, the words rasping low as his mouth descended again.

She gasped as he trailed kisses along her belly, pressing them to her thighs, settling between her legs with a hunger in his eyes that terrified as much as it thrilled. Hot air ghosted across her wet slit, his hands steady on her hips.

"Tell me you want this."

His words struck her. Hard. Fast. She realized she was panting; short, quick bursts of breath that made her head spin. Willow swallowed, letting her head fall back, her words coming loose like a prayer.

"Milo, please, *I need you*."

Willow's fingers tangled in his hair, her back arching, every nerve in her body straining toward him. The bond cut through her like a current—every touch amplified, every brush of his mouth sparking low and deep.

His hand slid lower, between her thighs, spreading heat and pressure where she already ached for him. Willow moaned softly, thighs clenching tighter, her whole body alive with sensation. She could hardly think—only feel, only want.

"Milo…" Her voice broke on his name, half-plea, half-surrender.

When he finally slipped two fingers inside of her, curling them slowly. He dragged in and out, and Willow nearly lost her mind. Her moan was louder now, full of something akin to pain.

He lifted his head to watch her face, bringing his closer to hers, his fingers still working her with a slow, steady rhythm that unraveled her. "That's it," he growled against her neck. "Tell me how badly you need to be fucked, Willow. I want to hear it from that beautiful mouth."

She melted under him, giving herself over entirely—to his hands, to his mouth, to his heat pressing her down into the bed until she was certain she would break apart in his arms.

"You feel so—oh!—fucking *good*," Willow groaned, her hips rocking in perfect rhythm with his hand. The room lay cloaked in shadows, but the fire building inside her blazed brighter than any sun, flooding her senses and driving her closer—ever closer—to the edge.

Milo pressed a kiss to her cheek, whispering, "I'm going to make you come until you pass out."

It sounded like a vow, but it landed like a warning. The sheer power he held over her body, over her, was staggering. With nothing more than his hands, he could open her completely.

The thought of his mouth tracing that same devastation made her tremble.

She knew already, of course. Their dreams had given her glimpses, muted shades of this hunger. But this? This was something else entirely. This was reality stripped raw. What he did to her now bent reason, mocked the very idea of control, and thrived in the exquisite chaos of her undoing.

Her head fell back.

She came *undone*.

MILO

CHAPTER THIRTY FOUR

She was flying through space and time, caught in the orbit of his touch, her whole body answering to a single hand. Every flicker of expression that crossed her face shredded what little control he still clung to. Milo's cock twitched painfully. A growl tore through his teeth, low and guttural, as he descended.

She whimpered for his attention. In that moment, there was no question.

Willow *belonged* to *him*.

Slowly, he dragged his tongue, flat and rough, against her glistening slit. Her arousal, now hovering in front of his face, had a scent both rich and undeniable, a force that consumed everything else. Time seemed to fracture, each heartbeat a point at which his mind broke. The edges of his vision blurred, darkened, until there was nothing left but her—laid out before him like the only meal he'd ever eat again. This was the feast he'd hungered for, denied and aching, and now it was finally within reach.

Milo spread her pussy with a deft hand, latching onto her swollen clit with gentle, insistent lips. The response was instant, a visceral jolt that sent her hips arching, trembling as they pressed up against his mouth with a desperate, fragile force. The sound that tore out of him was unrestrained, a guttural moan that betrayed just how undone he was by her.

"Fuck, baby, the way you taste," he groaned as he came up for air.

He followed through on his promise with

merciless dedication. Minutes bled away, and she was left glistening with sweat, fingers twisted deep into the sheets, spine locked in a desperate arch beneath his touch. Her breaths came ragged and shallow, each one dragged from her like it cost her everything; he was sure the exhaustion twined inseparably with the pleasure wracking her body.

"Milo, please…" she cried out, "I need you to fuck the next one out of me."

Those words shattered his entire reality. He felt himself coming apart at the seams, his mind scrambled, his vision blurry. Milo turned his gaze to meet hers, knowing that he looked every bit like the monster she was so desperate to hate.

But when their eyes locked, all he found staring back at him was a mirror of his own desperate lust. Not a flicker of hesitation. Not a hint of fear. She wanted this—wanted him—as badly as he did.

Milo rose up just enough to peel away his shirt, the fabric clinging before sliding free, baring the hard planes of his chest. Willow's breath caught. He knew she'd seen him shirtless before, but never like this, hovering above her in the flesh, gaze molten. Every inch of him was carved with strength that had been honed for war but now focused entirely on pleasuring her.

His hands went to his belt, the quiet sound of metal sliding free echoing in the stillness of the room. Willow's pulse stuttered, the sight both terrifying and intoxicating. When he unfastened his pants, her eyes followed the movement.

Milo noticed. The corner of his mouth curved in the faintest, most dangerous smile. "What are you staring at, naughty girl?" he teased, his voice roughened with restraint. He slid the belt free in one smooth motion, the leather whispering before snapping taut between his hands. The sound cracked through the room like a warning, sharp and deliberate, a promise delivered by a threat.

Willow flushed and turned her face into the pillow, but her body betrayed her, arching slightly toward him. Milo filed that reaction away for later; they would certainly be discussing limits soon. For now, he leaned back down, bracing himself on either side of her, skin hot against hers now.

The air between them thickened, charged, and Milo could feel it—how the world narrowed to this moment, to her, to the bond tightening invisibly around them with every beat of their hearts.

And then her hand found him, reaching between them so that she could stroke his pulsing length. Milo's breath hitched and he groaned, hips jerking into her touch. Willow's eyes were full of wonder…

Until her hand bumped into his swollen knot. "*Oh*—" she started, eyebrows shooting up, "Oh, wow?"

"That's my knot, baby," he panted, trying his

hardest not to spill himself prematurely. She wasn't making it easy for him; her hand wandering with shameless curiosity, brushing over the firm swell of his knot that would bind her to him in ways she couldn't yet comprehend. That single touch carried the weight of what came after, of what it would mean once he finally claimed her.

But not this time.

She wouldn't be able to handle it yet.

He felt her hesitation and leaned down, pressing a gentle kiss to her lips. "Sweetheart, it's okay. I would never knot you without your consent. You aren't ready for that."

That soothed the frightened doe inside her, loosening the tension in her body. Willow let her forehead press against his, their breath shivering between them. With trembling focus, she guided him to her slick, desperate entrance—hips rising instinctively, a small, broken sound slipping out.

His hips pushed forward, and Milo sheathed his throbbing cock in one, slow thrust. Their cries tangled in the air, a single sound born of shared surrender. Both of them shifted, bodies straining to match the rhythm of this new reality they'd built between them. For a breathless moment, nothing else existed—just their world, steeped in heat and bound by a pleasure that felt eternal.

"Oh, God, Willow," he breathed, the words hot against her hair as he buried his face into the crown of her head. Now that he was fully inside her, every muscle in his body trembled with restraint. He cursed the height that kept him from seeing her face; he ached to watch her unravel, to see her eyes glaze and cross when the pleasure became too much.

"Oh, oh," she whimpered, sounding like a wounded animal, "*Oh*, Milo, you're too big."

"Hush, sweetheart," he whispered. "You're going to adjust. I'll teach you how to take my cock."

With that, he began to move—slow, deliberate, no more than a whisper of motion inside her. And yet, it was still enough to break her wide open. Willow's cry tore through the room, a raw, piercing sound that rattled his bones and set every instinct in him ablaze.

"God, I just want to fucking pump you full of my cum, watch it drip out of that pretty pussy," he was growling desperately into the air, hips rolling in a smooth rhythm. He wasn't thrusting, no, just moving around. Milo wasn't convinced she could handle anything more than this.

Even so, this slow lovemaking was unraveling him, bit by fragile bit. Everything in his body screamed with the effort of restraint, his control stretched to breaking. Milo swore he'd spill himself each time her breath caught on a moan, or when it hitched sharp and sweet the moment he found that tender spot inside her.

And then, he felt it.

Milo felt her *come for him*.

Willow writhed beneath him, her cries raw and feral, a wild sound that rattled the bars of the beast caged inside him. Each sweet noise that burst from her threatened to let it free, to drag him past the fragile line between control and surrender.

A roar tore from his chest as the raw, electric need surged through him, drowning out reason. His rhythm faltered into something reckless, ragged—each thrust harder, faster, the heavy press of his knot battering against her entrance. Instinct screamed at him to give in, to claim her fully, to lock her to him in a physical bond she couldn't sever. It took every shred of discipline not to surrender to that pull, not to force that intensive intimacy on her.

Instead, Milo surrendered, letting himself crash over the edge. Release tore through him in violent waves, his hips grinding desperately into hers as hot spurts of cum spilled into her cunt. Each frantic thrust was met with her voice—his name spilling from her lips again and again, a broken plea, a tether keeping them both from being swept completely away.

After, the room was heavy with silence, broken only by the ragged sound of their breathing, lungs straining to catch up after the marathon they'd just endured. Milo remained braced above her, his forehead pressed to hers, sweat dripping from his temple onto her cheek. She didn't flinch—just let it mingle there, as if proof of what they'd done should stay marked on her skin.

After a long stretch of quiet, he shifted down and pulled her into his chest, strong arms wrapping around her as though the act of letting her go for even a moment was unthinkable. Willow melted into him without hesitation, their tangled bodies humming with the aftershock of what they had just shared.

Her voice was a whisper against his collarbone. "I'm sorry I pushed you into the pool."

Milo chuckled low in his chest, the sound reverberating through her, and tilted her chin up with his knuckle. His eyes were softened by affection, fixed wholly on her beautiful face. "Don't be. That's what I admire most about you, Willow. You don't back down just because of who I am. You're so gentle, sweetheart, but you've got a spine. That's why you're perfect for me."

Her breath caught, eyes searching his.

He pressed a kiss to her forehead, lingering there. "Your place—" he murmured against her skin, "—is to right me when I'm wrong. To rule beside me. You're not just some random woman I took, Willow. You're destined by fate to be my queen."

Willow didn't respond. Instead, she just curled in closer to him, sighing contentedly. He waited until her breathing was even before drifting off as well, his knot still rock-hard and throbbing for release.

WILLOW

CHAPTER THIRTY-FIVE

Morning crept in slow, the pale light of dawn spilling across the sheets, tangling with the scent of sex still thick in the air. Willow stirred, struggling against the weight of sleep, her body sore in ways that reminded her exactly how the night had gone. Heat crawled up her neck at the memory—his hands, his mouth, the way she'd clung to him as though she might die without his cock.

It had been reckless. And now here she was, lying in his bed with his arm heavy across her waist, his chest rising and falling steady against her back.

Willow swallowed hard, her throat dry. She knew she should roll away, put distance between them, rebuild the wall she kept patching together only for him to tear down again. This was dangerous. Getting too close, letting herself soften, giving a crime lord she didn't even trust pieces of her heart she wasn't sure she could ever reclaim.

But she didn't move.

Her fingers twitched against the sheet, aching to curl into his hand where it rested possessively on her lower belly. The quiet was suffocating and soothing all at once, her thoughts caught between regret and yearning. She hated how easy it felt. How natural. As if she belonged here, as if she hadn't been dragged into this life kicking and screaming.

Willow shut her eyes, willing her heart to still, but it betrayed her anyway—beating faster, syncing with his as though her body had already chosen.

Milo stirred behind her, the shift subtle at first, becoming heavier as he drew in a long breath. His chest pressed closer, nose grazing her hair. Willow squeezed her eyes shut, trying to even her breathing like she was still asleep.

It didn't work.

"You're thinking too loud," he murmured, voice rough with sleep, words dragging low across the nape of her neck.

Her heart leapt. She swallowed, unsure what to say, unsure what she even felt. "I wasn't," she whispered, defensive by instinct.

Milo's arm tightened around her waist, pulling her flush against him. "You were," he countered, softer now, like he could feel the panic rising in her chest. "Whatever it is, you can always share it with me, Willow."

She turned her face into the pillow, heat stinging at her eyes. She hated how much she wanted to believe him, how badly she wanted to just let herself sink. "It was just…" she muttered. "Last night. I wasn't thinking."

"Maybe not," he admitted, and she felt the rumble of his voice against her back. "But we're getting closer to the full moon, Willow. You're going to start experiencing some… new things."

She went still. His hand splayed wide against her lower stomach, warm and grounding, as he continued.

"The full moon matters, but not the way humans think. We don't sprout fangs and eat people. What it calls out in us is something different. It's tied to our fertility, our breeding. When the moon hits her peak, every instinct in me is to breed my bitch under that light, to bind us in the way nature demands."

Willow's mouth went dry, her mind fumbling over what he'd just revealed. She blinked hard, as if that might help her catch up, but it only left her more flustered. And then, like a trapdoor swinging open beneath her, an awful suspicion slithered in.

"Milo... what's a knot?"

The silence that followed told her more than she wanted to know. He just stared, broad shoulders stilling, before the corner of his mouth curved into that infuriatingly crooked smile. It was obvious he was fighting laughter.

Heat flared in her cheeks. "Don't be mean to me," she groaned, smacking his chest with the back of her hand. He was solid as a wall, barely budging, and the huff she let out only made him grin wider.

After a moment, Milo finally sobered, his chest rising and falling with a long, measured sigh.

"A knot is a kind of bulb at the base of my cock. When I start to come, instinct pushes me to, uh, shove it inside of you. It physically ties us together for up to an hour."

The silence was deafening.

"That's... absolutely horrifying," Willow said

at last, her voice slow, deliberate, like she was trying to parse his words. On the surface, it was grotesque, something out of a horror movie. But low in her belly, something twisted.

Not fear.

Not revulsion.

Desire.

The realization made her flush hot, her skin prickling as though she'd just knelt in a confessional. What he wanted to do to her, it was fucking unholy. It sickened and fascinated her in equal parts.

But then, the want bloomed in her like it had back when she was a virgin, before she'd ever been touched, before she knew anything beyond the hunger yawning in her core. That nameless, impatient need for something to be inside of her.

Willow hadn't known what it was to have something in that aching place. And yet, somehow, she just knew she needed that exactly.

She felt the same way about his knot.

Her thoughts were spiraling, tangled up in places she didn't dare go, when Milo cleared his throat. A sharp cough, like he knew exactly where her mind had wandered and wanted to yank her back before she twisted herself up any further.

"You hungry?" he asked casually, his voice threaded with amusement, like he wasn't really asking at all. "Because I know the kittens are. They're going to start crying soon."

Willow blinked, grateful for the interruption.

A small smile tugged at his lips as he pushed off the bed and offered her a hand. "Come on, then. Let's feed your little mistakes before they tear the place apart."

Willow gasped and threw a pillow at him. "Milo!"

***

The morning had drifted into something soft and slow, the rising heat making them both feel lazy. Breakfast had been messy—kittens darting underfoot, Milo teasing her about the way she burned the toast—but now the chaos had faded into this, quiet, easy stillness.

She lay curled against him in the hammock, his arm heavy around her shoulders, her cheek resting on the solid expanse of his chest. The hammock rocked gently with each lazy push of his foot against the grass, swaying them back and forth like the world had slowed just for them.

It was too comfortable. Willow told herself not to sink into it, not to let the steady rhythm of his heartbeat beneath her ear trick her into believing this was normal. There *was* a normal life she wanted to return to, when the danger was over, maybe…

And yet.

His hand stroked idly along her arm, fingertips

brushing over her skin with absent reverence, like touching her was as natural as breathing. He didn't speak, didn't fill the silence with heavy words or questions, and that silence did more damage to her defenses than any charm or charisma could. Because she realized she didn't need him to make those extravagant promises right now. She just needed him.

Willow's throat tightened. She shouldn't feel safe. She shouldn't feel cherished. But with Milo's warmth wrapped around her, the kittens watching from the slider, and the hammock rocking them in time with the breeze—she almost forgot to be afraid.

Almost.

"Careful," he murmured eventually, his voice a low rumble vibrating through his chest. "If you keep looking at me like that, you'll never look at a hammock the same way again."

Her lips twitched, betraying her even as her heart tried to crawl into her throat. "I wasn't looking at you any sort of way," she sniffed, turning her nose up at him.

His chuckle was deep, dangerous, and unbearably fond. The kind of sound that made her wonder—terrifyingly, traitorously—what it would be like to hear it for the rest of her life.

Milo leaned his head toward hers, whispering into her ear, "I'm beginning to think that your first punishment isn't going to be given over my knee." She flushed, eyes widening.

"Instead, Willow, I think you'll have to choke on my cock until I come down your throat so you can learn to better watch your mouth."

Her eyes fluttered shut, and the sound that escaped her throat was small, fragile—something she didn't even know she was capable of making. Milo's laugh followed, low and rich. He pulled her closer, his strength swallowing her whole. She didn't want him to see it—the ache, the hunger, the way she craved him not gently, but brutally.

Violent.

Overpowering.

Dominating.

She no longer pined for candlelight under the stars. Not since meeting him. No, Willow wanted to be *taken* under a swollen moon.

Although, it did strike her as funny that he had, in fact, taken her already under the full moon, and her reaction had been less than thrilled.

As though he'd reached into her head and plucked the thought straight from her brain, Milo dipped his face to her hair, his lips brushing the crown of her head.

"Sweetheart," he rumbled, voice carrying that dangerous tenderness that both soothed and inflamed, "we've got plenty of time to explore all of the ways in which we're sexually compatible. But right now…" His mouth lingered against her temple, a phantom kiss. "Right now, I want us ready for the full moon."

She sat with it for a long moment, turning the words over in her head, trying to piece together a clearer picture. Her throat worked, but her voice came out soft, almost hesitant.

"Is it... going to hurt?"

Milo's gaze softened, though his answer carried weight. "It's... complicated. Yes and no. From what I've been told, it's not pain in the way you think. It's overwhelming—stretching you further than you thought possible, holding you there for upwards of an hour, where you can barely move. But every woman I've ever spoken to says the same thing." His lips quirked faintly, and his eyes never left hers. "That it's the most intense, earth-shattering pleasure they've ever felt."

Her breath caught at the blunt honesty of it, her mind scrambling. And then a thought struck her, sharp and sudden.

"Milo, are there female werewolves?"

The look he gave her made her feel like she'd just grown an extra head. "Of course there are."

"Then why haven't I met any?"

He tilted his head, humming low in his throat as though considering it for the first time. "That's a fair point. You haven't. But this—" he gestured faintly to the walls around them "—is a bachelor house. My men won't take mates until their alpha does. That's how all packs operate. It has to start at the top. The alpha finds his match, and only then does the rest of the pack fall in line. That's how the next generation is born—new blood, new wolves. That's how the cycle continues."

She groaned, her head falling back so she could squint at the fluffy clouds hanging overhead.

"Werewolf culture sounds so complicated."

"Don't worry, sweetheart. You don't have to think. You just have to grow my babies," he growled into her ear. She gasped, whipping around to face him, eyes flashing with anger.

"I am not an incubator for your potential offspring, Milo," she growled, baring her teeth at him.

His smile was absolutely wicked. "We'll see how you feel come the end of the month. Bet you anything you're begging for me to pump you full of cum before night even falls."

She refused to dignify that with a response, even if she knew his nose would sense the one between her legs anyway.

MILO

CHAPTER THIRTY-SIX

The garden was overgrown, a tangle of weeds that had swallowed the beds whole and choked the pathways between them. Milo stood with his arms folded across his chest, boots planted in the dirt as he surveyed the wreckage.

It hadn't been touched in years—not since he had tended it as a boy and then a young man, hands raw from pulling weeds and learning which plants needed pruning, which needed patience. Back then, the garden had thrived. Back then, it had been something beautiful.

Now, it looked like a graveyard of all the dreams he had held while he was young.
Milo exhaled through his nose, shaking his head at himself. A soldier, a commander, a killer—and here he was, thinking about fertilizer ratios and whether or not the soil was too acidic to hold basil.

But maybe that was the point.

Milo crouched, dragging a broad palm through the dark earth, and for the first time in years, he thought about what it would mean to rebuild something instead of tearing it apart. The idea of starting the garden again settled strangely in his chest. Maybe Willow would like it. She deserved beauty. She deserved peace. And if he could give her that in the form of a garden, then he would.

His mind drifted—inevitably, always—to her. To the way she'd looked at him that night a couple weeks back when they'd first made love, hesitant but unafraid, to the tremor in her voice when she'd asked him what it would mean to be knotted.

She hadn't run. She'd listened, thought about it, and still, she was *willing*.

The relief that swept through him at the memory was staggering. The beast inside him, always so close to the surface when she was near quieted in that remembrance. She would let him claim her fully, bind her to him under the moon. The mate bond would no longer be a fragile thread but something unbreakable. Permanent.

Milo straightened, brushing the dirt from his hands, and looked over the tangled mess again. It would take weeks of work, patience, and persistence. But he could picture it already—sunlight catching on budding flowers, herbs spilling over wooden beds, Willow wandering barefoot between the rows with a watering can.

Milo left the garden behind, brushing the dirt from his palms as he stepped back into the house. The shift in air was immediate—cooler, quieter, but not without its own kind of chaos due to their newest additions. The kittens came barreling through the kitchen like tiny streaks of furry lightning, one skidding across the tile before regaining balance with a startled chirp.

He leaned against the counter, arms folded as he watched them tumble over each other. Already, they'd doubled in size since he and Willow had brought them home. Their paws didn't look so oversized anymore, their eyes sharper, more alert. A few more weeks and they'd start losing that fragile kitten clumsiness, turning into proper little predators.

His chest tightened in a way he wasn't ready to put words to. Too damn fast. Everything felt like it was moving too damn fast, and it all seemed to be going so well. His stomach tightened. It couldn't stay that way. It wouldn't. He hated that.

The back door clicked, followed by the sound of shoes scuffing on tile and the unmistakable scent of his packmate. Milo looked up just as Lachlan trudged in, peeling off his jacket with the sluggish motions of a man who'd gone far too long without real rest.

His hair was mussed, his purple scrubs wrinkled, and there was a shadow to his face that spoke louder than any words could.

"Long shift?" Milo asked, voice low.

Lachlan dropped the jacket over a chair, exhaling like the weight of the day was still pressing on his shoulders. "Thirty-six hours, I think. I stopped counting after the twentieth." He scrubbed a hand over his face, eyes half-shut, then glanced toward the kittens now attacking one another under the table. "At least someone in this house is thriving."

Milo let out a faint huff of amusement, though his gaze didn't leave Lachlan. He looked hollow, but grounded—same as always after a shift like that. Lachlan dropped onto one of the stools at the island, propping his elbow on the counter and letting his cheek sink into his palm. He studied Milo with that slow, heavy stare that came after too many hours engaging his brain.

"Any updates on Jenner? Or anything else I should know?"

Milo leaned back against the counter, arms folded. "Touched base with our friend in the shipping container."

Lachlan's lip quirked. "Still in the shipping container?"

"Yes."

"Y'know, I really think it's part of his charm."

A dry laugh passed Milo's lips. "Jenner's been… doing nothing. Which, honestly, is worse. He's pulled away from his pack, but no one can make sense of why. It's like he's on a vacation of some sort."

Lachlan's eyes went unfocused as he processed, expression flat but alive beneath the exhaustion. Always thinking, always pulling strings together in his head even when the rest of him was running on fumes. Milo felt a rush of relief having him home again. For all the sidearms they carried, Lachlan's mind was still one of their sharpest weapons.

"Think he had a falling out with McGarvey?"

"Doubt it." Milo's answer was immediate. "He wouldn't walk away from that alive. Jenner's the brains, sure—but at the end of the day, he's still expendable if McGarvey thinks he's going AWOL."

Lachlan straightened in his seat, fatigue pushed aside as his gaze sharpened on Milo. "Then what if it's deliberate? What if they're trying to split your focus?"

Milo's jaw flexed as he considered it, arms folding across his chest. His head tilted, weighing the words. It wasn't impossible. In fact, the idea slotted into place far too neatly.

"But what exactly are they trying to pull me away from?" Milo asked, voice low.

"Does it matter?" Lachlan countered, tone steady but edged with weariness. "You're pulled in a dozen directions already. That's the whole point—you won't see the primary objective if you're chasing all these offshoots. Jenner's little disappearing act feels like the biggest carrot, so to speak."

"Yeah?" Milo's lip curled. "Well, I'm about ready to shove that carrot straight up his weasel ass." Lachlan's laugh cracked the tension, soft but genuine, his eyes narrowing with amusement.

"Milo, you cannot still hate him for things that happened when we were kids."

"I sure can, actually."

"He was a little boy."

"He was a slimy tattletale."

"He's a grown man now."

"He's just a bigger, slimier tattletale."

"Oh, good lord. Here we go." Lachlan pressed his fingers to the bridge of his nose. "Let me grab a chair."

"You're already sitting."

"I'll need another."

Before he could retort, he felt her. But, milliseconds before that, he smelled her.

And so did Lachlan.

Both men froze at once, realization striking like lightning, their eyes widening in unison. Lachlan rose slowly from his chair, and together they moved toward her—silent, deliberate, almost predatory in the way they closed the distance.

To her credit, Willow didn't shrink back. But the shift in their energy had her stiffening, brows drawing tight as her gaze darted between them. The air was charged, heavy with something unseen, and still she held her ground, even when they leaned in, tentative and testing the air like hounds on a trail.

Milo hardly registered her sharp, impatient look. The annoyed confusion on her face drowned beneath the tidal wave of hormones and instinct. His body was taut as a nocked arrow, pulse stretching long and slow as he straightened, Lachlan mirroring the motion at his side.

"What are you doing?" Willow demanded at last, her voice tight with exasperation, though there was a thread of unease beneath it.

Milo's throat worked. The words didn't come easily, but his chest ached with the wonder of it. "Willow, sweetheart…" He paused, eyes alight, caught between awe and disbelief. "You're pregnant."

He would never forget the way her expression shifted in that heartbeat. Annoyance faltered into shock. And then, like glass fracturing, devastation exploded across her face.

WILLOW

CHAPTER THIRTY SEVEN

Willow lay curled on her side in the darkness, her arms wound tight around a pillow as if it could keep her from falling apart. The room was quiet but for the soft, uneven sound of her own breathing—hitching, stifled sobs pressed into the cotton so no one would hear.

She tried not to think about their superhearing, and the fact that they probably could hear her anyway.

Her body shook with the weight of it, a life inside her. The words plastered across her brain like a map of clues she couldn't make sense of. She hadn't asked for this, hadn't dreamed of it. And yet, there it was—woven into her blood, rooted in her uterus, threatening to change everything about her life once again.

Her fingers clutched harder at the pillow. She didn't even know what she wanted. The idea of a child was terrifying enough, but the thought of becoming a mother in this world—one filled with violence, betrayal, and monsters she hadn't even known existed a month ago—made her feel sick.

She loved Milo. Or at least, she was circling dangerously close to it. That was the problem. The thought of breaking him, of watching his face when she told him she didn't want this, that she wanted it gone, turned her stomach inside out. His entire being seemed wired for legacy, for pack, for bloodline…

But she wanted her freedom.

She buried her face deeper into the pillow, hot tears spilling freely now. If she kept it, she wasn't sure she'd survive it. If she ended it, she wasn't sure their bond would. Panic clawed through her chest, sharp and merciless, until she thought she might choke on it.

Her tears slowed but didn't stop. She stared into the darkness, vision blurred and eyes painful, thoughts circling like vultures.

Would Milo even *let* her have an abortion?

The question bled through her mind before she could stop it, and the horror of it nearly broke her. She'd heard stories—women trapped in situations where their partners decided for them. Bodies treated like vessels. Dreams discarded because a man's decision weighed heavier.

And Milo… God, Milo was *not* just a man. He was an alpha. His world ran on dominance, on control. If she told him she didn't want this, would he tighten the chain around her neck? Would he see her body as his to claim, his right to dictate?

The thought made her shake harder, clutching her stomach with trembling hands. Already, her mind replayed his protectiveness, his intensity, the way his voice roughened when he talked about mating and bonds. He was overwhelming at the best of times. How would he be now, with something that shared their DNA between them?

Willow buried her face in the pillow again, muffling a sob. She didn't want to lose him. But she didn't want to lose herself either.

The bedroom door opened with the faintest creak, soft enough that she might have missed it if not for the way her heart immediately jumped into her throat. Milo didn't say a word. His footsteps padded across the floor, steady, careful, and then the mattress dipped behind her.

A warm arm slid around her waist, slow and unthreatening, pulling her back against the familiar breadth of his chest. His breath fanned over her hair as he pressed his face to the crown of her head, just holding her, giving her time.

Willow trembled, fighting to keep quiet, but the moment she turned in his arms and met the solid wall of him, the dam broke. She buried her face against his chest and sobbed, her hands fisting into his shirt like she might drown without him there to keep her afloat.

He tightened his hold, murmuring into her hair, "Shh, sweetheart. I've got you. I've got you." He let her cry, his hands stroking down her spine, his chin resting atop her head. And then, when her body finally slowed in its shaking, he whispered, raw and unguarded, "I love you, Willow. That doesn't change. Not with this. Not with anything."

Her throat clenched painfully. She dragged in a shaky breath, her voice muffled against him. "I don't know what to do, Milo. I don't know if I can—" Her words broke into another sob, tears soaking through his shirt. "I don't know."

He exhaled slowly, like he was forcing himself to be calm when he wanted to be anything but. One of his hands cupped the back of her head, tilting her gently so he could look at her. His gaze was steady, fierce in its softness. "Then you don't have to decide right now. We'll figure it out together. But listen to me, Willow…" His thumb brushed her cheek, wiping away the tears that wouldn't stop falling. "What matters is what you want. No one else. Not even me."

Her chest heaved, a ragged sob escaping as she collapsed against him again, clinging to him as if she were afraid he'd vanish. "I don't know," she wailed into his skin, the words breaking on every syllable. He held her through it, strong and unyielding, whispering the same words over and over into the darkness. "It's okay. I've got you. Whatever you decide, I've got you."

Her tears finally ebbed into hiccupping breaths, her body still trembling but no longer wracked with sobs. Milo's warmth surrounded her, his chest rising and falling in steady rhythm beneath her cheek. The silence stretched, weighted but safe, until Willow forced herself to lift her head, blinking at him through swollen eyes.

Her voice was raw, quiet but resolute. "I don't want this, Milo. I can't… I want an abortion." The words cracked at the edges, but she held onto them, bracing herself for the fight she expected to come.

But it didn't.

Milo's expression softened instead of hardening, his thumb brushing the damp trail of tears from her cheek. "Okay," he said simply, his voice low and steady. No judgment. No hesitation. "Then that's what we'll do."

Her throat closed up, disbelief written across her face. "You're... you're not angry?"

He shook his head, pressing his forehead gently against hers. "No, sweetheart. Never at you. This is your body, not mine. If this is what you want, then that's what happens. Lachlan will make sure it's safe, and I'll be with you every step of the way." His hand came to rest against her side, grounding her, steady as stone. "It's going to be okay."

Willow's lip trembled, her chest clenching with something sharp—relief so strong it hurt. She stared at him, wide-eyed, as though trying to see if there was some hidden condition in his words. But there wasn't.

He *meant* it.

She collapsed back into him, her face pressed to his chest again, a sob breaking free—not of fear, but of gratitude. "Thank you," she whispered, the words muffled but soaked with every ounce of her shaking relief.

Milo only kissed the crown of her head and held her tighter. "Always, baby. Whatever you need."

Willow's sobs quieted again, her breaths finally finding some fragile rhythm against him.

Milo smoothed a hand down her back, the tension in his chest easing as he felt her start to steady. He kissed her temple, lingering there a moment before murmuring, "You've had enough heaviness for one day, sweetheart."

He shifted just slightly, the hint of a grin tugging at his mouth. "Let's get cleaned up," he purred, the words low and edged with meaning. His tone promised more than just a shower—it was an invitation, a reminder that he wanted her, not out of duty, not out of circumstance, but because she was his and he adored her.

Willow bit her lip, nodding slowly, already being swept up by the heat building in her body.

***

Milo scooped her up as though she weighed nothing, his arms steady, his chest unshakable against her cheek. Willow clung to him out of instinct more than need, her tears drying into his shirt as he carried her into the en suite. She felt the sway of his stride, the grounding calm of him, and by the time they reached the bathroom, her body had relaxed in his arms.

He set her down gently, making sure she was steady on her feet before letting her go. His hands lingered a second longer than necessary, brushing down her arms, reassuring without words. Willow watched as he reached for the hem of her shirt, lifting it slowly. His movements weren't urgent, weren't hungry. They were careful, tender, deliberate—as if each button, each sleeve, each shift of fabric was some small act of devotion.

Her breath caught as he knelt briefly to peel her socks from her feet, pressing a kiss to her knee before standing again. There was no shame in it, no heat beyond the warmth of his love. Just Milo, her Milo, taking care of her.

He turned to the shower, twisting the handle until steam rose, then tested the water with his palm. A frown, an adjustment, another check, until his features softened in approval. Only then did he begin tugging off his own shirt, his belt, setting each piece aside with quiet efficiency.

When he was finished, he reached for her hand. His fingers twined with hers, tugging her gently toward the spray. "Come on, sweetheart," he said softly, his voice rich and grounding.

She went with him, letting the heat of the water and the warmth of his presence wash over her at once, her body and heart caught between comfort and ache.

The heat of the water cascaded over her shoulders, washing away the remnants of her tears from her scrunched face. Steam curled around them, softening the edges of the world until it felt like there was only this—her and Milo, cocooned together.

Willow let her eyes wander, drinking him in. The water clung to him in rivulets, sliding down his thick neck, tracing the ridges of muscle across his abdomen, catching in the dark trail of hair that disappeared lower. Every inch of him seemed carved with purpose, forged by strength and discipline, but softened now in the intimacy of this moment.

She couldn't stop herself from staring, from marveling at how someone could look both dangerous and inviting at once.

Milo caught her gaze and smiled, that slow, crooked expression that always undid her. He stepped closer, lifting a hand to cup her cheek, his thumb brushing lightly over her damp skin. "You're staring," he teased, as though he didn't mind at all.

Her lips parted, but no words came. Instead, she leaned into his touch, her body moving of its own accord. Their mouths met softly at first, tentative, the kind of kiss meant to soothe rather than ignite. She tasted water and warmth and him, steady and familiar.

But as his hand slid to cradle the back of her head and hers pressed against the solid plane of his chest, the kiss deepened. Not hurried, not desperate— just lingering, tender, as if both of them were afraid to break the fragile peace that had settled over them.

Willow sighed against him, her body melting under the spray, and Milo kissed her slower still, savoring, steadying her as the world slipped away.

LORE

Some animals are reactive if
they come across their owner
in a shifted form.

If you've ever seen an animal
react to their owner in a
mask, it's kind of like that.

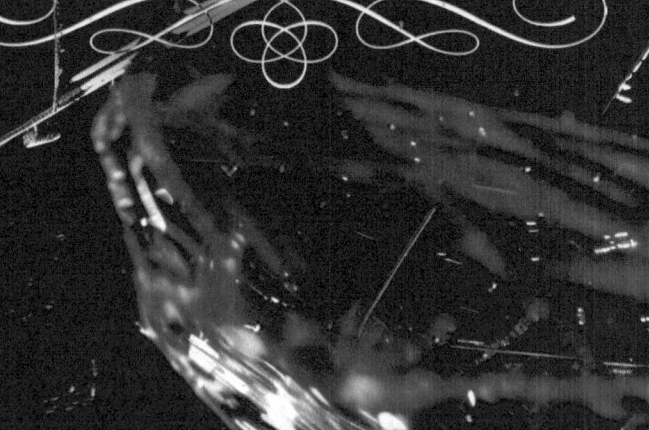

MILO

CHAPTER THIRTY EIGHT

Milo could hardly believe his eyes. This gorgeous, complicated, maddeningly perfect woman was his. After all the time he'd spent watching from a distance, calculating his every move, biding his time with the patience of a hunter waiting for the right moment, Willow was finally here.

In his arms. In his life.

His.

Steam wafted around them in hazy ribbons, water streaming down their bodies as their mouths moved together in a kiss that felt like home. Milo held her face gently in his palms, thumbs brushing across her wet cheeks as though she might break if he pressed too firmly. He wanted her with a ferocity that made his chest ache, but he didn't let it rule him. Not now. Not when she was in such a raw, delicate state.

She leaned into him, her body softening as if she belonged there, and he fought the urge to deepen the kiss, to take everything he craved. His wolf snarled at the restraint, but Milo forced himself to stay grounded, to hold back. She needed tenderness, not hunger. She needed the man right now, not the beast.

Still, his heart thundered with disbelief. Willow. His Willow. After everything—the endless hours of waiting, the dark plans, the blood and violence that had paved the road to this moment—she was kissing him like he was worth trusting.

Milo let out a slow breath, resting his forehead against hers between kisses, steadying himself against the weight of it all. He didn't deserve her, not really. But he would spend every last breath proving that she was safe in his arms, that he could be more than the monster he had been trained to be.

And as her lips brushed his again, featherlight and sweet, he thought he might die from the sheer wonder of it.

The steam wrapped tighter around them, clinging to their skin, making every bead of water shimmer like little stars under the bathroom light. Milo braced a hand against the tile, trying to steady himself, because Willow was shifting in front of him, lowering slowly, deliberately, until her knees met the slick shower floor.

For a heartbeat, he thought he'd imagined it. His chest tightened, his breath caught. But then she looked up at him with those wide, doe-like eyes, lips parted just enough to undo him.

"Willow…" His voice was roughened by restraint, the single word catching in his throat. "You don't have to—"

"I want to," she whispered, water dripping from her hair, trailing down her cheeks like the diamonds he wanted to shower her in. Her hands slid over his thighs, teasing, feather-light, nails grazing just enough to make his muscles twitch. She was all shy determination and quiet bravery, and it nearly broke him entirely.

She didn't know, couldn't know, how close he

was to grabbing that beautiful face and fucking her throat until she was choking around his cock.

The sight of her like that—on her knees, hair plastered to her shoulders, mouth hovering near his rock-hard length with such devastating intent—waged war on his control. The wolf in him wanted to make his claim, to fist her hair and guide her exactly where he needed her. But Milo forced his hands to remain at his sides, fists clenched, every instinct screaming as he gave her the space to lead.

She toyed with him first, fingertips gliding down the length, brushing against the head, testing the edges of his composure. Her smirk—soft but wicked—nearly made him lose his balance.

"*Willow…*" He choked out her name like a plea, tilting his head back against the tile with a groan. He was undone already, and she had barely even started.

He dared a glance downward, meeting her gaze again. The look she gave him—half tender, half sinful—made his pulse erratic. She had no idea what she was doing to him. Or maybe she knew exactly.

Either way, he hoped she never stopped.

Milo did his best to stay still. This wasn't about taking. This was about letting her—his mate—explore, taste, claim him in her own way. She needed the freedom to familiarize with him.

The first brush of her lips against his shaft made him groan, deep and raw, echoing in the small space. His hand slid into her wet hair, not pulling, just anchoring himself against the storm she stirred in him. She kissed her way up toward the head in maddening little patterns, and every nerve in his body lit up like fire.

"God, Willow…" he rasped, the sound of his own voice startling him. He hadn't known he could sound so broken. His hips quivered with the effort of holding back.

She looked up at him then, eyes bright with mischief and devotion, and it nearly dropped him to his knees beside her.

Willow parted her lips and finally took his cock between them, her tongue warm and teasing as she worked him deeper down her throat. She choked and gagged, eyes filling with tears, and the beast inside him roared. Milo's hand tightened in her wet hair, every muscle in his body trembling with restraint.

Water streamed over her shoulders, glinting in the light as she set her rhythm, slow at first, deliberate. He let out a sound that was half-groan, half-growl, the noise bouncing off the tile.

"Easy, sweetheart…" His words came rough, even though she clearly wasn't listening. She pushed herself further, daring to take more of his cock. When she gagged softly, a wet, choked sound, he nearly lost his grip on his control. The sight of her, water dripping down her cheeks, determination in her eyes, undid him more than anything.

She moaned around him, and the vibration shot straight through his body like lightning. Milo swore, head slamming gently back against the wall, vision blurring at the edges. The sound of her pleasure did something inexplicable to him.

And then, she did something that almost made him lose his grip.

Willow lifted her other hand, wrapping both of them around the thick swell at his base. Her fingers trembled slightly, but the squeeze was intentional, deliberate. The pressure made his vision spark white.

Milo's head snapped back, shoulders crashing into the slick tile as he let out an unrestrained howl that tore from deep in his chest. The sound cracked midway, unraveling into a guttural groan that echoed hard against the walls, reverberating back at him like proof of his own undoing.

Every nerve lit up at once, his body jerking under her touch, hips twitching despite his desperate attempt to stay grounded. The water pouring over him only heightened it, sluicing down his chest in hot rivulets as his pulse thundered in his ears. He had never felt so close to breaking—so entirely at her mercy.

Willow's eyes flicked up to him, wide and luminous, watching the way he came apart for her. The sight alone nearly undid him a second time, his chest heaving as he forced air into his lungs, clutching the back of her head as if she were the only thing tethering him to the ground.

"Fuck, Willow, I'm going to—I'm—" His hoarse voice faltered, cracking beneath the weight of everything she was pulling out of him. The warning tangled on his tongue, too broken to finish, because she was relentless, merciless in her devotion.

His body lurched forward, hand braced hard against the slick tile as his hips bucked helplessly. He couldn't hold it back, couldn't bite down the guttural sounds spilling from his throat as she dragged him past the point of no return. The effort to restrain himself was obliterated in a heartbeat, replaced by the firestorm of release tearing through his chest and down his spine.

His head fell back, jaw slack as he lost himself completely in the wet heat of her mouth. A growl escaped him, half-snarl and half-moan. He tried to look down, tried to focus on her, but his vision fractured at the edges, his world narrowed to the sight of her lips stretched around him, her throat working to take every bit of him she could manage.

Unfortunately, he hadn't filled her in on one important aspect of werewolves and knots.

His pleasure came hot and fast, filling her mouth and then spilling out over her swollen lips. Willow pulled back in surprise as his cock continued to spray a seemingly endless supply of cum, covering her cheeks, nose, and chin in thick jets.

Milo was still trembling, chest heaving, every

muscle twitching as he tried to keep himself upright. His hand stayed braced hard against the shower wall, forehead pressed to his bicep while he dragged in ragged, uneven breaths. The world around him was blurred at the edges, nothing but steam and the lingering aftershocks firing through his veins.

When he finally dared to look down, the sight rooted him to the spot. Willow was still on her knees, motionless, eyes wide as if she wasn't sure what to do next. The evidence of his pleasure was smeared across her lips and chin, clinging in places she hadn't had the chance to wipe away, startled and horrified.

Milo's throat tightened as a laugh tried to claw its way out. He slapped a hand over his mouth to keep it in, shoulders shaking—not because it was funny in the traditional sense, but because the image was seared into him. Forever.

"I'm sorry," he rasped, still catching his breath, water running down his face as he tried not to so much as smile. "I should've warned you."

Willow's daze cracked, her eyes snapping up at him as she barked, "Warned me? What the fuck do you mean, warned me?"

He rubbed the back of his neck, suddenly sheepish. "About... the other thing knots do."

Her glower intensified. "Which is?"

"It, uh... stores semen."

For a moment, she just stared at him, lips parted, still covered in his cum, as if the words themselves refused to register. Then the full weight of it hit her, leaving her looking half shell-shocked, half betrayed.

"Milo," she said slowly, her voice trembling with deadly seriousness. "I thought I was gonna die."

That did it. His composure shattered. A laugh exploded out of him, raw and uncontrollable as he braced himself against the wall. He shook his head, water spraying from his hair, shoulders heaving with amusement. Not at her discomfort, never that, but at the absurdity of it all.

"It's *not* funny," Willow whined, starting to get up. Milo reached down and helped her, pulling her close. He ran a thumb through the sticky, white glob on her cheek.

"Oh, sweetheart, you made such a mess of yourself," he murmured, mesmerized by this woman who had made such a mess of him, as well.

LORE

Knots store excess semen. It's thought that this is an evolutionary adaptation to ensure impregnation.

WILLOW

CHAPTER THIRTY-NINE

Willow sat at the kitchen island, her hands wrapped around a mug she hadn't touched, staring down into the lightened coffee like it might give her answers to what plagued her.

Lachlan stood opposite her, sleeves pushed up to his elbows, his expression calm in that steady, clinical way she knew he must carry at the hospital. She had become a patient, in his eyes. There was no judgment in his eyes, no pity—just quiet assurance.

"It's all taken care of," he said gently, setting a folder on the counter but not opening it. "You're scheduled for tomorrow. First thing."

Her stomach clenched, but she nodded faintly.

He leaned forward a little, lowering his voice as though they weren't already alone. "It's a very straightforward procedure, Willow. Medically speaking, it's called a dilation and curettage, or D&C. What that means, simply, is that we'll dilate your cervix and use suction to clear the tissue. It doesn't take long. The whole thing will be maybe fifteen minutes, tops."

Her throat worked, but she still didn't speak. Lachlan gave her space, his tone calm, like he'd explained this a hundred times before to patients who needed the same reassurance.

"You'll be in and out in a few hours. It's safe. You'll cramp afterwards, like a heavy period, but nothing you can't handle. And both Milo and myself will be there the entire time." His words had finality, like a promise he wouldn't allow himself to break.

Finally, he tilted his head, studying her with those kind, tired eyes. "Do you want to be under twilight anesthesia for it? It'll keep you calm, take the edge off, and you won't remember much. Some people prefer to stay awake, some don't. It's entirely up to you."

Willow swallowed, blinking down at her untouched coffee. The words sat heavy, clinical but softened at the edges, and for the first time since last night, she felt the faintest stir of relief.

She sat in silence for a long moment. Finally, Willow nodded once, her voice quiet but steady.

"I want to be under," she said. Her fingers tightened on the mug, knuckles pale against the ceramic. "I don't... I don't think I could sit through it awake. That sounds like *torture*."

Lachlan gave her a slow, understanding nod, the faintest curve of sympathy tugging at his mouth. "Of course." He straightened, brushing an invisible speck from his shirt sleeve before continuing. "And for now, I can prescribe you something mild for the anxiety. Nothing heavy, just enough to keep you comfortable."

Her eyes lifted to meet his, and though she managed a small, grateful smile, it didn't quite reach her eyes. "Thank you, Lachlan."

He reached across the island, resting a hand briefly over hers, warm and grounding. "You don't

have to thank me. It's my honor to look after you."
Then, as though sensing she needed space, he stepped
back, gathering his folder. "I'll get the prescription
filled today. Make sure you take one tonight and
another in the morning."

She nodded again, and he offered her a
quiet, brotherly smile before leaving the kitchen, his
footsteps fading down the hall.

When the silence settled back in, Willow
let out a long, shaky breath and pressed the heels
of her palms against her eyes. It all felt surreal, like
her life had been dragged into fast-forward without
her permission. Only weeks ago, Milo had been a
presence at the periphery of her world—dangerous,
magnetic, terrifying. And now she'd woken in his bed,
tangled in his arms, carrying his child, and making
the choice to end it.

Everything had escalated so quickly.
Somewhere between his relentless pursuit and her
reckless surrender, she'd crossed a line she hadn't
known she was approaching. And now she was sitting
in his kitchen, staring down the aftermath, wondering
how everything could feel both so devastating and
inevitable all at once.

Willow was still sitting at the island, hands
curled around the cooling mug, when she heard the
quiet creak of the floorboards behind her. Milo's
presence filled the room before she even turned, that
heavy, grounding energy of his already filling the air

around her.

He came up behind her and set his broad palms gently on her shoulders, kneading the tension there before leaning down to brush a kiss against her temple. "Sweetheart," he murmured, voice low, steady, "you don't have to go through this alone. I'll be there. Every step. When it's done, you'll come home to me, and you'll recover in nothing but comfort. Luxury, if I have my way."

Her throat closed around the words she didn't want to say, but they spilled out anyway, fragile and raw. "Milo... I'm ending a little life."

For a heartbeat, he was quiet. Then he shifted, crouching in front of her so he could look into her face. His thumb brushed across her cheekbone, catching the trace of a tear she hadn't realized had fallen. His eyes were sharp, unwavering, but there was no judgment—only a fierce, unyielding tenderness.

"It might be alive, Willow," he said softly, "but it's not a life. Not the kind of life you're thinking of. Not yet." His hand settled over hers, large and warm, grounding her trembling fingers. "What you're doing isn't wrong. You're taking charge of your future. Our future."

Her chest hitched, torn between the ache of guilt and the swell of relief his words gave her. He leaned closer, pressing his forehead to hers, and the weight of his certainty settled over her like a blanket. "You're doing the right thing, Willow. You're always right to choose yourself. In the animal kingdom, female animals abort their fetuses and even kill their own young when they can't take care of them. Controlling your own reproduction is the most natural thing in the world."

And for the first time that morning, she let herself lean into him, her forehead pressed into his shoulder, breathing in the familiar scent of him until the panic inside her loosened its grip.

***

By afternoon, the heaviness of the morning had thinned into something bearable, though still weighing on her. Lachlan had pressed a handwritten list into Milo's hand before heading back to the hospital, his pen-strokes neat, medical, efficient— hydration salts, heating pad, electrolyte drinks, easy-to-digest foods, ibuprofen, thick pads. Milo had tucked it into his back pocket with care.

Now, the two of them moved side by side down the glossy aisles of a pharmacy, the blast of AC not quite enough to cut the summer heat still clinging to her skin. Willow had thrown on a white tank top and jean shorts, her hair falling over her shoulders.

Milo, infuriatingly, looked completely at ease despite the temperature, broad frame in dark jeans and a black t-shirt that stretched over his chest and shoulders. He had one hand resting on the cart handle, the other at his side, posture loose but alert. Willow knew Titan had gone in ahead of them, sweeping each corner. It was surreal, shopping for Pedialyte and crackers under the quiet watch of men who could dismantle a body in seconds.

Milo reached for the top shelf without hesitation, plucking down a mega-sized pack of overnight pads and dropping it into the cart. The muscles in his forearm flexed, and Willow caught herself staring before dragging her eyes away.

"You okay?" he asked without looking at her, tone casual but carrying that undertone—him checking her pulse in ways that had nothing to do with her physical health.

Willow smoothed her palm against the hem of her tank top, nodding. "Yeah. Just hot."

His mouth tilted, faint amusement cutting through the otherwise cool mask of his face. "Yeah, you are." He winked.

She rolled her eyes, cheeks warming, but couldn't fight the small smile tugging at her lips.

***

The house was quiet, the kind of silence that felt thick, as though it knew what tomorrow would bring. Willow lay tucked into Milo's chest, his arms wrapped around her like steel cables softened by warmth. The sheets were cool against her bare legs, but his heat made her feel cocooned, tethered to him.

He pressed his lips into her hair, voice low and steady against the back of her skull. "You're making the right choice, sweetheart. Don't let yourself carry shame that doesn't belong to you."

His words eased something inside her, but only for a breath. A thought crept in, fast and unrelenting—the calendar.

The full moon.

Her stomach clenched.

"Milo," she whispered, pulling back just enough to see his face in the dim light. "Tomorrow's the full moon."

She hadn't realized how much she'd been counting on it, how much she'd pinned her security on the bond they were supposed to complete. Her pulse skittered as panic welled in her throat. "You're supposed to knot me tomorrow and—"

"Shh." His hand cupped her cheek, thumb brushing softly across her skin. His expression was calm, measured, even as her own turned frantic. "Listen to me. Your health comes first. Always. Knotting you before surgery could cause complications. Infection. Bleeding. You'd be going in technically already injured, and we can't risk that."

She blinked at him, struggling to process, but his certainty grounded her. He was so matter-of-fact, so immovable.

"It's one or the other, Willow," Milo

murmured, leaning his forehead against hers. "And between my knot and your life, I'll choose your life."

Her breath caught, tears stinging her eyes. He said it so simply, like it wasn't a choice at all.

Willow swallowed hard, still tucked against his chest. The weight of his words sat heavy in her mind, like smooth stones she couldn't quite stack without everything tumbling down. Her fingers toyed absently with the hem of his shirt, the question slipping from her lips before she could stop it.

"What happens if we don't... finish it? The bond?"

Milo shifted, the low rumble in his chest brushing against her ear. For a moment, he was quiet, considering his words carefully, choosing which edges to soften and which to leave sharp.

"There are consequences," he said finally, voice low and certain. "Without the bond, the pack will always feel unsettled. They'll sense the gap, the unfinished connection between us. They'll still follow me, but there'll be hesitation in them. Doubt. There's also the matter of their inability to find their own mates, which can be devastating for morale."

Willow tilted her head back to search his face, her brow furrowing. "And for me?"

His mouth quirked faintly, not unkind, but almost reverent. "Once it's done, you're more than just my mate. You'll be their queen. Every wolf beneath me will feel it, and they'll submit to you as natural as breathing. Even though you're human, you'll hold authority they can't ignore. No one could challenge you. No one could touch you."

Her breath caught. She thought of Lachlan, Titan, the others—grown men with violence in their nature—bowing their heads, not out of choice, but instinct.

"Lachlan and Titan seem so quick to listen to me already," she said, her voice quieter this time. Milo's gaze softened. "That's because they're good men. But you haven't met any other wolves for a reason, Willow. I can't introduce you to my empire in full until you've accepted my knot."

Willow let his words sink in, her chest tightening with every revelation. Her decision was already made—had been the moment she'd let him share her body—but that didn't stop the flicker of annoyance sparking in her eyes. He hadn't told her any of this before.

Of course, she would still have said yes. That wasn't the point.

It was the ease with which he left things unsaid that rankled her, the way he measured out truths only when pressed. Like he couldn't, or wouldn't, hand her the whole picture until she was too far in to turn back.

Willow shifted against him, biting back the sharpness rising in her throat. She didn't want to pick a fight, not now. But a part of her still simmered, a low burn beneath her ribs.

She was his mate. His queen, apparently. She wasn't some fragile piece on his chessboard to be moved and protected without explanation. If he expected her to stand beside him, then he needed to start treating her like she belonged there.

LORE

The first time a female is knotted,
there can be some tearing.

This grows easier with time, and
the overwhelming pleasure helps
distract from the pain.

MILO

CHAPTER FORTY

Milo could see it plain as day, the terror in Willow's eyes. She was bracing for war, except this wasn't a battlefield, it was her own body. It gutted him that he couldn't fight this one for her, even though he'd been the one to do it to her in the first place.

He cupped her cheek with a hand that had broken bones, spilled blood, and ended lives—but now it trembled, not from violence but from love. "You're going to be okay," he told her, his voice low, steady, commanding in a way that left no room for doubt. "Lachlan's got this covered. He handpicked the team, and my men will be at every door, every exit. Nothing touches you. Do you hear me? They're going to replace your IUD too, so that's taken care of."

She nodded, attempting a smile, but the tears shining at the corners of her lashes betrayed her. She still couldn't believe she'd forgotten her IUD had expired, but, with everything happening, it had just slipped her mind.

Milo swallowed hard, pulling her into his chest, burying his face in her hair. She smelled like floral soap and fear, a combination that made his chest hurt.

The clinic wasn't some sterile public hospital where strangers could whisper and judge. Lachlan had pulled this together with his connections—a network of underground doctors who owed him favors, who worked quiet and discreet, where no questions were asked and no records could ever trace back. Milo had made use of the underground regularly since he'd been back, but never for something that mattered this much.

He tilted his head, brushing his lips over her temple. "You're not alone in this. Not for one second. I'll be with you every step of the way."

And he meant it. Even if it killed him to watch her go through it, he wasn't letting go.

"Milo, we have a problem."

The sound of Titan's voice cut through the air like a blade, sharp enough to turn both Milo and Willow's heads at once. The kid stood in the doorway, shoulders tight, eyes wide in a way Milo didn't like.

Milo rose from where he'd been holding Willow, his body already shifting into that familiar battle-readiness. He didn't need to ask what kind of problem. The tension in Titan's stance told him enough. This wasn't small.

Titan jerked his chin toward the hallway. "Need a word, boss."

Milo brushed a kiss over Willow's cheek, murmuring low in her ear, "I'll be right back, sweetheart." He forced his body to move steady, unhurried, but every nerve in him was already wired hot. He followed Titan into the other room, and the moment the door shut behind them, the kid let it out.

"McGarvey's making a move. Everywhere." Titan's voice was clipped, urgent. "Reports are flooding in—multiple places hit, wolves dead. Some of ours, some of theirs. It's chaos. Nobody knows what to do."

The words lit Milo's blood on fire. His jaw locked, shoulders straightening, mind already snapping into formation. "Where?" he demanded.

"Fucking everywhere, dude. It's coordinated. He's everywhere."

Before Milo could answer, his phone buzzed violently in his pocket. One glance at the caller ID had him moving without hesitation. Arlo.

He answered, voice dropping into command mode, every ounce of softness from moments ago with Willow gone.

"Talk to me."

"Milo," Arlo's voice came in hard and ragged, the sound of an engine in the background, "McGarvey goons came for us. Condo's been breached. Poppy and I barely made it out. We're on the road now."

Milo pinched the bridge of his nose, pacing, his pulse roaring in his ears. "Stay moving. Don't go to ground unless you have to. Titan and I will coordinate an extraction route."

Poppy's faint voice echoed through the line, panicked, but alive. That alone steadied Milo enough to press on.

"Arlo, listen to me. You keep her safe, you hear? Get her out of sight until I can send backup. McGarvey wants us scattered. We need to regroup as quickly as possible."

Arlo exhaled hard, but there was iron in his words. "Copy that."

Milo's eyes flicked to Titan, who was pale with fear. His chest tightened. Willow in the next room, likely terrified. Poppy in the wind. Wolves dead. McGarvey hitting every border.

War had just landed on his doorstep.

***

Milo's hands lingered on Willow's shoulders longer than they should have, his thumbs brushing against her collarbones as though he could etch strength into her spirit through touch alone. She was pale, nervous, but trying so damn hard to be strong. Lachlan sat in the backseat beside her, face set into that doctor's mask he wore when he needed to be steady for someone else.

"You'll be safe with him," Milo murmured, leaning in close. "I'll meet you after. Nothing will touch you, I swear it."

Her fingers clutched at his shirt like she didn't want to let go, and for a split second, he almost said fuck it to everything—McGarvey, Jenner, all of it. But war wouldn't wait. With a gentle press of his lips against her forehead, he pulled back. "I love you, sweetheart. You're doing the right thing."

Willow's eyes shone, glassy and fearful, but she

gave him a small nod. Milo stepped away and closed the car door, watching until the driver he'd assigned pulled away. The SUV disappeared down the long driveway before he turned back toward the house.

Titan was already waiting, shoulders squared, jaw tight. No backtalk, no grin. Just a wolf ready for blood to defend his land.

They didn't speak as they moved into the library. Milo reached for the thick manual in the bookcase, pulled it outward, and slid the bookcase over. Once the door was open, the faint scent of gun oil and metal hit his senses like a homecoming. The armory yawned open, a cold, shadowed space where he felt more at home than anywhere else.

Except, of course, in her arms.

Milo stepped inside, shrugging out of his t-shirt and tugging on a slim Kevlar vest that would pass under his hoodie without drawing stares. He clipped spare mags into the inner webbing, deliberate and quick. No wasted movement.

"You don't want to be bulked down," he told Titan, his voice low and even as he adjusted the straps. "If humans spot you decked out like a Green Beret, they'll lose it. Blend in. Civilian, but ready."

Titan nodded, already mirroring him, tugging on a dark jacket over a vest that fit snug against his frame. His hands moved a little shakier on the buckles, but Milo stepped over and tightened them down with efficient pulls, clapping him once on the shoulder.

"Good."

They moved along the racks, loading backpacks with compact carbines broken down into parts, sidearms tucked in holsters, suppressors wrapped in cloth. A pair of rifle bags leaned against the far wall—Milo tossed one to Titan. "Carry it like it's nothing special. Just another hunter with his gear."

Titan zipped it closed, testing the weight before slinging it over his shoulder. "Feels light."

"Won't when it's full," Milo said, grabbing his own bag and sliding a shotgun inside, the action smooth and practiced.

When they stepped back into the library, the air felt heavier, as though the house itself knew what they were walking into. Milo closed the bookcase behind them, sealing the armory away again, and looked at Titan—really looked at him. The boy was gone. A soldier stood in his place.

"Stay sharp. We don't have the luxury of mistakes. Take your car. Get to Poppy and Arlo. I'll head into the thick of things."

Titan nodded once, and together they strode toward the door, the weight of oncoming battle slung across their backs.

LORE

It is thought that the knot collects
semen during mating in order to
ensure insemination of the female.

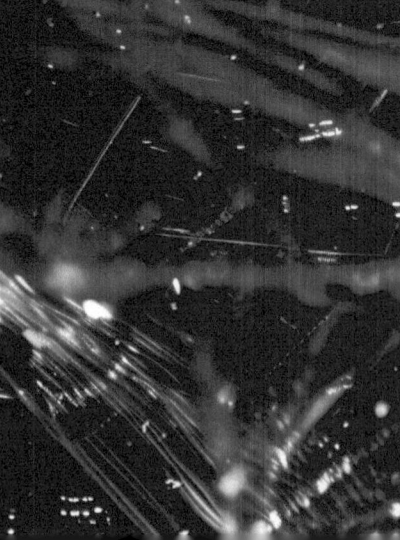

WILLOW

CHAPTER FORTY ONE

The quiet thrum of the tires against the road was hypnotic, steady and low, a lull that settled in her bones. Willow sat in the backseat, buckled in, her knees drawn close together, hands folded in her lap. Lachlan glanced at her, his voice calm and professional.

"How are you feeling? That benzo kicking in yet?"

She wet her lips, shrugging faintly. "A little... floaty. Like my head's a balloon." Her words slurred just slightly, and she gave a soft, nervous laugh. "I guess that means it's working."

"Good," Lachlan said. "It's supposed to take the edge off so you aren't nervous for surgery. Just ride it out and let yourself breathe."

She nodded, settling back against the seat as a strange, slow warmth threaded through her veins. It wasn't happiness, not really, but the sharp screaming of panic had dulled into something muffled, as if her head were wrapped in cotton.

The car grew quiet after that, silence falling like a heavy blanket. The world outside blurred into patches of green and gray, unimportant compared to the ache inside her. Almost without thinking, Willow's hand drifted down to rest against her lower stomach. Her palm pressed lightly, as though she could feel the truth of what was there with just the weight of her touch.

What if she let it grow? What if she gave it

a chance to become something more than cells and possibility? She tried to imagine it—the tiny kicks, the curve of her belly, Milo's arms wrapped around her with that proud glow in his eyes. A life growing inside of her that tied her to him forever.

The thought hollowed her out as quickly as it filled her. Fear and longing twisted together until she couldn't tell them apart. She swallowed hard, forcing her eyes away from her hand.

The SUV descended into the underground garage, the sudden shift into shadow jarring after the light of day. The tires echoed against concrete, the air cooler, more sterile. Lachlan parked near a nondescript door with no signs, no markings. Just another gray wall hiding something monumental.

He got out first, circling to open her door. Willow slid out on shaky legs, her body heavier than she remembered, as though the consequence of her choice pressed into her muscles. Before he could take a step, she reached out, fingers clutching the sleeve of his coat.

Her throat burned, tears already spilling before the words made it out. "Lachlan… will you be mad if I change my mind?"

Her voice cracked, raw and small in the cavernous garage.

He turned immediately, his face softening, no judgment in his eyes. He placed his hand over hers, steady and grounding.

"Willow," he said gently, "this is your choice. Only yours. Nobody will be mad. Not me, not Milo, not anyone. Whatever you decide, we'll stand by you."

The reassurance broke her, her sobs rising again, but softer this time, as though his words had carved out space for her grief instead of adding to it.

Lachlan squeezed her hand, his smile tired but warm, like the kind of smile a parent gave to ease a child's fears. "We can go home right now, if you'd like," he said softly. "Or we can take a few minutes and talk it through before you do anything. Whatever you need, Willow. This is at your pace."

Her chest trembled with another sob, relief flooding her veins. She nodded faintly, lips parting to speak.

And then the world shattered.

A deafening crack split the air, sharp and final. Lachlan jerked violently, his smile ripped away in an instant as his body twisted. His blood sprayed hot against her cheek.

Time stopped.

Her hand flew up, touched her face.

Red.

Wet.

Wrong.

Lachlan staggered back against the SUV, clutching his shoulder, breath caught in his throat. Her own body wouldn't move. Wouldn't listen. She stood frozen, staring, until the sound of boots and gunfire dragged her back into the moment.

"Lachlan!" she screamed, voice raw, her throat tearing.

Masked men flooded into the garage, monsters with rifles, shouting to each other over the ringing gunshots. The driver barely had time to draw before his chest bloomed red, his gun clattering uselessly to the concrete. He crumpled, lifeless, as his blood seeped across the floor in a dark pool.

Willow stumbled back a step, her vision tunneling, the urge to run screaming through every nerve in her body. Her legs twitched, muscles ready to bolt—but hands were already on her, rough and unyielding.

"No— *No!*"she shrieked, thrashing, nails clawing at fabric, skin, anything. But she was dragged backward, her shoes skidding uselessly against the floor.

A van door yawned open behind her, black and gaping like a mouth. She was shoved hard, her body slamming against cold metal as she landed in the back. The door slammed shut before she could catch her breath, sealing her inside.

The last thing she saw of the outside world was Lachlan bleeding on the ground, his face pale, eyes still locked on hers even as she was stolen away.

Her chest heaved, lungs burning as the van jolted forward. The metal walls rattled with every turn, every bounce of the tires. She pushed herself upright, clutching the side of the van with trembling fingers, her eyes darting—

Two men loomed over her. Masks half-pulled up, their faces rough, eyes glinting with cruel amusement.

One of them stepped forward, tilting his head as he looked her over. "What a quick, little slut," he sneered. "Looks like he knocked her up. She's pregnant."

Her blood ran cold.

The other man barked out a laugh, cruel and sharp. "Not anymore."

The words barely registered before his boot connected, hard and merciless, with her lower stomach.

White-hot agony ripped through her. Willow folded, curling instinctively around the pain, a choked scream tearing from her throat as she hit the floor. She couldn't breathe. Couldn't think. Every nerve lit up with fire, her arms wrapping protectively around her middle even as her body convulsed from the impact.

Laughter rang in her ears, echoing, blurring with the roar of blood rushing through her head. Tears burned her eyes. She couldn't move, couldn't fight—not through this pain. Her body shook, sweat beading on her skin as her vision smeared.

Willow could feel something wet between her legs, a sickening gush.

She forced her head up, blinking through the

haze. Another figure shifted in the shadows of the van, sitting further back, too still. Too familiar. Her stomach dropped for an entirely new reason, icy fear cutting through the heat of her pain.

Her lips trembled. The word scraped out of her, broken, disbelieving.

"You?"

And then she was kicked again.

Harder.

And then the world slipped from her fingers, blackness pulling her under as the van thundered down the road.

THANK YOU
FOR READING

I am endlessly grateful to you for
choosing my book... and finishing
it, too! From the bottom of my
heart, thank you, reader.

Ready for the next? Don't forget
to follow me using the QR code
provided on the next page.

You'll be able to find
me everywhere!

I'll be releasing updates primarily
through my Discord, IG Channel,
and newsletter first and foremost.

Juniper Hartmann

CONNECT

Want to see more of Junie?

Find her shitposting on Threads or
check her socials for the latest.

JuniperHartmann.com
@JuniperHartmann

ABOUT

Junie is a woman in her early 30s from the frigid but beautiful Northeast region of the USA. She lives with her husband, sister, and too many animals.

You can find her running The Red Fox Creative when she isn't writing.

ACKNOWLEDGEMENTS

This book has been... an experience. It's my first time focusing on plot rather than sex. I just hope I did it all justice! You read this far, so I'm guessing I did a pretty alright job at doing so.

First and foremost, I have to shout out my incredible team. To be clear, I could not do *ANY* of this without the support of the group of people behind me. From my Discord mods to my business partners to my service providers, you all make this wonderful author life of mine possible.

My husband has provided immeasurable support that I fear I'll never be able to reciprocate. Without him, I wouldn't be able to pursue my dreams.

And, of course, my editor, Ana. She's pushed me to be a stronger writer, revealed my bad habits, and has thoroughly worked the kinks out of this book. You should have seen the hot mess it would have been otherwise!

EARLY READERS

I have a tradition of including early
reader reviews in my book. These are
selected (and used with permission!)
from my ARC team usually.

This little book baby wouldn't have
gotten nearly so much love without
them. I am forever grateful!

Enjoy the reviews over the next pages.

"Willow has closed herself off from romance, devoting her life to caring for her disabled sister—until she meets Milo Schwarz, a former soldier turned ruthless werewolf pack leader. Their collision sparks passion, danger, and moral conflict.

This is a solid paranormal romance with mafia-like power dynamics, supernatural action, and heavy emotional stakes. It's not aiming for subtlety, but fans of intense, edgy werewolf romances will find plenty to sink their teeth into."

NORMA FISCAL

@nfiscal94

My heart is in my throat, and I believe I've forgotten how to breathe. That's how this book left me.

If you enjoy a sweet shifter romance with the blush of new love and fairy tales, this is not it. But if you find yourself longing for something more raw, intense, and downright infuriating at times, welcome to your new favorite book!

Juniper Hartmann has written a story that will make you question everything you ever thought you knew about wolf packs, knotting, and even consent. Definitely check out those trigger warnings, but even they won't prepare you to be completely undone by the ending. I'm preparing you now, you won't come away unscathed.

ALICIA NELSON

@mycellicroots

This book delivered it all: spice, grit, dark edges, and even moments that made me laugh. What really stood out for me were the characters. Milo is the perfect mix of dominant, protective, and patient, while Willow is sweet but also determined and unwilling to bend too easily to their bond. The side characters shine as well—Titan, Lachlan, and even the cats add depth and charm.

I'm especially excited to see more of Poppy and Arlo in future books. And that cliffhanger? Brutal. I regretted reading so fast because I wasn't ready to let go of these characters yet.

TAYLOR SHEPPARD
@library_of_wandering_words

A gripping mix of romance, suspense, and supernatural intrigue. Willow and Milo's alternating POVs shine, with fresh werewolf lore, mafia twists, and a slow-burn romance that pays off beautifully.

Memorable, witty, and steamy — a must-read for fans of fated mates and high-stakes paranormal romance

LAUREN H.

@thatonebookgirl2

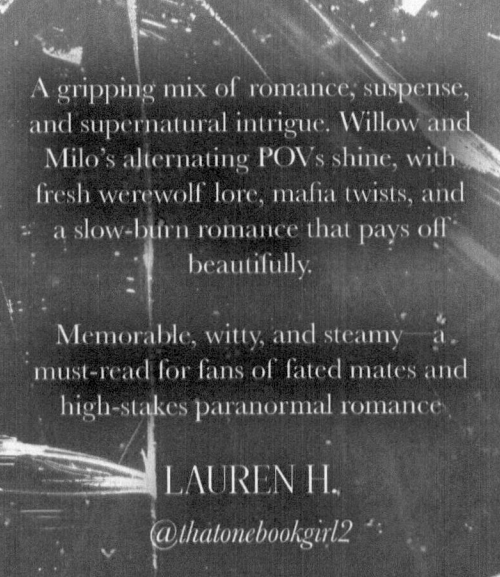

The writing balances gritty darkness with moments of tenderness, and Hartmann doesn't shy away from morally gray characters or high-stakes romance. And then… that ending. A nail-biting cliffhanger where many important details remain heartbreakingly unclear.

This was such an intense, edge-of-your-seat read, and I can't wait for book two to see where the story picks up. If you love dark paranormal romance with mafia vibes, heavy tension, and a cliffhanger that leaves you desperate for more, this one's for you.

MEGAN METCALF
@that_bookstagramgirl

I'm left speechless. This book shattered
my expectations the way it shattered
my heart and left me aching for more.
The chemistry between Milo and
Willow had me rooting for them all
the way through, and the banter had
me laughing loudly.

I'm going to lose my mind waiting to
find out what happens next!

BRITTANY BAILEY

no socials yet

I could not read this forced-proximity, werewolf mafia tale of fated mates fast enough! From the very first chapter, the story pulled me in and refused to let go. The blend of werewolf lore, giving off True Blood vibes, with a fresh mafia twist made for such a unique and addictive read.

Milo and Willow's chemistry was electric, and I adored every moment between them. This is a five-star read that's equal parts thrilling, romantic, and unputdownable.

REBEKAH PRICE

no socials yet

I absolutely devoured this book. It was beautifully written; with lines that made me pause with awe, wonderfully descriptive narration, and thoughtfully done points of view.

This author has a true gift of words, layering them in strokes like a painting. She let the characters tell the story and allowed it unfold in a way that felt so real and vivid. This book truly read like a movie in my mind.

MELINA LEPE

@next_chapter_mama